Welcome to Shady Gulch, Dakota Territory.

Savannah is the first book of the Silver Dollar Saloon series.

SAVANNAH

Silver Dollar Saloon

Paty Jager

Windtree Press
Hillsboro, OR

This is a work of fiction, Names, characters, places, and incidents either are the product of the author's imagination or are used fictitiously, and any resemblance to actual persons living or dead, business establishments, events, or locales, is entirely coincidental.

SAVANNAH: SILVER DOLLAR SALOON

Copyright © 2017 Patricia Jager

All rights reserved. No part of this book may be used or reproduced in any manner whatsoever without written permission of the author or Windtree Press except in the case of brief quotations in critical articles or reviews.

Contact Information: info@windtreepress.com

Windtree Press
Hillsboro, Oregon
http://windtreepress.com

Cover Art by Christina Keerins
CoveredbyCLKeerins

Published in the United States of America

ISBN 9781942368274

Disclaimer

Shady Gulch is not a real town in North Dakota nor was it a town in the Dakota Territory at the time of this book. I took information about railroad towns along the Northern Pacific Railroad and made my own town and populated it with the ethnic groups that traveled to the area to set up new lives.

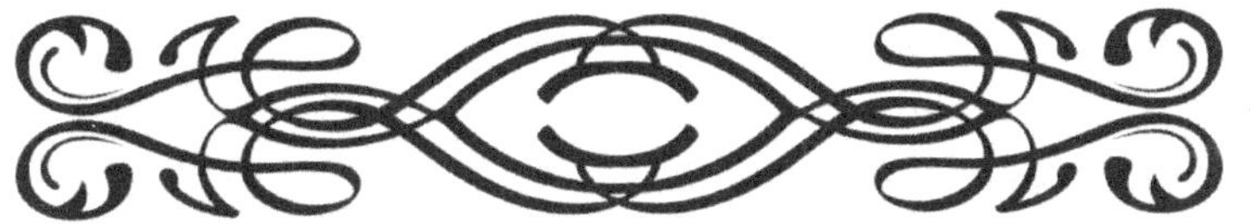

Chapter One

Shady Gulch, Dakota Territory
1878

"Shady Gulch!" the conductor hollered.

Savannah Gentry brushed the soot from her canvas travel coat and peered out the blurry, soot-coated window at the same scenery she'd watched since boarding the train that afternoon in Bismarck. This was the final leg of her nearly two-month long trip.

She sighed. "Please let my half-brother see me as family and not as a pebble in his shoe." If not for finding the letters from a woman in New Orleans to her father, she would have never known she had a chance to be an independent woman. She only hoped her half-brother would take her in until she found a way to support herself.

If she had known whether or not her half-brother would take her in, she could have spent more and had a padded seat on this last part of her trip. Her backside was sore from the hard bench. The rocking of the train made walking impossible to do on her fashionable pointy-heeled boots, and so, she had not moved from the hard, wooden seat since embarking on the train.

She thought about the old Creole woman she'd found in New Orleans instead of Marjolaine, the woman who wrote the letters to her father, or her son, Beauregard. She'd thought the Creole woman crazy at first with her wild clothing and chicken legs hanging around her neck. But once she'd heard Savannah's story, she'd said her son, Jules, and his friend, Beau, had taken roots in Shady Gulch, Dakota Territory.

Looking out at the small town coming into view, she hoped they had. After using most of her money traveling to reach her brother, she would need his assistance for living expenses.

The train whistle blew, announcing the train's arrival. The other passengers pulled their belongings out from under the benches and onto their laps.

She'd held her satchel all the way from Bismarck. All the money she'd hidden away after discovering her mother had bankrupted the family was sewn in the lining of the bag. As well as the jewelry her daddy gave her. The day after Daddy's funeral, the banker, Mr. Cartwell, had sent collectors to their home. The two men had taken everything but two sets of clothing, her jewelry, and money she'd hidden under hay in the horse stables. Mr. Cartwell had thought she'd have to marry him when she was left with nothing.

She smiled. She'd fooled that pasty-faced banker. The minute the men had left with everything but the house, she'd dug her hidden stash out of the hay and caught a ride to Atlanta where she'd set off on her search for her half-brother.

Everything she owned, she either wore or had in the satchel. And to think, only a year ago she'd spent hours trying to pick the right outfit to wear to the opera from a closet full of dresses.

The train slowed; the wheels grated on the metal tracks, black smoke chuffed by the window, and she peered out at the town that would be her new home.

Tears burned her eyes. She pulled out a white handkerchief and dabbed the corners, soaking up the sorrow. Daddy was dead. She'd never see him or their home in Georgia again.

Her mother's selfishness had left her husband and her daughter penniless. "I hope no man with money falls to your charms," Savannah said under her breath. It was wrong to wish her mother the same fate she'd chunked upon her daughter, but she found little affection in her heart for the woman who brought her into the world. Daddy had helped Savannah with her school work and took her to the plays and social events her mother attended with society people. She'd learned early on her mother was self-absorbed. Daddy had indulged his beautiful and much younger wife. And all it did was put him in the poorhouse and a grave much too soon.

The train stopped. She waited for the others to leave the car before she stood and moved on wobbly legs down the aisle.

The man she'd noticed hopping on the train as it rolled out of Bismarck, stood by the door as if waiting for her to leave. He had on a blue chambray shirt and a white bandana around his neck. He shifted. The glint of sunlight off a shiny gun in a holster hanging on his right hip made her wonder if he was a lawman or an outlaw.

He tipped his hat as she approached. "Ma'am." His deep voice had a soothing quality.

She nodded and held her satchel in front of her as she passed. That was when she noticed he had a valise in his left hand.

Her mind wandered to thoughts of what he could be carrying. She stepped off the platform and onto the step. The pointed heel of her boot caught in the metal grid. The weight of the satchel pulled her forward.

The moment she realized she was about to take a tumble, an arm snaked around her middle, holding her suspended in air. Her satchel hit the ground and popped open.

A boy ran toward her bag.

"Lord a mercy! No! Stop! Get away!" she shouted, struggling against the arm that held her on the stairs.

"Joshua, close the lady's bag and guard it," the deep voice behind her said.

The boy did as asked, snapping the bag shut and standing with a leg on each side of it.

"Can you get your heel unstuck?" the man asked, his arm still circling her.

"I could if your arm wasn't wrapped around my body like a Georgia crossvine." She hadn't meant for the words to come out as haughty as they had.

"Sorry. I didn't want you to fall." He released her and remained on the platform above her.

The conductor appeared. "May I help you?"

She raised her skirt enough to show her foot. "My heel is holed up in this grate."

The man started to reach out then pulled his hand back.

"Lark, you better do this."

The man behind her chuckled. "You afraid Lee will find out you touched another woman?"

The man called Lark eased by her, his tall body brushing her arm.

He set the valise between his legs like the boy stood over her satchel. "May I touch your foot?" His gaze met hers and she couldn't breathe. Brown eyes, rimmed with copper, peered at her. One dark eyebrow rose as if waiting for her to answer.

"Y-yes," came out much to breathy.

The handsome man smiled, a dimple appeared on his left cheek.

She stilled her racing heart as he gently, but efficiently, dislodged her boot heel.

"There you go. Miss—"

"Gentry."

He rocked back and stared at her. "Gentry?"

Why was he repeating her name? "I declare, do you need your ears cleaned? Even with my southern drawl you couldn't have misheard me."

"I did hear you." He walked over and patted the boy on the shoulder. "That was a good deed you did, son."

The boy grinned up at him and took off at a run toward what appeared to be stockyards.

Lark Webster smiled. He'd known the boy had been about to pilfer the woman's satchel. Putting him in charge of guarding it with others around to see would give the boy more confidence, something his father didn't seem fit to do.

He shifted his attention to the beautiful woman. "Are you here to see Beau?" Lark picked up the satchel.

The woman made a grab for it, but he held it away

from her. "I'll carry it. Where do you want to go?"

"I can tote my own bag." She glared at him with eyes as blue as a Dakota summer sky. Her hair was the color of wheat, ready to harvest. Judging from the fancy coat, bustle, and high heeled boots, she was a woman of means.

Funny, Beau never mentioned any relatives.

"While you may prefer, I'm not about to let a lady carry her own bag when I have a free hand." He nodded toward town. "Where are you going?"

"To the Silver Dollar Saloon." The words came out of her bow-shaped mouth as if they soured her tongue.

"Then you are related to Beau."

She nodded, bouncing the feather on her fancy hat.

"This way." He led her down the street. As they passed the Altman Hotel, he tipped his head toward the two-story building. "You want to get a room and freshen up?"

The pair of deep blue eyes narrowed. "No."

She was a woman of few words. He liked that. And made him more certain she was a relation of Beau. He was a man of few words.

"Mind if I drop my valise off at the bank?" he asked, stopping at the door of the bank.

"Just hand over my bag and I'll not be frett'n you anymore." She held out her hand.

"You're not fretting me. I just need to finish my job." He put both bag handles in one hand and entered the bank. From how she'd yelled at Joshua when he started for her satchel, he had no doubt she would follow him.

The hollow thud of her heels on the wood floor let him know she was right behind him.

"Larkin, I see you made the trip successfully," his brother, Owen, said, walking out of his office as bank manager.

"Here's your dispatch." Lark handed off the valise and spun on his heel, nearly bumping into Miss Gentry.

"Who is this?" Owen asked.

His brother was married, but he had an eye for money, and it was clear he'd pegged this woman as a potential patron of the bank.

"Miss Gentry, my brother, Owen Webster, the bank manager." Lark stepped back and watched the woman's interaction with his brother.

"Mr. Webster, it is my honor to meet you," She held out her hand, limply.

Owen shook hands with her, which put a blush on the woman's creamy skin.

"If you need to open an account, come see me," Owen said.

"Bless your heart. I'll give it a thought." She glanced at Lark. "Shall we wander?"

He grinned and winked at his brother, who grinned back and shook his head. Lark held out his arm, hoping the woman would slip her hand through the crook at his elbow, but she walked to the door and waited for him to open it.

Back out on the boardwalk, he started across the street. While he'd wanted to escort her properly, it was apparent she had other ideas. He stepped into the street, causing dust to puff up around his legs. The June sun and unending wind had dried what was mud not a month ago, to four inches of dry powder.

He glanced back. Miss Gentry stood on the edge of the wood boardwalk, looking like a person afraid to jump into a river.

"Ye have to pick up yer skirt and not be too proud ta

walk these streets," Mrs. Cleary said, hefting her wool skirt up and stepping into the dust. She glanced over her shoulder at Miss Gentry.

The younger woman heaved a heavy sigh and raised the front of her skirts. The only problem—the back was longer and she wasn't raising it up at all.

Lark doubled back and picked up the tail of her skirt, following along behind the woman. At that moment, Sheriff Tyson Blake stepped out of his office. He whistled and hollered, "I knew you were good for something other than a preacher!"

Miss Gentry stopped, and he ran into the back of her.

Ty roared with laughter.

Lark's face and ears heated up hotter than Manfred's forge.

"Y-you're a preacher man?" Her gaze traveled from his dusty boots up to his wide-brimmed hat.

"Yes, ma'am. Every day of the week but Wednesday. That day I'm the bank courier."

She spun around and hurried to the boardwalk in front of the mercantile. Once she set foot on the planks, she said, "Land a mercy, take your hands off my dress."

He dropped the fabric as if it had caught fire. He didn't like holding up her skirt any more than she liked him doing it. "I might suggest you dress for easier getting around."

She glared at him and continued down the boardwalk. The Silver Dollar Saloon sign swung in the wind at the end of the block. She grasped her hat as a gust whipped down the street, spinning curls of dust into the air.

"Does the wind always pick up like this?"

"Nope, this is a mild day."

She stopped and stared at him. "Reverend Webster, I'll

tote my own bag. I'm sure you have better thangs to tend to."

He grinned. "Nothing to do the rest of the day. I'm looking forward to seeing the look on Beau's face when you walk through his door."

Chapter Two

Savannah studied the man. He was handsome. And he was a preacher. She'd let him touch her foot and tote her skirt. The humiliation made her stomach twist in knots. Either that or the fact she was about to come face to face with a half-brother she'd never met.

Reverend Webster winked and motioned for her to walk through the big wooden doors with frosted glass and the words: SILVER DOLLAR SALOON.

She inhaled, steadied her heart, and pushed the doors open. Noise, color, and smoke were her first impressions of the interior of the saloon.

The music stopped, the chatter stopped, and all eyes gazed at her. She swallowed, scanning the room for the brother she'd traveled nearly two thousand miles to find.

She spotted him in a tall, broad-shouldered man with black hair and her daddy's face right down to the cleft chin and piercing hazel eyes.

"Beauregard Gentry?" she asked, walking toward the man.

Several of the men around her chuckled. Someone shouted, "Hey, Beauregard!"

"Yes. Who are you?" He stood with his legs spread, arms crossed, and staring her down like their father had treated business adversaries, but not his wife or daughter.

She held out her hand. "Your sistah, Savannah."

His face turned white before quickly taking on a crimson hue. "My what?"

Savannah started to take a step back but felt a presence behind her.

"Perhaps you and your sister should go over to Mrs. Dearling's and visit," Reverend Webster said, stepping up beside her.

At that moment, she was happy the pushy reverend had insisted he come with her.

A darky with skin as shiny and brown as the finest chocolate in the confectionary, walked up to Beauregard. He spoke in a language that resembled French but more foreign. His words seemed to push her brother into action.

He reached out to the reverend. "Lark, give me her bag."

To her surprise, Reverend Webster shook his head. "I'll join in this conversation. To keep things civil."

She stared at her brother. Surely, he wouldn't hurt her? Would he?

"Have it your way." Beau shifted his attention to the darky. "Jules, take care of the bar." He scanned the room, and said loudly, "If any of you touch one of the girls, Jules has my permission to throw you out or shoot you, his choice."

At his words, Savannah noticed the four women dressed in bright colored skirts that showed off too much leg and tops that covered only as much as a corset. She seethed thinking her brother allowed men to pay to have their way with one of the women.

Beauregard stomped to the back of the establishment. Reverend Webster motioned for her to follow. Her heart thudded in her chest from anger and fear. She didn't know either of these men, even though there was no denying the man ahead of her was her brother. They could take her out in the alley and … Her thoughts, lack of food, and being tuckered from the trip caught up to her. The world went black.

Lark had been staring at the woman's straight back and the gentle sway of her bustle when he noticed her body start to crumple. He dropped her bag and caught her before she slithered to the ground.

"Beau!" he called to his friend, who had stepped out the back door of the saloon.

His large form hurried back in. "What happened?"

"I don't know. She was walking along and, all of a sudden, she collapsed." He shuffled her around in his arms and stood. "I can carry her, if you want to grab her satchel."

Beau picked up the bag and they hurried across the alley to Mrs. Dearling's boarding house. She only boarded the women who worked for Beau.

"Oh dear! What have you there?" the gray-haired, plump woman in her fifties asked, holding her back door open.

"Beau's sister," Lark said.

"Supposed sister," Beau countered.

Lark placed Miss Gentry on the settee in the parlor and faced his friend. "From the time I've been with her, she has your stubbornness, brevity of speaking, and quick temper.

I'd suggest you wait for her to come around and listen to what she has to say before putting that big foot of yours in your mouth."

Beau glared at him as Mrs. Dearling entered the room with a small vial of smelling salts.

"This should bring her around. My, but she has nice shoes and clothes, though they won't do her much good here." The woman leaned over Miss Gentry, waving the salts under her nose.

The young woman's hand came up first, shoving the vial away. Her eyes opened, the blue dimmed with confusion.

"Miss Gentry, you fainted," Lark said, dropping to one knee next to her. He started to reach for her hand, but she shoved both hands into the cushion and raised her body up. This was the same reaction he'd expect from Beau coming out of a faint. Ready to do battle even when there was no threat.

Mrs. Dearling pushed between Lark and the woman. "There, there dear. You fainted. Reverend Webster brought you in here to recover. I'm Mrs. Dearling. I run this boarding house."

"I don't faint." Miss Gentry shoved up to a sitting position and quickly swung her feet off the horsehair cushions.

"Maybe not before, but you would have hit the ground hard if I hadn't noticed your body slumping." Lark wasn't going to let her push this off as if it meant nothing. He knew a woman didn't faint for no reason. Either fear, their health, or heat did it to them. It wasn't an overly hot day, and she had nothing to fear from them. Had she sought out her brother because of an illness?

"Lark, go get Doc Nolan," Beau said as if he had the same thoughts.

Lark stood.

"There's no need to fetch a doctor. I'm healthy as y'all." She stood, wobbled a bit, and Lark grabbed her by the shoulders.

"That doesn't look fine to me," Mrs. Dearling said. "Stay put. I'll brew up a pot of tea." The older woman left the room.

Miss Gentry's gaze flashed from Lark to Beau. Did he see fear in her eyes? Was that why she'd crumpled? She was scared of them.

"Why don't you settle back down on the settee and tell us why you sought your brother." Lark eased her back down on the cushions and then sat on a foot stool. He motioned for Beau to sit. There were a couple of small chairs.

Beau eased himself into one. It creaked a bit.

Savannah licked her lips and watched the two men. They'd brought her to a boarding house. The woman, Mrs. Dearling appeared harmless. The last time she'd fainted was during a Fourth of July picnic. She'd participated in the sack race against her mother's wishes.

Beauregard had the same intense gaze and twitch in his cheek as their father when he was unhappy with circumstances. She hoped her fainting didn't make him think she'd be a problem.

"I come here, to you, Beauregard—"

"Don't call me Beauregard. I'm Beau." His hazel gaze grew darker.

"No need to get tetchy. Our granddaddy was always called by Beauregard. I figured you would be, too." She studied him. Talk about their grandfather made him uncomfortable. His gaze dropped to the settee beside her and his face became a ruddier hue.

"I wouldn't know. I was never allowed to meet my father or my grandfather." He glared at her. "How did you learn about me?"

"When Daddy passed, I was go'n through his things. He had letters written to him from your mother. I learned your name, where you and your mother lived. I fetched myself to Nawlens, looking for you two. Mrs. Mathieu, told me you were here." The old woman had scared her at first. And had spoken a strange language. The same one Jules had used while talking with Beau. However, once she understood Savannah's plight, she'd spoken in broken English. Her Jules…the darky Beau had told to take over the bar and watch the girls…and Beau, were in Shady Gulch, Dakota Territory.

"Jules momma had no right telling you where I am." Beau's face closed as if he'd slammed a door.

"Beau, she's family. From what you've never said, I believe you thought you were alone." Reverend Webster waved a hand. "Looks like you do have family and your sister came looking for you."

"I've been just fine all these years with Jules and Momma Mathieu. I don't owe my father anything. He shunned my mother and me."

Savannah stared at the big man. His face was a stone, but she saw the glint of a tear in the corner of his eyes. She hadn't spent the money she did and endured the lowly accommodations to be tossed aside.

"I've been rid'n on steamships and trains for two months and I've used up purt near all of the money I hid from the conniving banker who came the day after I put our daddy in the ground and took everything that wasn't attached." She leaned forward, wagging her finger at her brother. "And hell will freeze over afore I'll let you chunk me away like some burr in your britches." Her finger shook, as did her body. She'd never been as angry and frustrated as she was at this moment.

Mrs. Dearling entered the room with a tray. She glanced at each person and set the tray down with a clatter. "It appears to me, you men should leave and let Miss Gentry rest. She's had a long trip."

"I didn't come here to be a bother to no one," she said. She'd hoped her brother would allow her to stay at his home.

"Put her in one of the rooms," Beau said to Mrs. Dearling. His gaze landed on her. "I'll be by at breakfast to speak with you." Without another word, he stomped out of the room and the kitchen door slammed.

Reverend Webster held his hat in his hands. "I'll be by after dinner to see if there is anything more I can help you with."

She nodded unsure what to say.

He peered at her for a few seconds then spun on his heel and left as well. But without slamming the door.

Mrs. Dearling handed her a cup and saucer of tea and smiled. "Now, tell me all about what brought you here."

Savannah sighed. She wasn't up for any kind of conversation. "I'm all give out, how about after I've rested?"

The woman nodded. "Drink your tea, and I'll show you to your room."

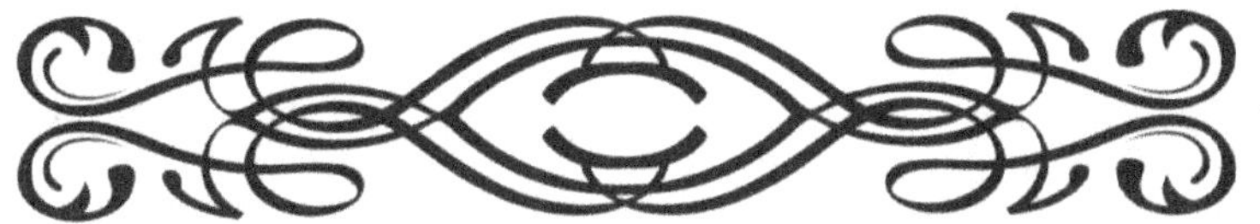

Chapter Three

Lark entered the Silver Dollar through the back door, the same way he'd left earlier. Beau was confronting Jules behind the bar. He hurried over to make sure the owner of the Silver Dollar didn't take his frustration out on his partner.

"She said your momma told her where to find me. Didn't you tell her not to let my father's people know where I was?" Beau's voice was growing louder and the bar noise had grown quieter.

"Beau, save this for later," Lark said, nodding toward the men and even the saloon girls leaning a bit toward the two men's conversation.

"Play some music and take these gossips' minds off my trouble," Beau said to Jules.

The big black man nodded and walked over to the piano. He sat down and rollicking music filled the air.

Lark stood at the bar watching the owner of the saloon scan the interior. He knew Beau was checking to make sure none of his saloon girls were being bothered. The man was a walking contradiction. It was evident his sister needed help, yet, he'd walk away from her and help out any other woman who needed it.

"Did you really not know you had a sister?" Lark asked, as Beau placed a beer in front of him.

"I figured I might have some half brothers or sisters, knowing my father had followed his family's wishes and wed the woman they picked rather than my mother." Beau let out a heavy breath. "What the hell am I to do?"

"Go to breakfast in the morning without hostility. There must be a reason she came to you. It sounds like your father is dead. Perhaps she was curious about you and is only here for a visit." As he said the obvious, his heart lurched. While she hadn't been sweet and unassuming, there was something about her that he liked. Liked a lot. Her strength, her conviction to take on a task. Admirable traits in a minister's wife. He set his beer down so hard it sloshed over the rim. Where had that thought come from?

"Hey, you're making a mess." Beau wiped up the spill. "You really think she needs my help?"

"She came here for a reason. I'm going by the boarding house after dinner, maybe I can learn something for you." He finished off the beer. "I better go see what I missed today." Lark left the Silver Dollar and headed to his small house next to the church and cemetery.

When he first arrived in Shady Gulch, at the request of his brother who'd wanted to make the town more family oriented by bringing in a preacher, he'd been sure he couldn't fit into such a small community. But his past never came up. That was the way he liked it.

The edges of three papers fluttered under the rock on

his threshold. This was how the community contacted him when he was away.

He picked up the notes and carried them inside. His gaze barely saw the scrawled writing as his mind conjured up Miss Gentry. Why was she here? What had driven her to find her brother?

Savannah was pleased to find a small bathtub in a room off the kitchen. Mrs. Dearling carried several buckets of hot water in, dumping them into the cooler water Savannah had pumped with a hand pump. Once she immersed her whole body, head and all, into the warm water, the tension that had made her body ache for the last two months, eased. She scrubbed her hair and body, emerging from the bathing room feeling more like herself.

Roasting meat, yeast bread, and cinnamon met her as she stepped into the kitchen. "That smells delicious. When is supper?"

Mrs. Dearling turned from the stove. "Freedom and Belle will be in to eat soon. When they leave Liesa and Lottie Mae will come in. You're welcome to eat with any of them."

Savannah noted the two plates set on the table in the kitchen. "Who are the ladies you mentioned?"

"The other boarders. They have to take shifts eating so there's always a couple of girls at the saloon." The woman set a steaming pie on the top shelf of the cook stove.

"I'm stay'n in a house with ladies of the even'n?" Savannah couldn't believe a preacher would leave her in a place such as this.

The older woman turned to her, her fisted hands on her ample hips. "Watch your mouth. There will be no name calling in my house. This is not what you think. I only take in good girls. My boarders fall on hard times. Beau gives them work at the saloon and they board here. He pays for their rooms."

She narrowed her eyes. "What all do they do in the saloon? I saw them stairs lead'n to rooms on the second floor. I've heard stories about the saloons and bawdy houses in Atlanta." When on walks in the park, her chaperone would always steer her and her friends clear of one street. Her friend, Darilee, had told them it was the street where the women sold their bodies.

Mrs. Dearling shook a finger at her. "You don't know your brother at all. No one is allowed to handle the women and they don't go upstairs. That's where Beau and Jules live, and they have two rooms they rent out when a judge or official comes through town." She turned back to the stove. "Your brother helps young women get back on their feet or out of tough situations." She glanced over her shoulder. "Go get dressed and you can eat with Freedom and Belle. I can hear your stomach grumbling clear over here."

Savannah wandered out of the kitchen and up to the room she'd been given. The window in the room overlooked the next block with four houses. Mrs. Dearling said the one on the corner was Doctor Nolan's. She was still trying to figure out what Mrs. Dearling had said about Beau helping young women, when she sauntered back downstairs and heard happy voices in the kitchen.

She stepped into the room and the conversation went quiet. Mrs. Dearling sat at the end of the table. Two young women, one a darkie, sat on one side of the table. Their plates were piled high with food.

"Miss Gentry, this is Freedom and Belle." Mrs. Dearling motioned for her to sit at the plate across from the two women.

Savannah nodded to each one. "How do you do."

Freedom, the darkie, smiled. "Welcome to Shady Gulch and Mrs. Dearling's house." She had beautiful golden eyes and skin the color of coffee that was half milk. Bright red bows that matched the color of her dress tied a pile of black ringlets on top of her head.

The other woman had light brown hair and a smattering of freckles across her nose. "I don't know what you said to Beau, but he's been biting everyone's head off since you showed up." Her brown eyes were narrowed, adding to the suspicion in her words.

"I can't help it if my appearance has made him sour." She didn't like knowing Beau was still upset. That didn't bode well for his helping her.

"He'll get over it. He riles easy, but smiles just as easy," Freedom said, forking another bite toward her mouth.

"It would ease my mind to know more about him and y'all," Savannah said, putting her first bite of the roast in her mouth. The meat melted on her tongue. She hadn't had anything so delicious in a long time. Not since, they had to let all the help go.

"Why do you want to know about your own brother? Shouldn't you already know everything?" Belle's protectiveness of Beau was admirable, but annoying.

"Until two months ago, I didn't know he existed." She'd keep it at that until she and her brother had a long chat.

Freedom nodded. "I can understand that. I didn't know

I had brothers and sisters until my daddy told me about the other women he'd bedded." She frowned. "I'm never gonna be that way."

"But the clothes y'all wear, men could think you are that way." Savannah couldn't let their working in the saloon go unmentioned. She'd never sat at a table or discussed such things with a woman not of the upper class. The one thing she'd learned while traveling, west of the Mississippi, everyone was treated the same. No one was a class above anyone else out here. While the two looked healthier and less painted up than the painted ladies she'd had pointed out to her on occasion, she was still ill at ease knowing where they worked.

"We dress like this to help draw in customers. They aren't allowed to touch. We sing and dance and deliver drinks. Nothin' else." Freedom's friendliness was gone.

"Miss Gentry, why don't you save your thoughts for another time." Mrs. Dearling was upset with her questioning as well.

She kept her mouth shut other than to fork another bite in. The other two finished eating, gave Mrs. Dearling a hug and left through the kitchen door.

Mrs. Dearling picked up the two place settings and set down two clean sets. She'd no sooner placed two glasses of water by the plates than two more women entered the kitchen from the back door.

"Miss Gentry, this is Liesa and Lottie Mae." Mrs. Dearling motioned to the two women.

Liesa was blonde and pretty, like a porcelain doll, and just as fine boned. Lottie Mae was a full-figured red head.

"Hallo," Liesa said with a definite accent. Savannah wasn't sure what her nationality could be.

"So, you're what's got Beau acting like everyone is his enemy." Lottie Mae sashayed around the table, her gaze on Savannah before she sat in the spot next to Liesa.

"We're not going to have another discussion about Beau and his temperament," Mrs. Dearling said.

"I don't have a reason to discuss anyth'n with anyone other than Beau." Savannah finished her meal and stood. "I'm go'n to retire to my room. What time should I appear for breakfast?"

"Breakfast around here is at nine. The girls and Beau work late, causing them to get up late." Mrs. Dearling piled food onto two plates.

"Are there more women com'n to eat?" Savanah asked, realizing too late how nasty her tone sounded.

Both Liesa and Lottie Mae frowned at her.

"The ladies will take these plates to the saloon for Jules and Beau. This time of day they can't get away. The all-day drinkers and night-time gamblers will be filling the place up and causing trouble." The boarding house owner set the two plates with cloths draped over them on the end of the table.

It appeared the woman took care of everyone connected to the saloon. She didn't understand any of it, but then she was tired and as she'd proven by her cattish comments, out of sorts. She wandered down the hall and was halfway up the stairs when a knock sounded on the front door. Knowing it couldn't be for her, she continued up the steps.

Even though she had no idea where she'd end up, Savannah had taken the two blouses and a green skirt from her satchel. She wore the least wrinkled blouse and the skirt. She'd hung the other in the small wardrobe in the corner of the room. That one would require a hot iron to rid the garment of all the wrinkles. She'd had to work to get the two sets of underdrawers, two blouses, skirt, stockings, and her toiletries into the satchel. All those items had caused the bag to pop open so easily when it dropped at the train station.

She'd kicked off her boots and was tugging off her stockings when a soft knock on her door had her gaze snapping that direction. What could Mrs. Dearling possibly need to say that couldn't wait until morning?

The cool wood floor felt good on her bare feet. She opened the door, "Yes?"

"Reverend Webster is here and wondered if he could have a word with you." It was apparent by the disapproval on the older woman's face, she found it inappropriate for the reverend to be visiting her.

Savannah wiggled her toes. She was tired, but the handsome preacher had been friendly from their first meeting. After all the suspicious looks from the women, she couldn't think of a better way to settle her down before she went to sleep than a discussion with the reverend on how her brother lived his life.

"I'll follow," she said, stepping out and pulling the door closed behind her.

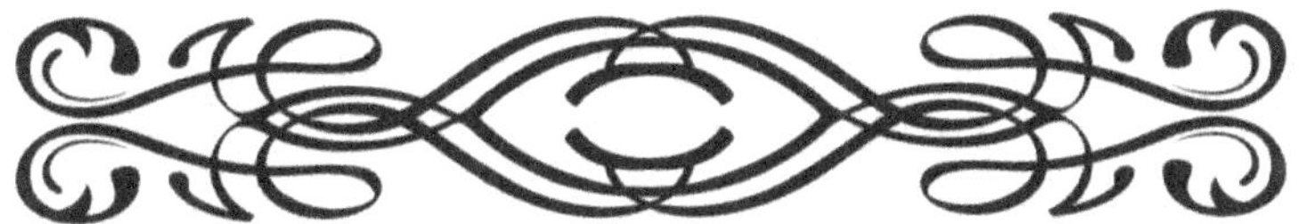

Chapter Four

Lark sat in the parlor waiting for Miss Gentry to appear. He wondered if Mrs. Dearling would return without the headstrong woman. The older woman had said Miss Gentry went up to bed. He glanced at his pocket watch. It was barely past seven. The town of Shady Gulch was just coming alive. And all the more reason he should be home writing up the Sunday sermon instead of feeding his curiosity by talking with Miss Gentry.

Mrs. Dearling entered the parlor first. She sat in the rocking chair and picked up her knitting in a basket to the side of the chair. He knew the woman wouldn't let him see Miss Gentry alone in her parlor or her house for that matter. That was why Beau had asked Mrs. Dearling to board his saloon girls. He knew the older woman would not allow for any shenanigans.

His gaze shot to the doorway as Miss Gentry entered. She no longer wore the fancy dress with the bustle. She had on a pristine white blouse and a dark green skirt. He caught the faint image of pink toes as she walked across the room. She *had* been retiring for the night, and he'd pulled her from her rest.

He stood. "Miss Gentry, I'm sorry if this is an inconvenient time. I can wait and come back tomorrow."

She took a seat on the settee and waved for him to sit in the chair. "You're here, I'm here. Why did you come call'n?"

"I thought if I learned more about your circumstances, I could relay them to Beau, and he could have the information digested by morning when the two of you meet." He was concerned how his private friend planned to deal with his sister. He was also curious about the woman.

"Reverend, while I understand you feel a need to protect your friend, and possibly me, I'd rather tell my problems to my brother." She leaned back. "Perhaps you could answer a question for me."

He nodded, enjoying the way her chin tipped up as she peered down her nose at him. Any other woman he would have thought she were being haughty or derisive to him. But he could see by her eyelids at half-mast she was merely trying to stay awake.

"I'll do my best to answer your questions."

The clicking of knitting needles stopped. He glanced over at Mrs. Dearling. She leaned forward, trying to catch the conversation.

"Why are you friends with my brother? He clearly has the morals of an alley cat which you, as a preacher, cannot condone."

Lark watched her eyelids slowly lower. "Miss Gentry, your brother has some of the highest morals of any man

I've ever met."

Her eyelids flew up and her blue eyes pierced him with indignation. "How can you say such a thing? He owns a saloon and has young, half-dressed women wander'n among the men."

"I told you, those ladies do nothing more than sing, dance, and deliver drinks." Mrs. Dearling said, with a huff.

"Bless your heart, you did. But I find that hard to believe. And if this is true, why would my brother even have those women in the saloon if he's so righteous?"

Lark stood, it was clear the woman needed her rest, and perhaps, by morning her good sense would come to her. "Miss Gentry, I'm sure you have led a sheltered life. There are few ways a woman on her own can live. Your brother provides a means to keep women who have been put out by their families and society to pick themselves up. You should ask the women where they would be without your brother." He bowed to Miss Gentry and smiled at the older woman. "I'll see you for breakfast to make sure Miss Gentry and Beau don't tear up your kitchen."

"I'll set a place for you," Mrs. Dearling said, picking her knitting back up.

Lark let himself out the front door of the boarding house. Miss Gentry's morals and the way she carried herself, told him she would make a wonderful addition to the town. But would she be able to fit in as a farmer's wife? He doubted it. There, however, were many railroad and cattlemen who spent time in Shady Gulch. She would definitely turn their heads. The thought of her being wooed by the likes raised his hackles. From the moment he'd watched her wobble down the train car aisle and he'd wrapped his arm around her to keep her from falling head first from the train, he'd become fascinated with her.

He walked around the block and found himself standing outside the Silver Dollar Saloon. The piano carried a rollicking tune. One of the young women was singing. He wasn't sure which one as he tended not to frequent the saloon during the evening. Many of his parishioners wouldn't understand he was there to visit with a friend.

Not quite ready to call it a night and face the sermon he'd started the day before, he walked across the street to see what Ty had to say about anything.

Savannah woke to sunshine streaming through her window. The brightness had her covering her eyes and slowly opening her fingers to adjust to the light. It appeared to be much later than she normally woke. Which didn't surprise her. She'd been exhausted. She barely remembered her conversation with Reverend Webster. But the sight of him in a black suit, vest, and white collar had wiped away the image of the man when they'd first met. He had looked the part of an outlaw on the train, and in the parlor last night, he'd appeared the epitome of virtue as a preacher. Her heart had skipped a beat as she'd entered the room and spotted him watching her entrance.

Softly spoken words in the hall reminded her she wasn't the only boarder. Savannah washed at the pitcher and bowl sitting on the wash stand and donned the white blouse and green skirt she'd worn last night. The only shoes she'd brought with her were the boots that would be completely useless in this country. She put them on and made a mental note to ask about a place to purchase a more reliable pair.

Once dressed, she opened the door and discovered Liesa and Belle walking down the hall toward her. They both wore pretty calico dresses, giving them the appearance of respectable young women. Reverend Webster's words came to her. He'd said her brother provided a service and to ask the women about themselves. His comments had her curiosity piqued.

"Good mawnin," she said, smiling.

They nodded and ducked past her.

Would they warm up to her and speak about their lives? She followed them down the hall, the stairs, and into the kitchen. The table was set for seven.

The women fell in alongside of Mrs. Dearling, helping with the meal. Feeling like an interloper she stood for a minute unsure what to do.

"Grab that pitcher and fill the glasses with water," Mrs. Dearling said.

Thankful for a task, she grabbed the pitcher and started pouring. A knock sounded on the front door as the back door opened. She stared at the way her brother filled the door opening. Where had his size come from? Their father had been tall, but not like Beau. And their father had a slender build. But there was no denying the similarities between the two men.

"Take your usual spot, Beau," Mrs. Dearling said, hurrying down the hall to answer the front door.

"Good Mawnin'," Savannah said to her brother.

He grunted and filled a cup with coffee before sitting at the head of the table.

She wondered if it was because his shoulders wouldn't fit well alongside others or because he believed himself the lord of this harem of women. The later thought soured her attitude.

Mrs. Dearling appeared with Reverend Webster following behind. He said, "Good morning," to everyone and sat at the corner of the table furthest from Beau.

Freedom and Lottie Mae wandered in, both apparently not happy to see the morning. Both poured cups of coffee before taking the two seats across from the reverend.

"Miss Gentry, take the seat on the other end," Mrs. Dearling said.

"What about you?" There were eight people and only seven places set.

"I'll be too busy serving, and I ate earlier."

Savannah sat. She had Reverend Webster on her right and Lottie Mae on her left. The other two women finished placing bowls and platters on the table and sat in the last two seats between the two men.

"Grace." The reverend held his hands out. She clasped the one nearest her and held her hand out to Lottie Mae. The hand being held in Larkin's became warm and sweaty. As he said grace, she peeked at the others present and watched as they all mouthed the prayer, even Beau.

"Amen," they all said in unison.

Lottie Mae released her hand, but the reverend held on a bit longer and squeezed. She glanced into his eyes. It was as if he were saying, "I'm here if you need me." He released her hand, and she wiped her sweaty palm on her skirt.

The food was passed around. Hot cakes, ham, and eggs. Everyone but Savannah piled their plates high.

Once the noise of the food being passed diminished, Beau cleared his throat. "Savannah, tell me about you and why you're here."

She stared at him before glancing around the table. "In front of everyone?" Humiliation had been her partner since Daddy told her he'd lost everything. She wasn't about to share it with people she didn't know.

"We're all one big family. What bothers one, we all take on." He nodded around the table. "Right ladies?"

They all agreed and kept eating as they watched her.

She shifted in her chair. Why was he doing this to her?

Reverend Webster spoke up. "Maybe if one of you told your story, Miss Gentry wouldn't feel as if she's been thrown to the lions."

Beau frowned but nodded.

Belle put her fork down. "My pa had plenty of girls and needed money worse than he needed another mouth to feed. As soon as I was old enough to make babies, he sold me to a man his age who wanted sons to help him in the field." She picked up her water and drank half the glass. Liesa patted her shoulder in silent unity.

"I became with child, and I bore a girl." Tears streamed down her cheeks. "He drowned my baby like it was a dog and then beat me for giving him a girl."

Savannah had only heard of this treatment to the slaves in the plantations before the war and a few places afterwards. "He was a vile monster to do such a thing!" she said, unable to contain her horror.

Reverend Webster grasped her hand and held it on the table. She glanced at his face. He'd heard the story before, was there more? Was that why he was holding her hand in comfort?

"I wrote to my pa and asked him to come get me. He refused. I went to the local preacher." Belle's gaze landed on the man holding Savannah's hand and flit away. "He told me I was bound to the man and had to do his bidding."

Savannah peered into Reverend Webster's face. The anger in his eyes made it clear he didn't hold the same beliefs as the man Belle had sought for help.

"What happened?" Savannah glanced at her brother. His jaw was twitching, his eyes were ablaze with anger.

"He near beat me to death when I refused to climb in his bed one night when he was drunk." Her eyes slipped from angry to adoring as she smiled at Beau. "When the man passed out, I crawled out of the house and stumbled down the road toward town. Beau came along the road, picked me up, and brought me here. Doc Nolan patched me up. I've stayed here ever since, working in the saloon and living here with the girls and Mrs. Dearling."

Savannah watched her brother reach out and pat Belle's hand. He'd saved the young woman from possible death.

Liesa spoke up. "He have save us all." Even though she spoke broken English, Savannah understood what the woman meant.

The other two heads nodded.

"Your story is safe with everyone in this room," Beau said, talking to her in a normal tone for the first time since they'd met.

"My story isn't as horrific." She peered around the table wondering what other horrors had happened to the women meeting her gaze.

The reverend squeezed her hand, reminding her he would give her strength.

"My mother was much younger than my daddy. She is beautiful and selfish. She squandered all of Daddy's money, leaving both he and I penniless. She ran off with a man with money and left us hav'n to pay off her debts. Daddy passed on two months ago. I'm still ponder'n if it was from a broken heart or humiliation." She glanced over at Beau. His face was a blank mask.

"The day after Daddy's funeral, the banker, who'd been hound'n us for months, sent men to take our belong'n's. A friend had mentioned the scoundrel's plan. I hid the money I'd managed to fetch over the last year, two sets of clothes, toiletries, and my jewelry in the stable." She withdrew her hand from the reverend's. "The bank manager had made sure the men who came took everything. There wasn't a morsel of food to eat or a pot to cook in. He also sent along a note. It said he would marry me to keep me in the wealth I'd known my whole life." Anger lit in her belly. "The man is noth'n but a coward who uses his bank as a way to take things from people. I crumpled the note and chunked it on the floor of the empty house. Then I grabbed the things I'd hid and headed by train to Nawlins. After daddy's death, I'd learned about my brother." She smiled at Beau. He stared back at her, not grinning, but not scowling. "In Nawlins, I learned he was here. I boarded a steamship to travel up the Mississippi, and then I took one up the Missouri, and then the train from Bismarck."

Mrs. Dearling asked, "What do you plan to do now?"

Savannah stared at her brother. "My skills are runn'n a house and plann'n parties. I hope y'all can help me reckon what to do."

Beau leaned back from his cleaned plate and crossed his arms. "All I can do is offer you a job at the saloon and a room here."

She smacked the chair with her backbone as if he'd

slapped her in the face. He wanted her to work in the saloon?

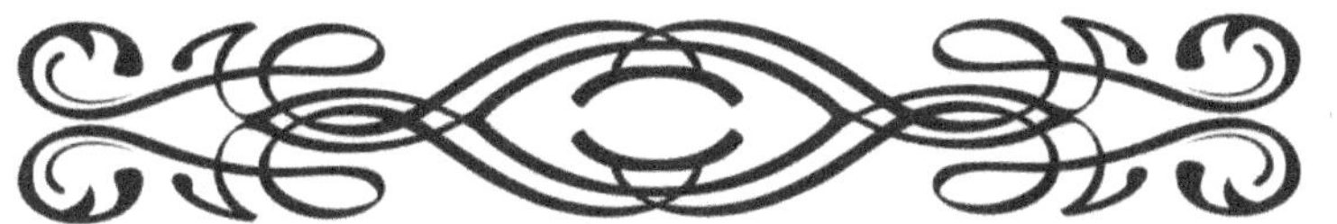

Chapter Five

"I-I can't work in a saloon. What would people be say'n about me?" Miss Gentry said, staring at her brother as if he'd just asked her to kill someone.

Lark couldn't let the woman down. He'd stepped in when she was about to fall on her face getting off the train and needed to come to her rescue again. "You'll find these ladies have a much better acceptance by the community than the women at the Mad Dog Saloon."

Her blue eyes peered into his. "I'd be one rung up from the bottom class of woman in this town? That's where I could have landed if I'd have stayed in Georgia. Well, bless your heart for making me feel better."

The anger and despair he witnessed made it hard to keep from wrapping his arms around her. The way she'd said Georgia and New Orleans, with the slow drawl and her voice dripping with honey, had him hanging on her every word.

"That's not what I meant." He glanced to the end of

the table where Beau watched all this with a gleam in his eyes. The man probably hoped his sister would return to Georgia. However, Lark could tell by the tone of her voice, she planned to stay here and make the best of things.

Beau cleared his throat. "While these ladies work in my saloon, the community knows they don't give favors to the men and they aren't allowed to have men in the house without Mrs. Dearling present." He smiled at the older woman. "I asked Mrs. Dearling to run this boarding house because she is a pillar of this community and everyone respects her and knows she will instill good morals in the woman who live here."

"We've already had three girls find husbands and now they have wonderful lives in other parts," Mrs. Dearling said.

Lark turned to Miss Gentry. "This home has helped each of the women who lives here become stronger and move on to a new life. They work in the Silver Dollar to help them pay for their lodging and meals and it gives them a chance to change their future."

She shook her head. "I can see where liv'n here and hav'n a job is good for someone like Belle with little experience. I only need a place to live. I'll find work. I'm educated."

"Educated. That doesn't mean a thing." Lottie Mae sneered. "I was a school teacher until two of the older boys caught me one evening after dark when I was walking home and…" She choked back an angry sob. "When I accused them of attacking me, I was called a whore, shunned by my family, and told I would never teach again." She smiled at Beau. "I was out of money and no one would take me on as a teacher without a recommendation from my past school." She shook her head. "I knew I couldn't get one. Then Beau came along."

Lark knew each woman's story as Beau had told it, but hearing it in their own words, he heard the hurt, mistrust, and anger in their voices. And the reverence they gave their boss. Beau was a saint, though the man would never allow anyone to say as much.

Miss Gentry reached out, touching Lottie Mae's arm. "I'm sorry for what you went through. But I don't see why I can't find a job." She glanced around the table.

Beau leaned forward. "You can continue to stay here. Look for work. But if you don't have anything by Monday, you'll work in the saloon to pay for your keep."

Miss Gentry scowled at her brother. "You'd make family pay?"

"I have yet to see proof you are my sister, and if you don't want to work in the saloon, you'll help Mrs. Dearling with the household chores and cooking. I don't know how you were raised, but I was raised to work for my keep. If I hadn't, I wouldn't have had anything to eat or a roof over my head." Beau stood, smiled at the women around the table and Mrs. Dearling. "Thank you for another good meal, Mrs. Dearling. Ladies, I'll see you in the saloon after noon."

Lark caught Miss Gentry's attention as the other women started clearing the table and washing the dishes.

"If you would like, I can take you around town and introduce you. But unless you care to work in the flour mill or the warehouse, I doubt you'll find work fit for a woman."

She studied him a moment. "Thank you for your offer of assistance. I'll be fine on my own." She turned her attention to the women. "Would one of y'all be will'n to help me purchase a new pair of boots? I've discovered the only pair I have aren't fit for rural liv'n."

Her dismissal of his offer knocked his pride and revealed his attraction to her wasn't something he should pursue.

"I'll see you all at Sunday Service," he said, standing and heading down the hall to the front door. He reached for his hat on the rack by the door and felt a presence behind him.

"Reverend Webster, I do appreciate your offer. I'm just not ready to look for work today. I need proper attire for my feet, and I'll need to write up my qualifications." Miss Gentry stood so close he caught a whiff of a floral scent.

"Miss Gentry—"

"Savannah. You may call me Savannah when we're alone." Her blonde lashes fluttered a bit before her wide blue eyes peered into his.

"Savannah, if you have qualifications to find work, why didn't you stay in Georgia?" His heart thudded in his chest at her request he call her by her given name.

Her gaze dropped. "I feared, no matter where I went, Mr. Cartwell would make sure no one gave me work."

He studied her face. Fear dulled her eyes and tugged on the corners of her mouth. "Why would he do such a thing?"

"He asked for my hand many times. Daddy always told him no. He didn't want me to be in a loveless marriage." She wrung her hands. "Mr. Cartwell has lots of money and many acquaintances who would do whatever he wanted for the right price. That was one of the reasons I wanted to find

Beau. I wanted to make sure if Mr. Cartwell come look'n for me, I would have a family member he'd have to ask for my hand."

Lark grasped her fingers. "You need to let Beau know this. You've seen how he takes in women who have suffered. He will keep you safe." He wanted to add, he would also keep her safe, but didn't want her to know how she affected him.

"I will, when the time is right." She squeezed his hand. "Thank you for com'n to my aid yesterday and for bein' here this mawnin'."

"I am always available to anyone who needs to talk." He donned his hat, released her hand, and stepped out the door. It was going to be another hot day, but his body was heated from the inside. Holding Savannah's hand and peering into her beautiful face, he'd had stirrings that he'd never thought he'd have for a woman.

Savannah stood by the door, watching the reverend walk away. Her heart raced, reliving his touch both during grace and while standing here discussing her fears. She'd never experienced the same intensity with a preacher before.

"Are you ready?" Freedom walked down the hall, a bonnet on her head and a small reticule dangling from her gloved hand.

In Georgia, even though the darkies were freed after the war, they had their own stores and communities. She'd never gone shopping with anyone of color before. "Are you sure you want to go?" she asked.

Freedom crossed her arms and glared. "You, southern girl, too good to be seen with the likes of me?"

"No. I mean. Where I come from, your people have their own stores and don't mix with…" she knew she'd stuck her foot in her mouth by the scowl on the other woman's face.

"My people. What is my people? My color? I bleed red just like you and I have feel'n's just like you. If you don't want me to show you where to purchase boots all you have to do is say so." Freedom spun on her heel.

"No. I mean, don't go."

Freedom spun back around.

"I want you to take me. That is if'n you can get into the store." There she went again saying something that appeared to give the woman a sour stomach.

"People here don't care about where you come from or what you are. If you have money to buy and don't steal, they treat everyone the same." She stepped to the door. "Get your things. I'll be on the porch enjoy'n the fresh air."

Savannah let out a sigh and hurried up the stairs. She opened the hole in the lining of her satchel and pulled out two dollars, placing them in her reticule. The only hat she had was the one she'd worn the whole trip. She plucked the feathers from the band, pinned the more sedate bonnet on her head, pulled on a pair of gloves, and picked up her reticule.

Freedom stood on the porch, her eyes closed, basking in the sunshine pouring down from the bluest sky Savannah had ever seen.

"I'm ready."

The younger woman startled. Her body pitched forward a bit as if taking off in flight. She regained her composure and nodded, stepping off the porch and onto the dirt.

Savannah wondered about her story, but realized this was not the time to ask. "The little I saw of the town yesterday there seemed to be a pile of stores."

Freedom nodded. "With Shady Gulch being a train stop, we can get anything we want. There is the general mercantile which will have boots, but they don't fit as nice as the ones made by the bootmaker, Mr. Markov."

The young woman walked down the street alongside the boarding house, across the alley, and beside another building. When they turned the corner, Savannah noticed the building on the corner was The Silver Dollar Saloon.

"Which place, the mercantile or the bootmaker, has the better price?" she asked, knowing if she didn't find a job and was at the mercy of her brother, she would have little money for necessities.

"The bootmaker will be twenty cents more, but the shoes will be more comfortable and last longer." Freedom stopped at the door to the building next to the Silver Dollar.

Markov Bootmaker was printed in square letters on the window.

Freedom opened the door and walked in.

The smell of leather, linseed, and wax, along with pungent cigar smoke, met Savannah as she entered the building.

"Miss Freedom, you cannot have worn out your shoes so soon." A short stocky man with a cigar in his mouth looked up and grinned around the stogie.

"Mr. Markov, Miss Savannah needs a new pair of shoes." Freedom walked along a wall with readymade uppers. "Something like this." She plucked a dark brown pair of button shoes off the shelf.

"Miss Savannah, are you staying in our town or

passing through?" The man stood, revealing a three-legged stool. He walked toward them.

"I'm hope'n to stay." Savannah had learned that in a community this small everyone knew each other. Which would be good to discover more about her brother, but not as good to keep her life private.

"Take off shoes." He dropped a square of leather on the floor.

Freedom led her over to a stool. "He's goin' to trace your feet so the boots fit you well."

She nodded. Back in Georgia, before her mother spent all the money, she'd had several pairs of shoes custom made. Her favorite had been a pair of opera slippers.

When her shoes sat on the floor beside her feet, Mr. Markov waved her over with his wide hand. "Come. Stand here." He pointed to the leather he'd tossed on the floor.

She stepped on the soft hide and lifted her skirt just enough he could see her feet.

The bootmaker knelt in front of her and traced around both feet, never touching her.

"Done."

Savannah backed up and he lifted the leather as he stood.

"Did you like these?" Freedom asked, still holding the pair of uppers.

"Yes." Savannah really didn't care what the shoes looked like as long as they were comfortable and practical. While she loved fancy things, she'd learned they weren't necessary. Food and a roof were the only material things that mattered.

"I will have these for you this afternoon," Mr. Markov said, taking the uppers from Freedom.

"Thank you. How much do I owe?" she asked, reaching into her reticule.

"New customer. One dollar and twenty cents." He held up a hand. "You pay when you pick up. If no like, no buy."

She nodded and followed Freedom out of the building. She'd never heard a dialect like his before. "Where did Mr. Markov come from?" she asked Freedom.

"He's Russian. He's a very nice man. He sends money to his family in Russia, hoping his wife and children can join him." Freedom glanced up and down the street. "Do you want me to show you where everything is?"

"Do you have time?" Not that Savannah wanted the woman to go to the saloon at all, but she didn't want to get her new friend in trouble with Beau.

"I do." They walked on down the street with Freedom pointing out the sheriff's office, Mrs. Cleary's Café, and the mercantile across from the bank. She'd missed that the day before because Reverend Webster had entered the bank with her satchel and she hadn't wanted it out of her sight. They turned to the left and down the next street was a hotel, attorney, another café, and the Mad Dog Saloon.

"Mrs. Polzin is a good seamstress," Freedom said, pointing to a small building on the end of the street.

Savannah noticed ahead of them was the church and cemetery. In a corner of the lot sat a small house. That had to be where the reverend lived. She scanned the area, wondering if she'd catch a glimpse of him.

"That big house there is a boarding house." Freedom pointed to a house across from the church. "Mrs. Malley runs it with her two boys. The single men live there. Sheriff Blake, his deputy, the attorney, Mr. Howard from the Land Grant Office, and Charlie, the bank teller."

"And is that the school behind the board'n house?" She didn't really care about the school but it kept her from gawking at the church.

"Yes. Mrs. Beal and Miss Walker are the teachers. Mr. Beal runs the train depot." Freedom walked toward the church. "This is the only church in town so far. Mr. Webster, the banker, he asked his brother, Reverend Webster, to come start up a church about three or four years ago. It was a year or so before I come." She glanced at the cemetery. "I know the cemetery ain't fillin' up near as fast since the preacher come."

"Is that because Reverend Webster is a good preacher?" Savannah stole a peek toward the house.

"Don't know if it's him or Sheriff Blake. Between the two of them, they's doin' a good job of settin' people straight." Freedom walked on by the house without saying if it was where Reverend Webster lived.

Savannah didn't want to ask and draw attention to her interest in the man.

"That house there, second one over is Mr. Webster, the bank manager's, house. He and his wife and baby live there."

That was an opening. "Reverend Webster doesn't live with his brother?"

Freedom grinned. "No. He lives in that little house by the church." She laughed. "The one you were staring at. I figured you were wonderin' but wanted to see if you was interested in him. He sure does touch you a lot."

Her face heated from embarrassment. She'd thought the man was just a caring preacher.

"Don't worry. If you work at the saloon, he won't treat you no different. Reverend Webster is different than most church men. There's gossip he wasn't a preacher long before he come here. Some say he was a gunfighter. Others say he was an outlaw. Something went wrong and he decided to make peace with his maker and become a preacher." Freedom stopped at the corner of the boarding house. "I showed you all the places for a woman to work in this town. You ain't gonna find a job. You might's well plan to start at the Silver Dollar on Monday. If you talk to Mrs. Polzin now, she can have a dress ready for you."

Freedom walked into the boarding house.

The thought of working as a saloon girl made Savannah's teeth grind and her stomach churn. Even if Beau didn't let the men touch, just parading around in the revealing dress would make her skin crawl.

"I forgot to fetch paper to write up my qualifications." She backtracked to the street in front of the saloon and walked down the boardwalk toward the mercantile.

This time, she peered into each establishment. There were more people milling about the streets as it was nearly mid-day. She glanced into the café and spotted Reverend Webster. He sat at a table with a young man and woman. Was he working with them to prepare a wedding or was he counseling them? She realized she'd stared too long when someone bumped her.

A mumbled, "Sorry," drew her attention to the board walkway. Three young men were walking abreast toward the saloon, making people step out of their way. As she continued to watch, a tall man, with a gun belt slung low on his right hip, crossed the street and confronted the three. Watching, she caught a glint of sunlight off a badge on the man's vest. He must be the sheriff.

The three young men waved their weapons. One

hollered, "What do you think you can do to us. You're one old man."

"I'm not asking you again." The sheriff's voice grew louder, but his stance remained firm and unmoving.

Fascinated by the confrontation, she continued in the wake of the three young men. She was no more than ten feet behind them, when a hand grasped her arm, pulling her into the saloon.

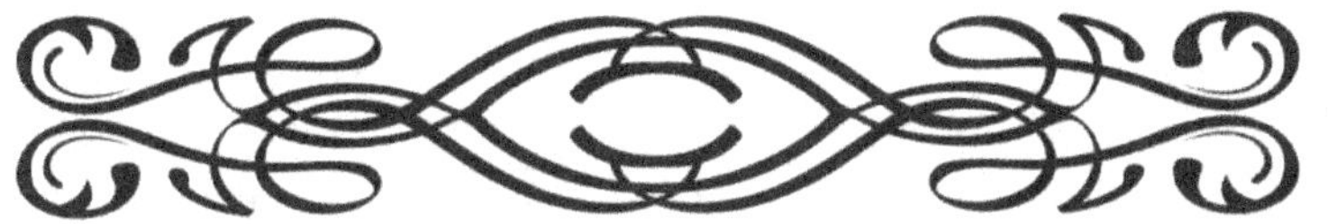

Chapter Six

A shriek caught in Savannah's throat at the same moment she recognized the hand. She knew who had dragged her into the Silver Dollar. Beau released her the minute the door closed behind her.

"Are you dimwitted, walking up behind those three?" he bellowed.

"They bumped into me. I was curious about them." She rubbed her arm where he'd grabbed her and glared back at him. "You had no right drag'n me in here like a catfish on a line."

"I wasn't fishing for you. But, if you are my sister, I am obliged to protect you. One of those men could have started shooting at Ty, and you'd have been behind them when he shot back." Beau scowled at her, then stomped to the bar.

"Shot?" Her blood went ice cold, sending shivers to her hands and feet.

"This isn't the east. If you haven't noticed, people out

here pack guns to use. And more times than not it's on each other." He picked up a rag and rubbed the top of the bar.

She wandered to the dark wood bar, noticing a man slumped over a table in a corner and another man sipping from a mug of beer. The place was quiet. A good time to look around. She walked over to the piano and tapped a couple of the keys.

"You know how to play that?" Beau asked.

"Yes, but not the type of music your d—Jules was play'n." She caught herself before calling what appeared to be a good friend to Beau by an unflattering word. After spending the morning with Freedom, she'd realized out here people with dark colored skin weren't treated any different than the person who could barely speak English or the person who ran the bank.

"We have patrons who would like to hear what you play." He nodded to the small stage. "If you played the piano, you wouldn't have to dance."

She spun toward him. "I'll not be work'n here. I was headed to the mercantile for paper when I became distracted." Savannah walked toward the door. "I need to finish my errand."

Beau was beside her in four long strides. "Let me check to make sure Ty has things under control." He opened the door and stepped out.

She didn't wait for his response, pushing the other door open and standing next to him. The young men had left.

"What was that about, Ty?" Beau asked the man standing on the walkway watching the three men.

The sheriff pivoted on a boot heel. His gaze slipped off Beau as if he had grease all over him and landed on her. "I believe I saw the preacher carrying the back of your skirt yesterday." He touched the brim of his hat and grinned. Sandy blond curls peeked out from under his hat. He had blue-gray eyes and a crooked nose.

"What is he talking about?" Beau asked, spinning toward her.

"My wobbly boots made cross'n the un-cobbled street a trial," she said, frowning at the sheriff. From the glint in his eyes, he wasn't about to let it go.

"We haven't been introduced." The sheriff pulled his hat off and held out his other hand. "Sheriff Tyson Blake, at your service."

She put her hand in his. "Savannah Gentry."

His gaze shot to Beau. "When did you get married?"

Beau took a step toward Sheriff Blake. "I haven't. This is my sister." His menacing voice and the way he'd made his body look twice its size, she was surprised the sheriff hadn't taken a step back or shown any fear.

Instead, he grinned bigger. "Sister. We can always use pretty, marriageable women in town. Welcome, Miss Gentry."

"Savannah, go on and get your items from the mercantile," Beau ordered.

Any other time she would have made exception with being told what to do, but while the sheriff didn't frighten her, the way he stared made her feel like she wore the skimpy clothing of the saloon girls.

She pivoted and headed toward the mercantile. The rumble of Beau and the sheriff's voices faded with each step she took. The door of the café opened. Reverend Webster, and the couple he had been seated with, stepped out. A smile spread across the preacher's face as his gaze met hers.

Lark couldn't believe his good fortune to have run into Savannah. "Miss Gentry, may I introduce you to Arvid Isberg and Maura Flanagan. We've been discussing the sanctity of marriage and how each person who comes into wedlock must be ready for the commitment." He'd been trying to keep the two young people from marrying for a month. It wasn't their completely different cultures that bothered him but Maura's immaturity. While Arvid believed he could provide for them, and most certainly would, Lark feared the young woman did not fully realize the duties that would be expected of her, and she would soon become weary of them and her husband.

"How do you do," Savannah said, nodding at Arvid and Maura.

"Thank you for speaking with us, Reverend Webster." Arvid shook hands with him and led Maura down the walk to the mercantile.

"They look awful young to be marry'n," Savannah said in a low voice.

"That is my fear. I have been counseling them in hopes the young woman will realize marriage isn't always good times."

Savannah's cream-colored skin took on a tinge of red. He'd embarrassed her. Her bold tongue made him forget she was a woman of proprieties.

"I'm sorry, I shouldn't have aired my concerns." He glanced up and down the street. Beau and Ty were standing on the far corner talking. Two women he knew walked down the boardwalk on the opposite side of the street. He nodded to them and asked Savannah, "Where are you going?"

"I'm fetch'n paper to write up my qualifications. Would you care to walk with me to the mercantile?" She started toward the building next door to the café.

He fell in step beside her. "I would have thought you'd have those written and passed out by now."

"Freedom took me to the bootmaker first thing and then gave me a tour of the town." She glanced his way briefly. "The church is nice. Do you like the small house you live in?"

He studied her a moment before opening the mercantile door. "I do like my house. It is better than living in a boarding house."

She entered the establishment, a frown marring her pretty face.

What had he said to have her thinking unpleasant thoughts?

"Reverend Webster, Maura told us she and Arvid were just talking with you." Mrs. Flanagan peered at the curtain blocking the view into the back room of the store.

No one walked through as Lark escorted Savannah to the stationary.

The storekeeper hustled over to where he stood and whispered, "It doesn't sound like you've been able to shake Maura's belief she is ready to marry."

He shook his head. Mrs. Flanagan and Mrs. Isberg were against the marriage. Both were concerned about the same thing he was, Maura's not being ready to take on the role and responsibilities of being the wife of a farmer. "I'm afraid I've said everything I can think of without coming out and telling them we don't believe Maura is ready."

Savannah faced him and Mrs. Flanagan with several sheets of paper and a quill and ink. "What if someone, like myself, were to sit down and have a chat with her? I can tell her how I had to go from fancy clothes and lots of social engagements to clean'n and cook'n. It wasn't how I had planned to spend my time, but someone had to do it." She touched Mrs. Flanagan's arm. "I can tell her of the chores she'll be expected to do on her own and how her husband will come in tired to the bone from work'n and won't even mention if the food was good or not, or that she starched the curtains."

Lark heard the hurt in her voice. She'd worked hard to help her father keep their house and land, and what she received in return was to secret away to keep from being the bride of a money-hungry banker.

"Miss Gentry talking with Maura might help. She's new to the community and Maura won't think anyone put her up to it if they meet somewhere." The more Lark thought about it, the more he liked the idea. Not only would it possibly save two young people sorrow down the road, but it would put Savannah in the good graces of Mrs. Flanagan, a woman of influence in the town.

"We've tried everything else." Mrs. Flanagan plucked the items from Savannah and strode to the counter at the back of the store.

Lark motioned for Savannah to follow.

The storekeeper said, "That will be ten cents." Then she leaned forward and whispered. "Maura will be at Mrs. Cleary's café this afternoon around three. She is meeting her friend Sigrid. I'll make sure Sigrid is late."

Savannah handed Mrs. Flanagan two nickels and picked up her goods. "I'll be there."

Lark tipped his hat to the woman and followed Savannah out onto the walkway. "You don't have to try to help me or Mrs. Flanagan," he said, falling in step beside her.

"I'm not do'n it for you or Mrs. Flanagan. I'm do'n it for Maura. I know what it's like to be starry-eyed and think your life is go'n to be one way, and out of your control, it becomes someth'n completely different."

"You're still reeling from your mother's betrayal and your father's death." The words came out before Lark realized he'd said them and not thought them.

Savannah stopped and faced him. The sadness in her eyes had him reaching toward her. She shook her head, stopping him from being seen holding a woman in daylight in the middle of town.

"You're right. I am still try'n to make sense of my mother, my daddy, and now my brother. I have the Gentry stubbornness and no matter what happens, I will not become my mother, nor will I let someone walk all over me as my daddy allowed my mother." Her shoulders slumped. "It was as if he didn't care what she did as long as he didn't have to be with her." Her blue eyes gazed into his. "I never understood their marriage. Read'n the letters Beau's mother wrote to Daddy. I don't understand how he left her when it was clear their love was real and my parents' love was only for society."

Lark cupped her elbow and turned her to continue walking. Given how closed-mouthed Beau was about his past, standing in the street discussing her family wasn't a wise thing to do.

"Even the best-intentioned parents don't always see the harm they do to their children." He'd seen it time and again, while growing up and then as an adult, how parents unknowingly put their unhappiness onto their children.

"A good reason to never marry and never have children," Savannah said, stopping at the corner of the street. "I thank you for walk'n with me to the mercantile. You have duties to attend, and I have qualifications to write." She picked up the front of her skirt and stepped into the street, heading toward the boarding house.

"I hope you don't truly believe that marriage is a bad thing, Savannah Gentry," Lark said to her retreating back. Since meeting the woman, he'd witnessed her kindness and loyalty. She'd make an excellent wife and mother for some lucky man.

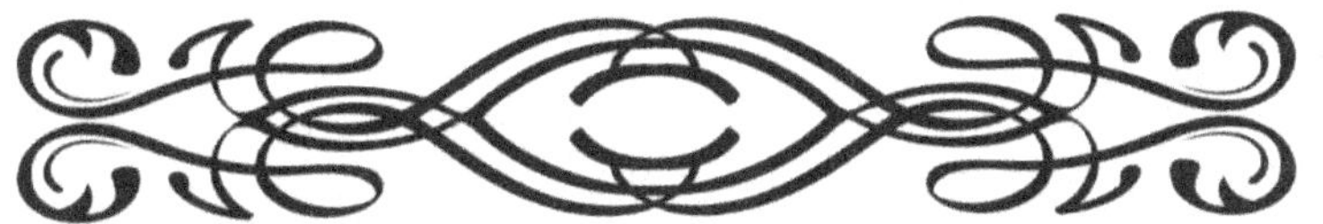

Chapter Seven

Savannah had six papers in her hand stating her qualifications for any type of work that could be found in Shady Gulch. She had decided to try the two cafes, bank, mercantile, and the two hotels. She'd rather clean rooms than work as a saloon girl. Her first stop was at Mrs. Cleary's café. She spotted Maura sitting at a table by herself.

Before sitting down, she walked up to the proprietor and handed her one of the papers. "How do you do, I'm Savannah Gentry. I've moved to Shady Gulch and would be tickled if I could work for you."

Mrs. Cleary barely glanced at the paper that Savannah had carefully scribed. "I'm sorry dearie, but I can't afford to take on help." She shook her head. "I doubt the Pedersens can either. When the trains come in, we're so busy my feet hurt but in between…" She waved her arms, showing there were only three people in the establishment.

"Thank you for your time." Savannah turned and

pasted on a smile for the young woman she'd offered to talk to.

"Gentry? Are you any relation to Beau who owns the Silver Dollar?" Mrs. Cleary asked.

Savannah spun back toward the woman. "His sistah." Hope surged that the woman had a soft spot for her brother. "Does that make a difference in me work'n for ya?"

"No, just wondering."

Her heart sunk, and she walked by the table where Maura sat. She nodded to a chair next to the young woman. "May I sit a spell?"

The young woman's brow wrinkled into a frown. "Why would you want to sit with me?"

"I wanted to congratulate you on your wedd'n and ask you about Shady Gulch. Since your parents own the mercantile, I'd imagine you've met purt near everyone in town and who live close by."

Maura's face lit up. "I do. That's how I met Arvid. He came to the store to purchase items for his family's farm." Her cheeks brightened when she mentioned her fiancé's name.

"Your face lights up like a noon day sun when you say his name." Savannah wondered if she'd ever feel that for a man. She mentally shook her head. While she didn't see the need for a husband, and didn't understand how a marriage could be good for both parties when it was evident that love between her daddy and Beau's mother didn't work and yet the arranged marriage between her daddy and mother hadn't worked either. Why *did* so many people marry?

"I can't wait to be married, so we can spend more time together." Maura's cheeks darkened in color and she leaned closer. "We can't wait to make babies," she whispered.

Savannah stared at the young girl. "Why would you want young'ns already? They're a heap o' work."

The girl wrinkled her nose and whispered. "It's not really the babies I want, it's the coming together as a man and woman."

This was something she had not experienced nor felt the desire to be that intimate with a man. But from the sparkle in the young woman's eyes, it was something she craved.

"I see. Do you think that's a good reason to get married? Just to satisfy a carnal curiosity?"

Maura leaned back. "That's not it. I love Arvid, and I want to be with only him."

"Have you been to his family's farm, seen the work that the women do every day?" Savannah was of a mind to tell her to bed the man, but should she become with child, the two would have to marry, giving the woman no recourse if she decided the life was too much for her.

"No."

"Before you take this desire any further, you need to spend a day or two at the farm and realize what Arvid would expect from you as his wife. That's figur'n he's go'n to continue on the family farm or purchase a farm of his own."

"Oh yes, he's put money down on a place not far from his family. He and his brother are building our home." Maura's gaze turned dreamy. "When they finish, I get to pick out all the furniture from a catalog in Papa's store."

The bell above the door jingled and a young woman walked in. She spotted Maura and headed to the table.

"I appreciate you talk'n with me." Savanah stood. "Reckon about what I said."

"I will." Maura smiled at her friend and they started chatting.

Savannah, with her papers in hand, left the café and walked to the mercantile. This time Mr. Flanagan was manning the store.

"Howdy." She went through her speech as before.

"What brought you to Shady Gulch?" Mr. Flanagan asked.

"My brother."

He glanced at the page again and glanced up. "Gentry. Related to Beau?"

"Yes."

"Funny, no one ever mentioned he had family." The storekeeper scratched at his head covered in thick salt and pepper hair.

"We're a family who likes to be private. Which would be good for work'n here, where I'm sure there are thangs your customers would like to keep hushed." She raised an eyebrow.

"That's true, but we really can't pay anyone to help out. My wife and children help me." Mr. Flanagan handed her paper back to her. "Good luck, but I've a feeling you'd be quicker to marry than to find a job around here."

She scowled at the man. She'd work in Bismarck, if she had to, rather than marry to stay in Shady Gulch. She'd left everything she knew rather than be in a loveless marriage.

Lark stepped out onto the small porch and stretched. He'd been working on Sunday's sermon all afternoon and needed a bit of fresh air. He spotted Savannah walking slowly along the opposite side of the street.

"Miss Gentry!" he called and walked toward her.

Savannah stopped. The sadness in her eyes told him her work seeking hadn't gone well.

"I need a bit of a breather from my sermon, care to see the inside of the church?" He knew to take her into his house would cause a stir, but the church would look as if he were extending her an invitation to church on Sunday.

She nodded but didn't say anything.

He was proud of the little building. He'd preached at the Silver Dollar for a year before the townsfolk decided he could stay and they would build the church. His brother paid for the small house he lived in.

The pride and joy of the congregation were the beautiful stained-glass windows Beau had ordered from a man in New Orleans. Lark's favorite was the conversion of Saul. A man with raised arms, his face pointed to the ray of light shining down. When he'd been at his lowest and felt a bullet from a Pinkerton, Marshal, or his own gang would surely be his death, he'd discovered the light. Letting the Topeka Kid fade into legends, he'd entered a college of theology.

His favorite window was one of seven different depictions across several denominations.

"All the churches in Georgia have gothic style designs," Savannah said, standing in front of each window, studying the images and colors.

"I give the sermons most Sundays, but if a traveling preacher of another faith comes through, he preaches." He waved at the two closest windows. "That's why there are different styles and depictions. Allowing other faiths to use the same house of worship has worked well to keep the whole community involved in the raising and upkeep of the church."

She faced him. "That's a good idea when a town isn't large enough for more than one church."

He didn't like how somber she acted. "Have you talked with all the businesses in town?" He led her over to a pew and they sat, facing one another.

She nodded and pulled neatly written papers out of her bag. "They all looked at the paper, asked if I was Beau's sistah, and handed it back, say'n they couldn't afford to hire anyone."

"I had a feeling that would happen. I'm sorry." He wanted to put his hand over hers, but restrained. The raw emotions he experienced when in her presence had his mind turned sideways. He wanted to act like any other man smitten with a woman, but he couldn't, given his profession, and he didn't want to scare her by being too forward.

Savannah peered into his eyes. "I won't work in the saloon. I'll move to Bismarck and find work there."

His heart leapt into his throat. Lark swallowed hard, twice, to get passage for the words he wanted to say. "Don't be hasty. If you're in Bismarck, you won't have anyone to help if you need it."

Her eyes narrowed as she stared at him. "You bein' a man of the cloth, why would you think I should work in a saloon rather than go to a town where I won't know anyone?"

"As Mrs. Dearling and I told you, the ladies who work for Beau are treated different. It's known that they aren't painted up ladies and only provide entertainment." He had talked with Beau earlier. "I stopped by the saloon a while ago. Beau mentioned you could play the piano, and I suggested that he could have you dress more conservatively and only play the piano, not serve or work the long hours the others do." He took a deep breath and spit out the rest of what he wanted to say. "And if you can play hymns, I'll see if we can get an organ for the church. You can play on Sundays. That would show the community that you are only at the saloon for your piano playing."

"How would you see that an organ was given to the church?" Her eyes brightened. "We could do a pie social and start raisin' money."

He held back the smile twitching his lips. "You know a thing or two about pie socials?"

"Yes! I raised enough money for the church back home to purchase a beautiful bell they rang every Sunday to call the community to service." Her enthusiasm brought the sparkle back to her eyes and straightened her back.

"I would be pleased to help you with the pie social to raise money for an organ." He didn't want to change her good mood, but he had to add, "Does this mean, you'll forget about going to Bismarck for work?"

"If all I have to do is play piano at the saloon." Her nose wrinkled. "I've slopped hogs and had to clean the chicken roost since Daddy's downfall, but there were a handful of men in the saloon the other day that nearly tossed my stomach. How do the others bear the stench?"

"It's amazing what a person will do when it's a matter of survival." He thought back to the time he'd hid in an outhouse for six hours waiting for darkness so he could creep out of town.

"I'm sure the good Lord didn't put whiskey on this earth so's a man would spend so much time in a saloon that their body reeks of liquor. Especially, if he has a wife and young'ns." Her eyes narrowed. "What are your ideas about that?"

"I agree. A man with a family should be with them and not hanging around in a saloon." He peered into her eyes. The irritation in her eyes melted, giving him a glimpse into her blue pools. He liked what he saw.

Their hands touched on the pew. He clasped her hand, holding it gently. "When do you want to start working on the pie social?"

"The what?" Her eyes had softened and her body leaned towards his.

He couldn't have drawn his body back if a lawman stood between them. He pressed his lips to hers, softly, a chaste kiss to not alarm her. He'd had his number of women, mostly prostitutes while riding with the Dellinger gang, but nothing had prepared him for a kiss that shook him to his toes and started his heart racing.

Savannah leaned back. "Lord a mercy," she whispered, pressing her fingers to her lips.

The door of the church banged open.

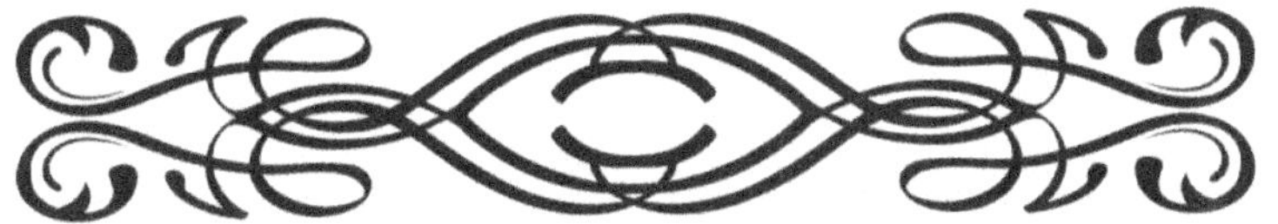

Chapter Eight

Savannah gasped as a man hurried down the aisle between the pews. He glanced at her but turned his attention to Lark.

"Reverend, my daddy is calling for you. He says the Lord has come to take him and he wants a word with you."

Lark stood, drawing her up with him. "Miss Gentry, we'll continue our conversation later. Eddie, I'll get my things and meet you at the ranch."

The man nodded and hurried back down the aisle.

"Where are you go'n?" Savannah asked, as Lark escorted her to the door.

"Mr. Cullen has been ill for several months. He asked me to be with him when he goes to our Lord." Lark closed the church door and faced her. "I may not be around for a day or two. When I get back, I'll look you up and we'll begin work on the pie social." His gaze sought hers.

She saw more in his eyes than working together, there was a promise of another kiss. "I could go with you." She waved her hand. "Give support." She told herself it wasn't to be with the man but to help him as he comforted the family.

He grinned. "Having you along would make the ride to and from the ranch more pleasant, but you would be bored as I wait for Mr. Cullen to take his last breath." He touched her cheek. "Knowing you will be here when I return will make this trip more bearable."

Her cheeks heated at his touch and words. "I'll be here. I won't go to Bismarck look'n for work."

"Good. If you were there I could only see you once a week." He nodded to the street. "I need to go. Would you like me to escort you back to the boarding house?"

"No, I need to see Mrs. Polzin about a dress." Savannah pivoted, feeling lighter than she had all day. The reverend wanted her to stay in Shady Gulch. She touched her lips and a pang of guilt caught in her chest like she'd swallowed a peach pit. Reverend Webster had kissed her. On the lips. How had she let herself be so brazen? She should have slapped him or stood up, not allowing their lips to touch. She brushed her fingertips across her lips. The soft touch reminded her of the kiss, stirring her insides again and giving her a warm, fuzzy feeling. She'd never felt this way before.

She glanced over her shoulder, catching a final glimpse of Lark as he entered his house. Did he ride a horse or use a buggy? She'd seen neither around his small house. There wasn't a pasture for an animal either.

At the door to the seamstress's establishment, she looked back and spotted Lark trotting toward town with a saddlebag over his shoulder. That answered her question, he would be riding a horse. The livery sat on the other side of town not far from the train depot.

Pushing the door open, the sound of chaos met her ears.

A young woman scolded a small boy, while a toddler cried. She didn't understand the language the woman spoke, but could tell she was unhappy with the boy.

"Pardon," Savannah said loud enough to be heard over the noise.

The young woman spun around. Her features were dainty, her body appeared frail. "May I be of help?" she asked in a soft voice.

The small boy ran into the back room and the little girl sniffed, her wide eyes full of tears as she stared at Savannah.

"I'm in need of a dress. I'll be play'n piano at the Silver Dollar Saloon." Savannah walked over to the bolts of fabric leaning up along a wall. They all appeared to be quality goods.

"I make dresses for Mr. Gentry's girls." Mrs. Polzin drew the tape measure from around her neck. "You will step behind screen. Take off outer clothing." Her accent sounded a bit like the bootmaker's.

"I won't have a dress like the other girls. Mine will go to the floor, have long sleeves, and a modest neckline."

Mrs. Polzin frowned. "You must be special to not wear same dress as others."

"I'm his sistah."

The woman's face lit up. "Welcome to Shady Gulch!"

Savannah smiled. "Thank you." This petite woman liked her brother. She wondered if he felt the same about her.

An hour after arriving at the store, she walked out

assured she would have a dress to wear by Monday evening. And Mrs. Polzin would deliver the dress to the saloon.

The sun cast a lazy evening glow on the streets as she headed toward the boarding house.

"Miss Gentry!"

She turned at the holler. The sheriff walked briskly toward her.

"I was hoping to get a chance to visit with you," he said, stopping in front of her.

"I need to get back to the board'n house. Mrs. Dearlin' will be wonder'n where I am." She made to step around him.

"I'll escort you there myself." He grasped her arm, looping it through his and leading her down the street.

"Well, bless your heart, but I can find my own way," she said, trying to pull her arm from his grasp.

"No need to throw a fuss. Any woman in this town would be pleased to have me escort them home." He shot her a grin she was sure melted most women, but she didn't care for a man who was full of himself.

"You can't bumfuzzle me. I am not any woman. Let me loose, or I swan, I'll start scream'n." She inhaled, getting ready to screech like an opossum caught by a hound when he released her arm and took a step to the side.

"You don't have to get all uppity." He frowned, touched the brim of his hat, and walked off.

She grinned and strode to the corner of the boarding house. There was only one man she'd tolerate touching her. Her lips tingled thinking of her kiss with Lark. She'd never cottoned to all the things she'd heard and read about kissing a man, but after this afternoon, she was wondering if she should have paid more attention.

Savannah entered through the front door.

"Where have you been? I didn't know whether to wait supper for you or not." Mrs. Dearling stood in the door of the parlor.

"Pardon. I lost track of time. I asked around about work, not a soul was need'n help. Then Reverend Webster called me over to gander at the church." She smiled. "It's beautiful. He talked me out of mov'n to Bismarck and suggested I play piano for Beau and the organ for the church."

"The church doesn't have an organ." The older woman stared at her.

"It will after we have a pie social, a Fourth of July picnic with auctioned baskets, and a Harvest dance." She hadn't mentioned the last two to Lark. She'd thought of them while being measured by Mrs. Polzin.

Mrs. Dearling grinned. "I think you're going to bring some life to this town. Count me in on helping."

"I can use all the help I can get. The socials will bring in more people if you help spread the word. I won't have any information to spread, though, until Reverend Webster returns from the Cullen Ranch." She wondered how far it was and when he would be back.

"Oh dear, that must mean old man Cullen isn't doing well." Mrs. Dearling led her down the hall to the kitchen.

"I believe he is dy'n and wished the reverend to be present." She took a seat, and Mrs. Dearling set a plate of food in front of her. "How far a piece is it to the ranch?"

"Several hours. I'm sure Reverend Webster won't return until Mr. Cullen is buried." The older woman stopped halfway when sitting in the chair across from

Savannah. "I hope he will return for Sunday Services."

Savannah nodded in agreement. After his kiss and parting comments, she was ready for him to return to learn more about the man and the emotions he conjured in her.

This was the part about his job, Lark liked the least, sitting beside a dying person, trying to give hope of the afterlife to them and console the living. Doc Nolan hadn't given Mr. Cullen as many months to live as the crusty old man had lingered. His family knew this day was coming months ago. They all appeared more relieved than sorrowful.

Mr. Cullen had grabbed Lark's hand the minute he walked up to the bed and clung to it like an eagle holding a slippery fish. As his grip lessened, Lark knew the man was slipping away. He softly spoke the prayers that would help the living and give the man peace with his maker.

One last short puff of air released from the man's wrinkled, dry lips and his hand fell limply to the bed.

Lark recited one more prayer and placed the sheet over Mr. Cullen's face. He turned from his spot by the bed and discovered a small child standing in the room. She had tears running down her cheeks.

"He will be strong and healthy where he's going," Lark said to the child.

She nodded. "But I'll miss him."

"Everyone will miss him. Your grandfather was one of the first people to settle in this area." He knelt beside the girl. "He'll be waiting for you in heaven and watching over you."

"Really? He can see what I'm doing?" She wiped at the tears on her face with chubby hands.

"He can. I'm sure he wouldn't want you to cry." Lark stood. His body ached, and he wished he could take up the family's offer to spend the night, but it was Saturday. He needed to get back to Shady Gulch, get some sleep, and be ready for Sunday Service.

Outside, the oldest of the Cullen boys had saddled his horse and held it ready for his departure.

"I can't thank you enough for staying here and making my pa feel at peace," the young, and soon to be called old, Mr. Cullen said, shaking his hand.

"I'm happy I could give your father and your family peace." He patted the man's shoulder. "I don't expect to see you at church tomorrow. You'll be burying your father."

The man nodded. "We surely appreciate you making this trip."

Lark swung up onto his horse and waved, before heading his mount toward town. He'd spent most of the night awake, praying with Mr. Cullen. As the warm sun beat down on him, his eyelids became heavier. He felt his body start to fall and woke quick enough to keep from toppling to the ground.

He slid off the horse and started walking, leading his mount. There had been many times in the years before he became a minister that he'd ridden all night, all day, and all night again to put as much distance between himself and the law. He shook his head. He'd been a boy looking for excitement and had picked the wrong type of people to follow. It was a wonder his brother used him as a courier for his bank, knowing his past. He'd killed a few men. He wasn't proud of it, but it had been him or them. He glanced up into the sun, staring beyond the bright glow to the heavens. Waiting out the law, in an outhouse, he'd promised God he'd change. While he hadn't found his new life exciting until Savannah Gentry arrived, he'd found being a preacher fulfilling.

The rumble of wheels coming down the road, moved him to the side. He glanced at the driver and was happy to see Roger Samson.

"Reverend, what are you doing walking your horse way out here?" the man asked, easing his horses and wagon to a stop beside Lark.

"I was out at the Cullen's putting the old man to rest. Sure could use a ride, I about hit the ground when I fell asleep on my horse."

"Tie your beast to the back of my wagon and hop in. You don't even have to keep me company, you can sleep. I was delivering implements to Rudolf Bader. He pert near talked my ears plumb off." Samson rubbed his left ear.

"Much obliged." Lark tied his horse to the back of the wagon and climbed up into the wooden box. He was pleased to see a pile of burlap bags to cushion him from the board floor.

Once he was settled, he barely remembered the jerk as the horses and wagon moved forward.

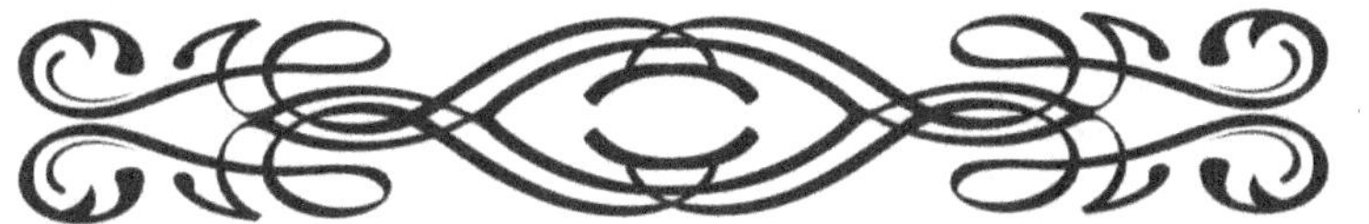

Chapter Nine

Savannah spent Saturday morning making a list of what needed to be done for a pie social. She couldn't write up a notice for the paper until she and Lark settled on a date. All the ladies in the house were excited and wanted to help, but she still didn't believe the community would want saloon girls at a church social. She kept her thoughts to herself because the girls were so excited about the event.

After they had all left to work at the saloon, she became fidgety with nothing to do.

"You can't sit still longer than a cat on a hot stove," Mrs. Dearling said. "Why don't you go talk to Beau about working there."

She stared at the woman. "Why would I want to set foot in that place other than to play the piano?"

"Because, one, he's expecting you to do more than play a piano if you don't go tell him different and, two, you need to learn about your brother." Mrs. Dearling waved her hand around the room. "If he hadn't asked me to run this boarding house for these women after my husband died, I don't know what would have happened to me. My husband was a gambling man who drank too much. When he wasn't losing our money, he would drink until he was mean. We had nothing. And he lost our home, this home, in a card game. When he'd realized what he'd done, he shot himself, leaving me homeless and husbandless all in the same night."

She narrowed her eyes and peered at Savannah. "There's not a woman in this town that doesn't know the kindness of your brother. And not a man who would cross him. If you want to be respected and live here, you'd best help him out. And you'll have a protector all your life."

In the few days she'd lived in the house, Savannah had grown to respect Mrs. Dearling. All the women living here adored her. She treated them as if they were her daughters, doling out love and admonishment like a parent. That the woman had come from such hard times surprised her. She didn't seem harsh or angry. That her brother had once again helped a woman, was becoming less surprising. What had motivated him to be the protector of so many women?

The only way she'd find out would be to spend more time with the man.

As she headed to the kitchen door, Mrs. Dearling said, "Go in the back door of the saloon. No one would expect you to walk in the front door."

She nodded and crossed the alley, her feet carrying her to the back door of the Silver Dollar Saloon. Her fingers shook with anticipation, rather than fear, as she grabbed the handle and gave the door a yank. She had to admit, there was a bit of a rebel in her that was interested in what happened in a saloon. The music, laughter, and loud raucous voices the day she'd arrived had piqued her curiosity.

Jules came through the blanketed doorway from the saloon into the back room. "Pleased to see you, Miss Savannah. Beau has been a bear not knowing what you're doing here." He picked up a barrel, set it on his shoulder, and nodded for her to follow.

Savannah followed behind him, piecing together what he'd said to her. His French Creole accent made her work to figure out what he'd said in his deep, rich voice.

It was Saturday afternoon and the saloon was rowdy. Men stood at the bar talking loudly over the drone of the men gambling and carrying on conversations at the tables. She spotted Freedom standing by the piano as if waiting for Jules to sit down and play. Belle carried a tray of drinks to a table of gamblers and Liesa had a tray of empty glasses walking back to the bar. Lottie Mae was behind the bar helping Beau fill glasses.

She wondered if this was the busiest time for the establishment. Not sure what to do, but not wanting to wander among the tables, she stood at the end of the bar, waiting for Beau to see her.

He glanced over, spied her, and frowned. He said something to Lottie Mae, and walked over to her. "What brings you in here?"

"I wanted to visit, but y'all look busier than a street cleaner after a parade." She raised her voice to be heard over the din.

He nodded to the back room. She understood, they could talk back there without having to shout.

Savannah walked back the way she'd come and turned when she heard a scraping sound.

Beau had placed two wooden chairs next to a box with a kerosene lamp. He lit the lamp and sat, motioning for her to take the other seat.

She sat and studied her brother. He appeared tired. "Do you ever take a break from here?"

"I have nothing better to do with my time." He leaned back. "Why did you pick now to visit the saloon?"

"I was fidget'n and Mrs. Dearlin' suggested we get to know one another better." She squared her shoulders. "I'll play the piano for you in the even'n, but I won't wear the scraps of cloth the other ladies wear. I've already asked Mrs. Polzin to make a dress." She studied him to see if he had any feelings for the seamstress.

He only nodded his head. "Lark told me as much. He seems to have taken an interest in your well-being." This time he studied her.

Savannah's cheeks warmed. "Reverend Webster is a thoughtful man."

A grin transformed her brother's usual glower into a strikingly handsome man. A man who should anyone from Atlanta walk through the door, they would know he was a Gentry.

"It appears you're both sweet on each other." He shook his head. "I've never seen Lark take a shine to a woman so quickly. You better not ruin his reputation." The grin was gone. The same stern expression she'd grown up receiving took away all merriment.

"I don't plan on ruin'n anyone's reputation. I have my own to worry about." She wanted to add, working for him would hurt her reputation but she held her tongue.

The sounds in the saloon grew louder.

Beau glanced at the door. "How about giving the

crowd a performance to show them what they'll hear starting Monday?"

"Play the piano now?"

"Might as well. I figure the music you play will soothe the beasts for a while." He stood and started for the blanket covering the doorway. "If they simmer down, you can stay behind the bar and help me pour drinks."

The man was a puzzle she wanted to piece together. Working beside him would give her a chance to see how he was with others.

She nodded and stood. "But I don't want anyone put'n their hands on me as I walk to the piano."

He grinned. "Not a problem."

Back in the saloon, Beau whistled. Everyone stopped and turned his direction. He motioned for her to step up beside him.

"This is my sister. She's going to play the piano. I don't want any of you lowlife braggarts putting your hands on her or jeering." He motioned for her to walk to the piano.

Savannah swallowed her apprehension and marched over to the upright, her head held high, and her gaze never leaving the black and white keys. Each man leaned back as she passed. Had it been Beau's threat?

At the piano, she sat and realized Beau had followed her through the room.

She did a few warm up exercises to get her fingers limbered up, then began playing the first concerto she'd learned. The crowd had grown quiet.

The music surged and faded in the room.

She held the last chord, allowing the sound to linger in the silence.

Clapping broke the silence and chairs scraped. She turned to her audience and every man was on his feet.

She'd never had such a reaction to her music before. A grin twitched her lips. She let the corners of her mouth tip up and bowed to her audience.

"Nicely done," Beau said, motioning for her to return to the bar.

"Thank you." She walked through the crowd, this time accepting compliments.

"That was something else. Where did you learn to play a piano like that?" Lottie Mae asked.

"I had lessons since I was a young'n. It was the one thing Mother paid attention to. She liked me to play for her parties." The realization struck. Mother had used her for entertainment when she should have been taking her around to social gatherings and helping her meet a husband. Instead, she'd kept Savannah at home, where she wasn't competition.

Beau touched her arm, pulling her from her recollections. "This is the beer. We pour it in these glasses. This is whiskey. It goes in the smaller glasses. Ten cents for a beer, two-bits for whiskey. A bottle of whiskey is a dollar."

She noted all the prices and information.

"You can watch me and Lottie Mae for a bit, then let me know when you want to take over."

She nodded and stood at the end of the bar, watching her brother and Lottie Mae talk and cajole with the men who stood at the other side of the large dark wood structure. The patrons came and went through the doors all afternoon.

Belle and Freedom set empty glasses and a tray on the

bar. "Ready to get supper?" Belle asked.

"Is it that time already?" Savannah had taken over serving at the bar from Lottie Mae twenty minutes after getting her instructions. She'd watched both Lottie Mae and Freedom sing and Belle and Liesa dance, all while keeping the glasses at the bar filled and filling the orders the women brought.

Two men had tried to grab Belle. Both Beau and Jules had approached the men, had words, and the men remained, their hands never wandering from the table again.

She'd noted many of the men's gazes drinking in the women in the scant outfits, but not a hand touched them. She understood what the girls, Mrs. Dearling, and even Lark had been telling her. The women dressed inappropriately, but their behavior was nothing more than a hostess at a restaurant.

Beau walked toward her. "Go get your supper. If you don't mind, I would like you to play again tonight. The men have been asking to hear another song."

She stared out at the crowd. "The men in here now have spent the whole afternoon here?"

"Not all of them. Some asked before they left if you'd be playing tonight." It seemed the grin he'd sported earlier wasn't a fluke. He had the same devilish grin on his lips again.

"I guess I can't deny my audience." She left the establishment, following the other women.

She stepped into the kitchen and was surprised and happy to see Lark sitting at the table.

"How was your trip?" She took the seat next to his as Mrs. Dearling placed filled plates on the table.

"Tiring. If Mr. Samson hadn't come along with his

wagon, I'd be sound asleep on the ground somewhere between Shady Gulch and the Cullen's." Lark couldn't believe his ears when Mrs. Dearling said Savannah was at the saloon. But here she'd walked through the door with Belle and Freedom, her cheeks glowing and eyes dancing.

"Lord a mercy, I'm glad he came along, too!" Her gaze traveled over his face.

Her interest in his welfare set his body humming. "I hear you were at the saloon."

"I played a song this afternoon. The men liked it so well, Beau wants me to play another one tonight." Her eyes sparkled.

"That's good. I take it you told him you are willing to play." He picked up his fork, noting the two women across the table were taking too much interest in their conversation.

"Yes. Land sakes! The saloon has been so busy, I haven't had a chance to tell him about the organ or the pie social." She placed a hand on his arm. "I've also come up with other ways to raise money for the organ."

He smiled. Savannah's enthusiasm and remarkable mind kept him on his toes. "And what are the other ways?" He forked a mound of potatoes into his mouth.

"We can have a picnic basket auction dur'n the Fourth of July celebration and a harvest dance later on. The men would have to purchase tickets to dance with the young women at the harvest dance." She stuck her fork into the chicken on her plate.

"Those are both good ideas. We'll have to run them past the congregation. Would you like to suggest them tomorrow after the service?" He hoped to get an invitation to dinner here after church tomorrow. He wanted to spend as much time with Savannah as he could.

"Do you think they wouldn't mind hear'n about this from someone new to the community?" She worried her bottom lip with her teeth.

The sight of her white top teeth sunk into her rosy lip had him whipping his gaze from her face down to the food on his plate. His body tensed and his shaft hardened. He hadn't been with a woman since becoming a preacher and this woman was testing his resistance.

"They'll be excited someone is willing to help the reverend make the congregation stronger," Mrs. Dearling said, plopping in the chair at the end of the table nearest Lark.

He glanced at the woman and wanted to hide under the table. The knowing expression in her eyes, said he'd already given away his attraction to Miss Savannah Gentry.

Chapter Ten

Savannah couldn't believe how tired and happy she was as she walked up the stairs of the boarding house. She wondered how the other women managed to work such long hours. They had started hours before she'd wandered over earlier in the day and would be there for two more hours. How did they stay happy, with their hours and standing on their feet all day?

The crowd had enjoyed her evening performance. She still couldn't believe that men who would frequent a saloon in Dakota Territory would be so enthralled with Beethoven and Bach. If the men enjoyed it so much, she must make sure she gave a performance for the women of the town as well.

She found the dress she'd arrived in cleaned and the hem taken up in the back, laying on her bed when she entered her room. Mrs. Dearling had cleaned the outfit and made the skirt shorter in the back so she could walk across streets without making a cloud of dust from dragging her skirt.

What would Lark preach about tomorrow? Her chest squeezed thinking about him dressed in his best suit, standing at the pulpit, advising the citizens of Shady Gulch how to live a good life believing in the Lord. Her visits to church the last few years had been few and far between. It was hard to sit through sermons when anger engulfed her. This trip had put distance between herself and her feelings toward her mother. She could sit through the sermon tomorrow with a new-found enjoyment in knowing her path was one she'd picked and not one that was preordained by her mother's excessive spending.

Lark stood at the door of the church. His hands were sweaty and his stomach churned. He'd lost these tendencies months after arriving in town. The town had liked his preaching and had accepted him. But today, the woman he wanted to impress would be sitting in a pew.

"Why is your hand sweating?" Owen asked as he shook hands before entering the church.

Lark shrugged at the same moment his gaze landed on Savannah.

Owen glanced over his shoulder and smiled. "I should have known." He patted his brother on the shoulder and entered the building with his wife and child.

"Good morning, Miss Gentry," Lark said, nodding to the woman he'd been thinking about all morning.

"Reverend. I'm as anxious as a dog wait'n for his meal to hear your sermon." She glided past, leaving her flowery fragrance in her wake.

"Reverend."

He turned his attention to Mrs. Dearling and the other

women staying at her boarding house.

"Mrs. Dearling, Ladies, good morning." They all smiled knowingly, and entered.

Lark continued greeting his parishioners until Mr. Beal tapped him on the shoulder. The depot clerk was one of the church deacons.

Squaring his shoulders, Lark walked up the aisle between the pews, nodding to the people. He noted Beau, Savannah, Mrs. Dearling and the other members of the Silver Dollar Saloon sat in the middle of the building.

During pauses in his sermon, he glimpsed Beau and Savannah exchanging glances and brief words. The brother and sister must have compromised on their differences. This was one of the things he enjoyed about being a preacher—bringing families together and helping them through their struggles.

He ended with a prayer and made eye contact with Savannah for the first time since taking the podium.

"Fellow citizens of Shady Gulch, may I present to you a new member of our community. Miss Savannah Gentry, Beau's sister, will be living here." He motioned for Savannah to stand.

She did and slowly turned, nodding to each member of the congregation before stepping past her brother and walking to the front, standing below the pulpit.

"How do you do. Y'all have a lovely community and church. When Reverend Webster learned I know how to play piano and organ, he suggested we try to come up with the funds to purchase an organ for the church."

Several people nodded in agreement.

"I thought we could start with a pie social." Savannah turned to him.

"The idea of a pie social is a good way to raise money for an organ. What do you think about next Sunday after church?" Lark asked the congregation.

The majority of the people nodded or agreed with the day and time.

"You can talk to Miss Gentry about any questions you have. She and I will be working with others in the community to have an area set up outside for the event." He noted the narrowing of eyes on some of the women. Two especially who had been fawning over him the last year.

"Have a blessed rest of your day," he said dismissing everyone.

Before he could walk out from behind the pulpit to Savannah, she had a half a dozen women surrounding her. Rather than look like a buck in rut, he walked over to Beau and several other business owners talking at the back of the church.

"This pie social, what's it all about?" Wallace Richards, owner of the Shady Gulch Hotel, asked.

"Women in the community bake pies. You can buy it by the slice or a select few whole pies will be auctioned." He wondered if Savannah would bake a pie or just run the event.

"My Sarah could bake a pie and sell slices?" Richards asked.

"Yes. Any woman who wants to bake a pie may."

"Once them men get a taste of her pies, they'll be flocking to our hotel for meals." Mr. Richard walked away rubbing his hands together.

Beau laughed. "Have you tasted Mrs. Richards cooking?"

Lark shook his head. "Can't say as I have."

"I hope you don't give refunds. Whoever buys her pie will want their money back." Beau slapped him on the back and left the church.

There were two young women still visiting with Savannah. They were Sigrid Pedersen, the daughter of Dagmar who owned one of the cafes in town, and Silvia Dentz, the daughter of one of the local farmers.

Lark approached the trio.

"Could my pie be one that is auctioned?" Sigrid asked.

"Why do you want your pie auctioned?" Savannah asked, smiling at the girl.

Sigrid glanced at Silvia and whispered, "I will tell Johnny Malley it is my pie, and he and I can sit together after he buys it." Her young cheeks flushed crimson.

Savannah glanced at Lark over the girl's head. "We'll put names in a hat and pull out a quarter of the pies to be auctioned. If your name is drawn, you may sit with whomever purchases your pie."

Silvia smiled and nodded. But she remained when Sigrid walked away. "Miss Gentry. Would you teach me to play the organ?" Her young gaze slid to Lark, and he cringed at the adoration softening the young girl's eyes.

Savannah smiled. "When the organ arrives, we can set up a time you can learn the instrument."

"Danka," Silvia said, her gaze on him.

"I think your family is waiting for you," Lark said, to pull the young woman's gaze from him.

"Yes. I must go." She hurried down the aisle and at the door spun around. "I'll bring a canned peach pie."

Savannah chuckled.

Lark had never felt so uncomfortable. The woman he had intentions for was laughing at him over a young girl's infatuation.

"She's starry-eyed over you, Reverend Webster," Savannah said.

He shook his head. "I haven't done a thing to encourage her."

"At her age, it doesn't take more than a how do you do to encourage a young heart to think they have found true love." She walked down the aisle.

He fell into step beside her. "Were you smitten at that age?" He wanted to know every detail about her life, but he'd discovered so far, she was almost as tight-lipped about her past as Beau.

"I had a hanker'n for a boy when I was about Sylvia's age." Her eyes narrowed. "However, my mother didn't like any male look'n at anyone but her. She seduced him into her bed and he could never look me in the eye again."

Lark stopped her before they stepped out into the sunshine and people. "That had to hurt. Did your father know, about the boy, his wife..." He was stumbling for the right words.

"Daddy knew mother bedded others. He didn't care as long as she did it discretely." She stared into his eyes. "Do you think it is discrete to walk into your daughter's room and announce what a lovely night you had with the boy she likes?"

Lark put a hand on her shoulder. "Your mother sounds as if she felt threatened by you. And with good reason, you are beautiful."

Tears glistened in her eyes. "I didn't want to compete with her. I wanted a mother to love me. I wanted that more than I wanted the boy to love me."

He pulled her into his arms, holding her. "Not all

women are meant to be mothers, but all women are meant to be loved." He wanted to kiss away her tears, but the sound of jingling harnesses and voices outside would only permit this one embrace. Lark held her away from him. "Dry those tears. You'll need to leave the church before someone comes looking for you. Being alone too long with the preacher could be worse for your reputation than playing piano at the Silver Dollar."

She grinned, pulled a handkerchief out of her sleeve, dabbed her eyes and nose, and exited the building.

Lark wandered up and down between the pews making sure everything was tidy before he headed for the door. It was his ritual to tidy up after service but today it was to regain his composure and allow his heated body to cool. If he hadn't known it before, his body had sealed his notion Savannah could be a woman he would happily marry.

He stepped out of the church and found Beau waiting for him. "I didn't expect to see you here." Lark closed the door and stopped beside his friend.

"When you go to Bismarck this Wednesday, I want you to send this telegraph, to this man." Beau handed him a piece of paper with the name of a solicitor in Atlanta.

"It's not my business, but why am I sending the telegraph from Bismarck when you could send it from here." He read the message. "Are you checking up on your sister?"

"I want to know about her claims of this banker taking everything, and I want to know where her mother is. Both sound like trouble for Savannah."

Lark's chest ached thinking of the pain Savannah's mother had already inflicted on her. "That's a good idea. But why not just send it from here?"

"I don't want Beal, or anyone else in town besides my girls and you, knowing Savannah's past. It will keep her safer." Beau flipped a silver dollar at him. "This should take care of the telegraph." He nodded toward the boarding house. "Mrs. Dearling said there's enough food if you want to come to dinner."

"I'd like that." Lark fell in step alongside his friend.

"That was a rousing sermon. Will there be more on forgiveness now that my sister is in town?" Beau laughed and stretched his stride.

Lark lagged behind. It was good to know Beau was listening. The forgiveness was for them all. Beau to his family and sister, Savannah for herself and her mother, the Silver Dollar ladies for their pasts, and the town for the individuals who worked at the Silver Dollar and anyone else that needed forgiveness to move on with their lives.

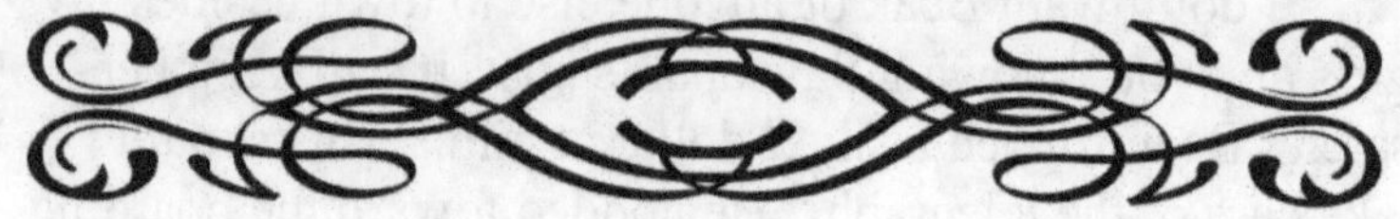

Chapter Eleven

Savannah sat across a table from Lark in Mrs. Cleary's café. They were both printing signs to put up around town about the pie social. She'd already asked the editor of the Shady Gulch Gazette to place the announcement in tomorrow's newspaper.

"Your printing is better than mine," Lark said, gazing at the lettering on her poster.

"That's because I take my time. Slow down. Do you have somewhere else to be?" she asked, teasing him.

"Not unless someone comes looking for me." He pointed with his quill at her block letters across the top. A blob of ink dropped on the paper above her lettering. "Look what I did." He grabbed up a blotter, and she shooed his hands away.

"Leave it be. Land a mercy, you'll make a mess because you're try'n too hard." She used her quill to move the ink around and make a flower. "There, no one will know you dropped ink on my poster." Savannah glanced at the paper in front of him. "You're slower than a turtle carrying a rock." She glanced over at Mrs. Cleary cleaning the counter and listening in. "I would love one of Mrs. Cleary's shugah buns."

"I can do that easier than make this poster." Lark shoved the paper to the center of the table and walked up to the counter.

Savannah studied his fine form as he walked away.

"Don't you worry about going to the devil for watching a preacher with such lust in your eyes?"

The words and vehemence startled her. Savannah peered up at a woman younger than her, but not a child. "I'm sorry, have we met?"

"I saw the way you watched him at the service yesterday and the way he watches you. He'll never marry a woman who plays piano in a saloon. Even if you try to wash away the sins by playing the organ on Sundays." The woman's eyes were narrowed and her face pinched in disgust.

"Bless your heart for care'n about me, but I don't know you, and I would suggest you watch your tongue afore a screech owl comes along and pulls it from your mouth."

Lark walked up to the table. "Miss Walker, have you met—"

"I do not care to meet the likes of her, and I can't believe you would sit in broad daylight with her. You being a preacher and all." The woman pivoted on her heel and marched out of the café.

"What was that about?" he asked, placing the sugar bun on the table and taking his seat.

"I've only played the piano twice at the saloon and

people are already call'n me names." Savannah didn't know whether to be amused or angry. The woman's words rang in her mind. Lark could never fall for a woman who worked in a saloon. Even though he stuck up for the other women who worked at the Silver Dollar, he would have to be careful who he married. The woman would be scrutinized by the whole congregation. This had to be the way the town felt about the other women who worked at the Silver Dollar even though Beau, Lark, and Mrs. Dearling said differently.

"I can't believe Miss Walker would talk that way or confront you. She's such a quiet meek person." Lark stared at the door.

Did he care for the young woman? Her heart lurched. Yesterday, standing in his embrace, inhaling his scent and the calm of the church, she'd felt at peace for the first time in years. She'd had a moment of wistfulness. What would it be like to be the preacher's wife? To help him in his tasks and run events like the pie social? While she hadn't planned on marrying, she could see herself happy with Lark, helping him in his duties.

"Eat your bun. I'll start hanging up the posters we've made already." He picked up the finished pages and headed to the door. Halfway there, he spun around and came back to the table. "Don't let her words worry you. After the pie social, everyone will overlook you're playing piano at the saloon." He disappeared out the door and she stared after him. Did everyone include him?

Lark had never been this antsy waiting for the train to take him back to Shady Gulch. He'd made his usual Wednesday run to Bismarck, dropped off Owen's bank notes, and sent the telegraph for Beau. He had barely sat down at the café near the telegraph office when a boy brought him the solicitor's reply. Even though he wanted to know what was in the message, he'd not opened it. It burned in his inside vest pocket. In his valise, along with the bank papers, were the nuts Savannah had asked him to purchase while in Bismarck. She said, she was going to make him the best pecan pie he'd ever tasted.

He grinned. It would be the best, because he'd never had a pecan pie before. The nuts would give him a chance to see Savannah when he returned. He'd also slip the message to Beau at the saloon.

While he waited for the train to get turned around and ready to head back east, he leaned against the side of the depot. A man with a familiar limp hobbled along the train platform as if in a hurry.

It had been ten or more years since he'd run with the bunch of outlaws led by this man. He couldn't take the chance Wild-Eye Ed Dellinger would recognize him.

Lark ducked his head, hiding behind the brim of his hat until the other man had cleared the platform.

The engine chuffed up to the depot and on by, slowing as the passenger cars paralleled the platform. Lark usually waited to get on until the train started to pull out of the station, today, he was one of the first people. He didn't like hanging around the depot knowing, Wild-Eye Ed was in Bismarck.

He took his usual spot at the back of the last car. With his leg stretched out across the seat, to avoid anyone sitting with him, he leaned his head against the wall right behind the window and pulled his hat down as if he were napping. He watched the people on the platform outside the window, hoping and fearing a glimpse of Ed. If he saw the man, he'd know where he was, but that also gave Wild-Eye the chance to spot him and see a resemblance to the Topeka Kid.

The train whistle blew and the last passengers walked down the aisle. Lark raised his hat and peered at the seated people. None were Wild-Eye Ed, but that didn't mean the man hadn't boarded. He'd have to be cautious when he left the train in Shady Gulch.

This was the first trip he'd made to Bismarck that felt as if he could have walked and returned to Shady Gulch faster. Finally, the train slowed, and the whistle blew, announcing the arrival of the train to the small depot.

Lark straightened, slid his hat back into place and scanned the people in the car, again. Still no one who resembled Wild-Eye Ed. He'd decided to leave the train with the others, to be concealed a bit more than getting off alone.

He didn't know if the old outlaw had even boarded the train, but he was going to be safe rather than sorry. Ty wouldn't be happy if Lark brought trouble to town, and he didn't want Savannah to get caught up in his past. What he didn't understand was why Wild-Eye Ed was in Dakota Territory. He'd always boasted he didn't go west of the Mississippi.

The train stopped, everyone gathered their belongings and started toward the doors.

Lark stood up as the last man leaving through the back door passed him. He followed the man off of the train, his gaze scanned the small depot. Memories of his departure of just a week ago, made him smile. He would much rather save a beautiful woman than be on the lookout for an outlaw.

"Lark!" He swung toward the voice, knowing it wasn't Ed. The outlaw never knew Lark's real name.

He spotted Ty waving at him. What in tarnation did the sheriff want with him? Lark sauntered over to Sheriff Blake. "Why are you yelling at me?"

"Did you happen to see any questionable looking men on the train?" Ty asked.

"Not on the train, but I spotted one walking around the Bismarck depot, why?"

"I received a telegraph that a group of outlaws have been robbing passengers on this line. I thought maybe I could stop them and get a little recognition for the town." Ty shined his star with the cuff of his shirt sleeve.

Lark liked Ty, but his head was bigger than his hat. "Best to let the Pinkertons or the U.S. Marshals deal with the likes of men who'd rob trains." He didn't want to be anywhere near if it was the Dellinger Gang robbing the trains.

Ty shook his head and wandered toward the train.

Lark hightailed it to the bank and the Silver Dollar Saloon. He'd make all his deliveries and get changed into his preacher clothes. One thing he knew about Wild-Eye Ed; he feared preachers and wouldn't look twice at a man with a white collar.

Savannah didn't have to go to the saloon until evening, but she had everything set up for the pie social and couldn't do anything more until Lark brought her the pecans to make her pie. She entered the Silver Dollar through the back door and held the blanket, that blocked off the storage room from the saloon, open just enough she could peek out and see if Beau was too busy to visit.

They'd started the habit on Monday night of her coming in early and he'd take a break. They sat here in the back talking, getting to understand the others life, and commiserate the wrongs handed them by their parents. But one thing they both agreed on, while a saloon didn't seem like the best place for a woman to find her strength, this saloon and the people in it, including Mrs. Dearling, was the best possible place for a woman in trouble to get back on her feet.

Tonight the saloon was packed. She watched Lottie Mae, Jules, and Beau all working like crazy to keep the thirsty men satisfied. Beau strode toward the back room, and she moved to the side.

"It looks busy," she said as he picked up a keg of beer.

"This is the third keg I've packed in. Do you mind helping out?" He stopped beside her. "Just pour behind the counter. That will let Lottie Mae help serve the tables."

"I can help." She followed him into the room, flinching at the noise. The building had never sounded so boisterous as it did tonight.

"Glad to see you came early," Lottie Mae said, sliding a mug of beer across the counter to a man of about thirty with eyes that looked as if he'd had more than enough beer already.

"Beau said he wanted me to take over so you can wait tables." Savannah looked around for the large white towel she'd tied around her waist the last two nights to keep her dress from getting soiled.

Jules walked up to her. "Mrs. Polzin, she bring this by for you today." It took her a minute to understand his words through his thick French Creole accent. He held up a full-length, white apron.

She grasped the shoulders and slid her arms through. "What gave her the notion to make this?"

Jules nodded toward Beau and Lottie Mae. "Those two, they think you should have one." With his impeccable manners and exotic way of speaking, Savannah no longer thought of Jules as a darky. He was her brother's best friend and had the same determination that no one treat the ladies of the Silver Dollar any differently than they would their sisters or mothers.

Savannah tied the garment and hurried over to give Lottie Mae and then Beau a hug. "Thank y'all."

"Get back to work," Beau said gruffly, but she saw the twitch of his lips. He was a bear of a man, but had a heart of cotton.

Supper time came and went, with her taking her meal in the back room like Jules and Beau. When she walked back out to tend the bar, Lark stood at the end in his Wednesday clothes. His gaze landed on her the moment she cleared the blanket.

Not wanting to attract attention, she took her time filling glasses and talking with the men at the bar as she made her way to the end where Lark stood.

"What brings you in here?" she asked.

"Mrs. Dearling said you were at work already." He glanced around. "I left your pecans with her at the boarding house."

"You were able to get them?" She leaned over and kissed his cheek. The second her lips touched his cheek, she realized what she'd done and straightened faster than a coiled snake could strike.

"Hey, I want one of those," said the man standing next

to Lark.

"If you're given out kisses, I'll take one, too," said the man next to him.

She couldn't believe she'd forgotten where she was and kissed a preacher, of all people, in a saloon. Her face blazed like she'd shoved it in a roaring fire.

Beau stepped between her and the men. "No one around here gives kisses."

"But I seen her kiss him on the cheek," said the one man, pointing to Lark.

"In all fairness, it was because I told her something that made her happy." Lark said.

"I can tell her something, too," said the other man.

Savannah wanted to run to the back room and hide, but she'd have to come out in thirty minutes and play the piano. It was best to move on and act as if she hadn't just humiliated herself.

She stepped out from behind Beau and moved to the other end of the bar, serving drinks until Beau tapped her on the shoulder and motioned to the clock.

Nine.

Time for her to play. She glanced down the bar as she untied her apron. Lark was still there, sipping on a mug of beer.

He'd get to hear her play. Knowing he would be listening, she straightened her shoulders, held her head high, and followed Beau over to the piano.

Jules stood. He'd been playing rollicking tunes for Lottie Mae and Freedom to sing along with.

She took her seat, did a quick warm up, and lost herself in the rippling notes and lightness of the Bach sonata. The other nights she'd played more serious music. Tonight, her heart soared, and she showed that in her song choice. Her audience sat silently as she played for fifteen minutes before coming to the end of the piece.

Clapping and shouting ensued when she'd finished.

Beau and Jules arrived at her side as men surged forward, begging her to play more. She would have never dreamed men who frequented a saloon would take such pleasure in classical music.

"Do you mind playing one more song?" Beau asked.

"I would play all night if you let me." She sat back down and the room went silent. A lullaby came to mind and she began playing. This song didn't last as long. Again, raucous applause exploded when she finished.

"You can hear Miss Savannah again tomorrow night," Beau said, escorting her back to the bar and the blanket to the storage room.

"I can stay and help at the bar," she said, riding the euphoria of such a wonderful acceptance of her music.

"Lark is in the storage room. He'll walk you to the boarding house," Beau said, pushing her behind the curtain.

She turned to give him what-for but a hand on her arm spun her around.

Lark stood an arm's length away. "I've heard talk of what a wonderful piano player you were but hearing you…it was like being taken to another place."

His compliment swelled her chest. "You felt that way? It's how I feel when I play."

"You, and your music, are breathtaking." He stepped closer.

She tipped her face up, hoping he'd kiss her, but he grasped her hand, leading her to the back of the storage room. Before they stepped out into the alley, she planted her feet and tugged his hand.

He faced her. "What's wrong?"

"When you're dressed like this, I can forget you're a preacher and hope you might like me enough to…" Staring into his eyes she lost her gumption to ask for a kiss even though that's all she'd been able to think of since their last chaste meeting of lips.

He took a step closer. "I might like you enough to what?"

"Kiss me," she whispered.

Chapter Twelve

Lark didn't need any more of an invitation than that. He'd been dreaming of kissing Savannah again ever since their chaste kiss in the church. He held her head in his hands and lowered his lips to hers. A soft brush across her bottom lip with his, sent heat coursing through his body and straight to his shaft.

She pressed against him as her arms wrapped around his waist.

He deepened the kiss, willing her to open to him. With a flick of his tongue against her lips, she did. His tongue touched hers and she moaned. He released her face, allowing his hands to trace her neck, arms, and press her lower back closer to him.

It had been years since he'd wanted a woman. Savannah had his body aching for release. He slowly drew his mouth from hers but held her close.

"I have never wanted a woman as badly as I want you," he whispered.

"You say that like it's a bad thing," she said, nuzzling his neck.

"Oh my!" He grasped her shoulders, holding her away from his heated body. "You don't understand what holding you and having you ask to be kissed does to me, my body."

She gasped. "How do you know what I do or don't understand about a man and a woman?"

"If you did understand, you wouldn't be coming on so strong. This—" he motioned between them with his hands, "—display is what causes women to tarnish their reputations."

Lark took two steps backwards. "I'll take you to the boarding house." He opened the back door and waited for Savannah to step through.

When she did, she glanced over her shoulder at him. "If you don't think I'm fit to court, don't ask me to help with any church doin's." She picked up her skirt and ran for the boarding house.

"Damn!" Lark took off across the alley after Savannah. She'd taken his remark the wrong way. By the time he pushed through the kitchen door, there wasn't a sign of Savannah. Mrs. Dearling walked down the hall toward the kitchen.

"What happened to Savannah?" she asked.

"I need to talk to her."

The woman's eyebrows rose and she crossed her arms. "I can bring her down to the parlor."

"I need to speak to her in private." He pulled his hat off his head and held it in his hands. "I didn't say the right words and she thinks…"

The woman continued to scowl at him.

"I need to speak to her alone. Could you just this once

allow a man upstairs?" His heart raced. How could he tell Savannah his real feelings without them ending up kissing again? He'd had few weaknesses in his life. He'd become acutely aware; this woman was one of them.

"I can't allow you to be alone in a bedroom with her." She must have seen his pain. "I'll bring her down and sit out on the front porch."

"Mrs. Dearling, you're an angel." A thought came to him. "You might not want to tell her it's me. Say an admirer of her music."

"And you, a clergyman, telling a lie." Mrs. Dearling tsked.

"It's not a lie. Her music can take a man's troubles away. But if you mention my name, she won't come down."

"Go wait in the parlor. I'll get her." The older woman's shoes tapped down the hall.

Lark found a spot in the parlor where Savannah wouldn't see him until she stood in the room. He waited, his palms sweating and his heart racing. He hadn't been this nervous the times he'd been in a shootout.

Savannah yanked the pins from her hair. The nerve of the man, kissing her like that and then saying she wasn't good enough for him. He was a man of the cloth, and yet, he was the one to set a fire in her loins and leave her smoldering. What had come over her? She had never felt this way for a man before. Yet her body and heart had been drawn to Lark since their first meeting on the train. What was she to do? It was clear he felt she was as wanton in her desire for him as she was for playing a piano in the saloon. Traits a clergyman could not have in a wife.

A knock on her door startled her. "Yes?"

"There's an admirer in the parlor that'd like to speak with you," Mrs. Dearling called through the door.

Her nose wrinkled thinking of the two men who had seen her kiss Lark's cheek and then requested a kiss from her.

"What does he look like? Did he give a name?" She opened the door, asking the questions.

"He's a handsome devil, no name." Mrs. Dearling turned to go. "Do you want me to tell him to leave?"

"No. I'll at least thank him for takin' the time to come see me." She didn't feel like being friendly to anyone at the moment, but it was bad manners to not acknowledge a compliment.

"You might want to put your hair up," Mrs. Dearling said, motioning to the hair hanging about her shoulders.

"Yes, tell him, I'll be right down." She hurried to the mirror, wound her hair on her head, and tucked in the ends with two pins.

She hadn't paid any attention to the men who weren't at the bar. Who could the man be? At the bottom of the stairs, she patted her hair, slid a hand down her front making sure all wrinkles were gone, and walked to the parlor.

A deep breath before tipping her lips into a smile and she stepped into the parlor. She didn't notice anyone. Had he left already?

"Savannah." Lark stepped out of the shadowed corner.

"You!" She pivoted to leave, but he crossed the room, grasping her arm. She searched for the ever-present boarding house matron. "Where is Mrs. Dearling?"

"I asked her to give us some time alone." He led her

over to the settee. "You took my words wrong. I didn't realize how they came across until you ran off." Lark drew her down onto the furniture next to him.

"I'm not a dummy. I understood what you said perfectly." She faced away from Lark. Gazing into his eyes would distract her from the truth she knew.

He put a hand on her chin, making her look at him. "No, you didn't." He glanced around and leaned closer. "I want you with an ache I've never had before."

She stared at him as his words started the fluttering in her nether regions. Keeping her mind on the words and not the feeling, she said, "Like a man craves a whore."

"No!" He stood, paced the room, and sat back down. "If that was the case, I would have taken what I wanted in the storage room." He picked her hand up in his. "I would like to court you, but until the congregation sees you for the warm-hearted, good soul that you are, I can't throw you, or me, to the lions."

Savannah laid her other hand on his knee. "You want to court me? You think I'd make a preacher's wife?"

He nodded. "We just have to wait for the congregation and community to understand you aren't a saloon girl."

She drew her hands back. "I'm not. They know I just arrived and have asked around for work."

"But your brother owns a saloon. He's never said anything about family. People are suspicious about you."

"What people?" She hadn't felt like anyone despised her until the encounter with Miss Walker.

He shrugged. "Mainly the marriageable women."

It didn't take a brick to hit her to understand what he meant. "There are women in this community that had their hats set on you." She narrowed her eyes. "These women are say'n things about me because they want you?" Her heart squeezed with indecision. Was this man worth getting her reputation torn to shreds?

Lark grasped her hand. "I've stopped all the unkind things being said, but I'm afraid until you win them over, these women will do whatever they can to shake your credibility."

She peered into his eyes. The desire burning in their depths triggered the flames that had engulfed her during their kiss. "Will we be able to meet alone?"

"We are working on the pie social and the July Fourth picnic basket auction." He grinned and squeezed her hand.

Mrs. Dearling bustled into the room. "Reverend, it's time for you to leave."

Savannah stood at the same time as Lark. Their bodies touched briefly before he released her hand. *He wanted to court her.* Knowing he wasn't allowing what others thought to change his feelings for her helped ease her anger at him from before.

"Ladies." Lark placed his hat on his head and left the house.

"You two are given off sparks hot enough to melt candles," Mrs. Dearling said. "Be careful you don't both get burned."

Before she could ask the woman what she meant, Mrs. Dearling hustled out of the room.

Lark whistled as he left the boarding house. He'd set Savannah straight about his feelings. The kisses they'd shared in the storage room still had him hotter than a randy buck. A dip in a cool stream would help. He stood in the street debating whether to walk or get a horse from the livery.

"Hey!"

He spun around, his hand going to the gun in the holster he still wore.

Beau trotted down the street toward him. "Were you going to draw on me?" he asked, stopping in front of Lark.

"Sorry. I saw a man from my past today. I'm a little jumpy." He hadn't told Beau everything about his past, but the man knew enough to understand.

"Yeah, so jumpy you forgot to tell me if the solicitor telegraphed back." Beau scanned the street as he talked.

Lark slapped his vest. "That was why I came into the saloon earlier, to give you the reply." He pulled the folded paper out of his pocket and handed it to Beau.

"Can I read this at your place?" Beau didn't open the missive.

"You aren't needed at the saloon?" He'd never known Beau to make anything more important than his girls and the saloon.

"They can handle things without me for a few more minutes." He shook the paper. "This is family."

He'd never known the man to care about family other than his mother and Jules. "Come on." Lark led the way to his house. Inside, he lit a lantern and took off his hat and holster.

Beau sat down at the table and slowly unfolded the paper, pressing it flat on the table with his hand. His gaze slid across the writing. "Everything Savannah has said is true." He scowled.

"That shouldn't make you look like you want to put a fist through someone's face." Lark hung up his hat and holster.

"The solicitor says that Mr. Cartwell, the bank manager, has been looking all over Georgia for Savannah." Beau glanced up. "He may come looking here."

Anger gripped Lark. He clenched his fists. "He can come, but we won't let him take her."

Beau stared at him. "We? She's my sister, I'll deal with him."

"By the time this bank man arrives, the whole town will help keep her away from him." He knew once the town saw how hard she worked to better the community, they'd fall in love with her.

"I think you have stars in your eyes. Why would this town protect Savannah?"

"When they see what she is doing for the church and the people of the community, they will want to keep her."

Beau grinned. "More like you're going to make sure the community likes her so you can keep her."

Lark grinned back. "You wouldn't mind having a preacher for a brother-in-law, would you?"

"I'll show them sin and you save them?" Beau raised an eyebrow.

"That's not what I was thinking." He frowned. "That might not sit well with a few people in the community, but dang if I'll let your sister get away. I'd stop being a preacher to marry her."

"And then what would you do? Go back to using your gun?" Beau shook his head. "I don't want Savannah ending up a widow."

His friend was too smart for his own good. What could he do besides preach and use a gun?

"I better get back. Don't say anything to Savannah

about this banker. We'll just keep it between us until he shows up." Beau stood and walked to the door.

"Best not to tell her, she may get the idea to move on." He didn't like the idea of her not being here where he and Beau could keep her safe. If the banker was looking for her, he must be a persistent cuss.

"That's why we won't tell her anything." Beau stepped out the door, closing it behind him.

Lark picked up the telegraph Beau left on the table. He slipped it into the back of his Bible and prepared for bed. If they were lucky, the man would never find out about Savannah's half-brother.

Chapter Thirteen

Savannah could barely sit still during the Sunday sermon. Earlier, she had instructed the people helping set up the area outside the church for the pie social and had found the men all easy to work with and amiable.

Lark's sermon was about welcoming new members to the flock. It was inspirational, and she felt had a bit to do with her.

"I hope the women of the congregation brought their best pies and the men are hungry," Lark said after the final prayer. "Miss Gentry and several of the deacons have tables set up outside. If those who brought pies would place them on the serving table, we have volunteers to cut them and take money. It will be a penny a slice with a whole pie going for ten cents. We will auction off a few whole pies. And remember, all the money made will go in a fund for a church organ."

Lark stepped down from the pulpit and nodded her direction.

Savannah burst to her feet and pushed by Beau. "I need to be at the table when the pies come."

"Me, too," said Mrs. Dearling, bustling down the aisle behind her. People stayed seated as they hurried out to the tables.

Women lined up in front of the tables, holding pies draped with towels or in picnic baskets. Mrs. Dearling wrote down the name of each woman who brought a pie. When everyone had dropped off their pies and the Silver Dollar Saloon ladies had brought their pies and Savannah's and Mrs. Dearling's, Savannah asked Lark to join them.

"I've put all the names of the women who baked pies in this here bowl. Reverend Webster will draw out the six pies to be auctioned." She mixed the names in the bowl and held it out to Lark.

He reached in and pulled out a paper. "Silvia Dentz."

The young woman squealed and stepped up beside her pie.

Savannah was glad Silvia's name had been picked. Maybe if a young man purchased her pie, she'd lose her infatuation with Lark.

"Miss Agnes Walker," Lark said, handing the slip of paper to Savannah.

This one she was torn. It would appease the woman's hostility toward her, if Lark bid on her pie, but it would also give the woman hope to be with him.

Agnes smiled and walked up to the table, picking up her pie.

"Mrs. Irma Ferst," Lark said, after pulling another name out of the bowl.

A robust woman with a big smile stepped forward and picked up a pie.

Lark plucked another slip of paper from the bowl. "Freedom."

Freedom was dressed in a pretty calico dress with a tatted collar and long sleeves. Her hair was twisted in a practical bun. She didn't look a thing like the woman with bows in her hair who sang lusty songs in the Silver Dollar. She smiled and stood beside her pie.

Lark reached into the bowl. "Mrs. Cleary."

"Oh my! Oh my!" said the middle-aged widow as she bustled up to stand with her pie.

"The last one," Lark said, reaching into the bowl. He pulled it out, glanced at it, and then at her. "Miss Savannah Gentry."

Savannah didn't know what to say or do. She didn't want to be in an auction against two women wanting Lark to bid on their pies. "I didn't put my name in there," she said, trying to grab the slip of paper from Lark.

"I did. You have a pie and your name went in the bowl," Mrs. Dearling said.

"I agree," said Lark. He turned to those present. "Don't you all agree, everyone, including the person who arranged the pie social, should have their name in the bowl?"

A cheer went up.

"Miss Savannah Gentry," Lark said, again, and motioned for her to stand by her pie.

"We'll auction the pies off in the same order as I called the names," Lark motioned for Silvia to step forward. "And to make sure we get as much money for the pies as possible, my brother, Owen Webster, will auction the pies." The crowd laughed.

Lark stepped away from the front of the tables and his brother stood beside Silvia.

Savannah scanned the crowd. If she was lucky Beau would buy her pie. She'd made sure he knew she'd baked a good ole Georgia pecan pie. She watched as Owen did a wonderful job of getting fifty cents for Silvia's pie. And the proud bidder was a young man. That made Savannah even happier.

Agnes and her pie were next. Owen started the bidding at ten cents. No one bid on it. Savannah glanced at Lark as he raised his hand. Her heart sunk. Was all his talk about getting the community to accept her before he could court her just talk?

Miss Walker's face lit up at Lark's bid. Then another man bid more. Lark didn't raise his hand again and the other man purchased Agnes's pie for fifteen cents. Miss Walker didn't look happy, but the man sure did.

Mr. Ferst bought his wife's pie for fifty cents. He received a kiss on the lips from his wife, which made everyone laugh.

"Now we have Miss Freedom's pie." Owen leaned down and sniffed the pie Freedom held. "My it does smell delicious. What kind of pie is this?"

"It's a shoofly pie. Bought the molasses fresh from Mr. Flanagan day before yesterday." Freedom smiled at the Flanagan family.

"Who'll give me ten cents for Miss Freedom's shoofly pie?" Owen asked.

He asked several times when Lark raised his hand. Knowing he had reacted the same when Miss Walker's pie wasn't being bid on made Savannah feel better about his actions.

Pretty soon there was a bidding war over Freedom's pie. It was between Beau, Jules, and a man in buckskin at the outer edges of the crowd. The stranger won with a bid of seventy-five cents, making Freedom's pie the highest price. She ducked her head and walked through the crowd to take her dessert to the winner.

Savannah noticed Beau and Jules also walking that direction. She wondered why, but turned her attention back to Owen.

"And here we have Mrs. Cleary's famous dried apple pie. I have a feeling this will cause quite a stir." Owen hadn't even asked for a bid and men started throwing numbers at him. When the bid was up to a dollar, he raised his hand. "Anyone wishing to pay one dollar and five cents for Mrs. Cleary's pie?" When no one did, he pronounced the blacksmith the proud owner of the apple pie.

"And now we have the last pie to auction. But don't forget we have a table full of pies and you can purchase a slice for a penny right after we auction Miss Savannah Gentry's pie."

She stepped up beside Owen.

He glanced at her pie and asked, "What kind of pie do you have?"

"This is a Georgia pee-can pie," she said, smiling and raising the pie for people to see.

"It looks delicious. Will anyone give me ten cents for this pie?" he said.

Three hands went in the air.

Savannah smiled. Beau, Jules, and Lark.

"I'll give fifty cents for that pie," Sheriff Blake said, walking to the front of the crowd.

Savannah knew she didn't have to eat the pie with the man who purchased it, like would happen at the picnic basket auction, but she didn't want the sheriff to taste her pie.

"Fifty-five cents," Lark hollered.

The sheriff faced him and said, "Sixty."

"Sixty-five," Lark countered.

"Seventy." Sheriff Blake narrowed his gaze.

"Seventy-five." Lark took a step toward the sheriff.

"A dollar-fifty," Beau said, pushing past the two and holding out the money.

Savannah grinned at her brother.

Owen took the money. "Sold to Beau. Everyone else come on over and buy a slice. It's all going for a good cause."

Beau plucked the pie out of her hands and held out a crooked elbow. "Care to share this pie with Jules and I?" he asked.

"I'd love to." She glanced over at Sheriff Blake and Lark still eyeing one another. "Should we invite those two to join us?"

"No. Make them pay for their own pie." Beau led her over to a spot shaded by the church.

Jules had a blanket spread in the shade. Three plates and forks sat in the middle of the blanket.

"Y'all had this planned all along," she said and laughed.

"We haven't had a good pee-can pie since leaving the South," Jules said.

Savannah spotted Freedom back at the tables serving slices of pie. She nodded that direction. "Why did you follow Freedom when she toted her pie to the buyer?"

Beau glanced at Jules before answering. "While most folks around here don't mind mixing with coloreds, there's a few who wouldn't mind teaching them they were once slaves."

Savannah peered into Jules' eyes and saw a hint of anger. "You think he bought her pie to hurt her?"

"He was a stranger, we didn't know what he wanted. Turns out, he was passing through, heard the commotion and came over. When Freedom said she'd baked a shoofly pie, he wanted it. His momma used to make that kind of pie." Beau sliced the pecan pie and put large pieces on two plates and a smaller one on the plate he handed to Savannah.

"He was dressed different. In what looked like buckskins." She waited to take a bite until the two men had taken a taste.

They both closed their eyes and rolled the pie around in their mouths.

Lark walked up to the blanket. "Mind if I have a seat?"

Beau opened his eyes and swallowed. "Shouldn't you be walking around thanking your congregation for bringing pies and buying what they could have had for free at home?"

"After Savannah and I eat our pie, we'll do just that." Lark questioned her with raised eyebrows.

"If you think I should."

"I do. You were the person behind the event. You should thank people for participating." Lark sat, even though Beau glared at him.

"Miss Savannah, this is the best pee-can pie I've ever had," Jules said, cutting another large bite with his fork.

"I'm tickled you liked it. Lark brought the pee-cans from Bismarck Wednesday. Without them, it just wouldn't have been a pee-can pie." She nibbled on a bite as Lark ate a piece of apple pie.

When they'd both finished, he helped her to her feet but released her hand as soon as she stood. She would have preferred he held her hand but knew they couldn't appear that familiar. They'd only known each other a few weeks.

They stopped at each family, thanking them for being a part of the pie social. When they stopped where Miss Walker and the man who'd purchased her pie sat on a blanket, the woman glared at her and didn't give Lark a friendly greeting. The man, however, shook Lark's hand and told her he couldn't wait until the picnic basket social.

When people began to leave and they had talked with everyone who attended, Savannah glanced around for Freedom, Belle, Lottie Mae, Liesa, or Mrs. Dearling. It appeared they had all left.

Three young men walked up to them. "Reverend, would you like us to help take down the tables?" Arvid asked.

"That would be a big help. Thank you." Lark left Savannah standing by herself as he directed the men where to put the sawhorses and boards they'd used for tables. Mrs. Dearling had already taken the tablecloths home with her.

"You think you can get into everyone's graces by holding pie socials and acting like the reverend's wife," Miss Walker said, her voice low enough for only Savannah to hear. "You aren't going to be his wife. I'll see to it. Reverend Webster won't want you when the community turns on you. He loves this town and his congregation, he'll choose it over you." She smiled and walked away.

"What was that about?" Lark asked, from behind Savannah.

She took her time before facing him. The woman's words had shocked and scared her. She'd never encountered anyone so vicious. Did she tell him of the woman's threats or hope the woman couldn't turn the town against her and if that did happen would Lark pick her over his church?

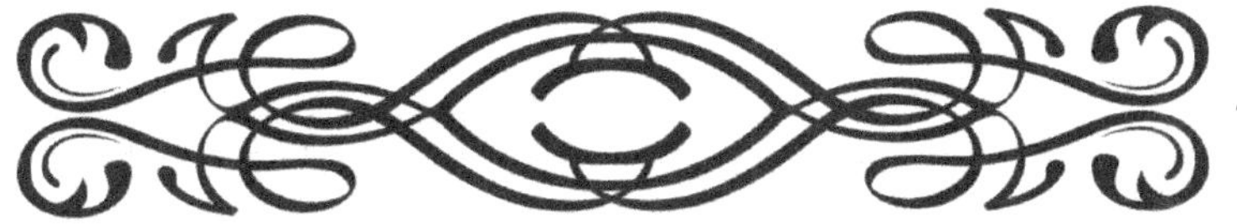

Chapter Fourteen

Lark hadn't liked the way Miss Walker had been talking to Savannah. The smile the school teacher had pasted on her face when she'd spotted him watching, made his gut twitch. What had the woman said?

Savannah took her time facing him. When she did, a forced smile barely curved her lips.

"What did Miss Walker say to you?" He wanted to reach out and touch her cheek, show her she mattered, but there were still enough people around, he didn't dare.

"She thanked me for put'n together the pie social." She waved a hand. "I'm tired. I'm go'n to wander back to the board'n house."

"I'll walk you." He wasn't about to let her get away that easy.

"No. You need to stay here and make sure everyth'n is put away." She gazed into his eyes. "I'll be fine. I just need to rest."

He didn't see fine lurking in the depths of her eyes. "I'll be by later."

She nodded and walked toward the boarding house. He watched her until she'd turned the corner at the end of the block.

He scanned the area where the tables had been. The young men had everything put away. The only families still lingering belonged to the men, except for Arvid. It appeared he rode into town on a horse. Maura stood by the wagons, holding a saddled gelding.

Lark walked over to Maura. "Did you make a pie?"

"Yes. And Arvid enjoyed the piece he had." Her gaze drifted to the young man walking their direction.

"Is Arvid staying for supper with your family?" Lark wanted to ask about her talk with Savannah. Since the girl didn't know it had been set up for Savannah to talk with her, he couldn't.

"Yes. He's going to ask if I may go back to his family's farm with him for several days." She patted the horse's neck. "Someone suggested I try the farming life and see if I understood what being married to Arvid would be like."

Happiness bubbled in Lark's chest. That had to have been Savannah. He hoped the trip would open the young woman's eyes. He couldn't see her as a farmer's wife, but then, he would have never thought he'd be a preacher either.

"I'll pray the trip helps you make the right decision."

"Thank you, Reverend."

"We have all the tables put away. Thank Miss Gentry for the pie social. We all enjoyed it very much," Arvid said, stepping up alongside Maura.

"I'll tell her the next time I see her. Enjoy the rest of your day." Lark walked to his house. He wanted to head straight to the boarding house and visit with Savannah, but they'd spent a good deal of time together already this afternoon.

The Silver Dollar was closed. Beau had never opened the doors on a Sunday, except for Lark's sermons before the church had been built. He was the unlikeliest of saloon owners between his keeping the saloon closed on Sundays and not allowing the women to be handled or bedded. He knew it had something to do with his mother, but that was all he'd ever been able to get out of the man. And Jules was as tight-lipped as his friend.

Without an invitation to dinner, Lark decided to see if he could get a meal at the Allman Hotel. It was a bit more money than he liked to spend on a meal, but it beat eating his own cooking. And if he was lucky, Mrs. Allman would tell him it was on the house.

Walking up the street, he glanced over at the Sheriff's Office. Ty sat in a chair beside the door.

"Where're you headed?" The sheriff stood, glancing up and down the street.

"The Allman for dinner." Lark stopped. "Did you get a piece of pie?"

"Yeah, but I bet it wasn't near as good as what Miss Gentry made." Ty frowned. "Didn't that beat all, the way Beau just shouted out a number and took the pie? We were still bidding."

"He can outbid both of us. And it was good for him to make a generous gesture toward his sister." Lark had been elated Beau bought the pie. He could have only gone five cents more and he would have had to concede to the sheriff.

"Yeah, what's the story with them two? Beau never said a word about having a sister. And a good looking one at that." Ty walked down into the street and stood beside Lark.

"It's not my family history to tell." Lark strode down the street.

Ty kept up with him. "But you know, don't you?"

"Only as much as they've been willing to share." He wasn't going to tell Ty anything. The man was tenacious at finding the outlaws and thieves, but that tenacity wasn't good for friendships or courting women. He'd witnessed Ty try to court several ladies in the last few years, and always his need to know more about them and their families had come between them. He'd arrested one's brother for stealing in Bismarck and another was still married to a man in Duluth. So far, Ty hadn't checked up on him. It helped having an upstanding banker for a brother.

"I heard she's quite the piano player. I can see why you want her to play the organ for the church."

Lark glanced over at the sheriff. His eyes were shaded by his wide brimmed hat, but the insinuation was in his words.

"It would make singing at Sunday Services more evangelical for the congregation."

Ty scrunched his face. "Evangelical. What the heck does that mean?"

"It will inspire the gospel into their hearts even more than just my words or the singing of hymns." Lark stopped at the hotel. "You coming in?"

"No. I can't afford to eat here." One eye narrowed. "How can you?"

"Mrs. Allman give me a free meal on Sundays." Lark opened the hotel door and entered. The lobby, as always, astounded him in its opulence. The massive wooden balusters up the stairway to the second floor and the dark wood desk that Mr. Allman stood behind, gave the place an air of money.

"Reverend. Excellent sermon." He patted his round belly. "And good pie. Mrs. Allman planned to bring a pie for the social but our little Astrid kept her busy yesterday and the pie didn't get made."

"I understand. Little ones can be a handful. Especially when your wife has so much work to do." A thought came to him. "Did Miss Gentry come to you about working in the hotel?"

"She did. But my wife feels we need to save our money and not pay someone to do the work she can do." He leaned over the desk and said in a quieter tone. "My Bertha likes to take care of things her way."

"Is she serving today?" Lark asked, understanding the man. Mrs. Allman was a woman who believed only she could do things correctly. He'd run up against her a couple of times when the church was being built.

"Yes, but only one meal on the menu-beef roast, potatoes, bread, and apple cake."

"That sounds good to me." Lark entered the small dining room that would be crowded and busy this evening after the train from Bismarck stopped. It was Sunday. The train would bring in the peddlers and salesman who wished to sell their wares in the morning. Some stayed at the Shady Gulch Hotel and the others would stay here.

He stopped at the door. A chill raced up his back as he stared into the face of Wild-Eye Ed Dellinger. The man ducked his head and stepped around Lark, darting out through the dining room door.

Lark spun around to see where the man went. Wild-Eye Ed climbed the stairs to the second floor.

Forgetting his growling stomach, Lark returned to the desk. "That man, the one who just went up the stairs, did he say what he was doing here?"

"He's looking for a relative." Mr. Allman scratched his ear. "His description fits Miss Gentry."

Lark's chest constricted with fear. What could Wild-Eye Ed want with Savannah?

Savannah sat at the dinner table not really hearing the conversation among the women, Jules, and Beau. Her mind was on the venomous words of Miss Walker and the kisses she'd shared with Lark. Could she or Lark survive any scandal the woman caused? She could move on, even if it meant leaving behind her brother, Lark, and the women. But would the jealous woman also ruin Lark?

"Savannah? Savannah?" Beau's deep voice broke through her thoughts.

"Yes?"

"Mrs. Dearling asked you a question?" Beau's brow was wrinkled and his dark brows almost touching.

"I'm sorry. I was reckon'n on the day." She smiled at the older woman.

"We made six dollars and seven cents today. I believe everyone at the service stayed for pie." Mrs. Dearling's face glowed with happiness.

"Yes, it was nice see'n so many stay." She'd been pleased with the response to the pie social and the Fourth of July picnic basket auction. But would she still be here for that?

"That nice gentleman who bought my shoofly pie said he'd be back through during the Fourth." Freedom's cheeks darkened.

"Are you sweet on the man?" Belle asked. "Bet you don't even know his name."

Freedom smiled. "Ben Hogan."

Belle sat back. "You know his name and he's coming for the picnic?"

"I invited him." Freedom took a drink of her water, her eyes sparkling over her glass.

"*Ma chérie* you do not know anything about that man," Jules said, leaning toward Freedom.

"I know he has a nice smile and he likes shoofly pie." She put the glass down firmly.

A knock at the back door was followed by Lark shoving the door open. His gaze landed on her for several heart beats then he nodded to Beau and walked through the kitchen and down the hall.

"What on earth?" Mrs. Dearling stood. "Tell Lark I've set a place for him," the woman said, grabbing another plate from the shelf.

Beau grunted and shoved out of his chair.

What could have made Lark look so dangerous? That was the word that came to mind. He'd had a look on his face as if he planned on doing harm to someone.

She glanced around at the other women. They were pushing their food around. Jules' brow was furrowed and his face blank of any emotion. She could see he leaned slightly toward the hall, trying to hear.

If the conversation was about her, she had a right to know and somehow, she had a notion it was. Savannah pushed back from the table and stood.

"Where are you going?" Mrs. Dearling asked, sitting back in her seat.

"To find out what has Lark so riled." She dropped her cloth napkin on her chair and walked out of the room and down the hall.

"You don't know for sure he's here looking for Savannah," Beau said.

"Who else could it be? Mr. Allman said his description fit her." The frustration in Lark's voice propelled her into the room.

"Who is look'n for me?" Fear that it was Mr. Cartwell constricted her throat.

"What are you doing in here?" Beau grabbed her by the arm and spun her so fast she would have toppled forward if not for his strong grip.

She stomped her foot and took a stance to keep from being propelled back down the hall. "I've a right to know what is happen'n in my own life."

Lark strode over to her. "You do." He extricated her arm from her brother's grasp and led her into the parlor, sitting her on the settee. "There is a man, an outlaw, at the Allman Hotel asking about a woman who fits your description. Do you have any idea why an outlaw would be looking for you?" He sat down next to her, his demeanor calm, quiet, unlike the stormy man who'd burst through the back door.

"I've no idea why an outlaw would be ask'n about me." She glanced over at Beau. The expression on his face, showed he was skeptical of her answer. "Can't you tell the sheriff about the man?"

"That's what I intend to do after I know you'll stay in

the boarding house or at the saloon with someone always around you until I can figure out what this man is doing here." Lark put his hand on her cheek. "Promise me you'll not go anywhere alone."

"I promise." She didn't know if the shiver was from his heated stare or the fear Mr. Cartwell had found her.

"Good." He glanced at Beau. "I'm going to tell Ty what I know." Lark peered into her eyes. "I wanted to talk to you about Miss Walker."

At his arrival, she'd forgotten the woman's threat. "There's noth'n to say." She didn't want to upset him any more than he already was. Having just witnessed his anger, this wasn't the right time to add to it.

"I saw the loathing in her eyes when she talked to you. She tried to cover it when I walked over. What did she say?" His hand slid from her cheek to capture her chin. He tipped her face up, making her gaze into his eyes.

The concern peering back at her stole her resolve. "She said I should stop playing your wife, it would only lose you the congregation."

He swore under his breath, and she leaned back. "Bless your heart, but those are not words that should come from a preacher's mouth."

Lark sprang to his feet and paced from the settee to the door and back. She could see his mouth moving but heard nothing. He'd become tetchy.

Watching him pace, she realized at some point Beau had slipped out of the room.

"Lark? Larkin Webster, sit yourself down and talk to me," she said, holding a hand out to him. Savannah didn't like the way his eyes were narrowed and his face muscles tensed. She'd never seen him so agitated.

He stopped pacing and stared at her.

She patted the settee. "Sit."

"Savannah, sitting isn't going to accomplish anything."

"Neither is wear'n out Mrs. Dearlin's rug." She patted the furniture again. "Sit. I can't talk to you if your pace'n back and forth. Can't tell if your listen'n to me or fum'n to yourself."

A half smile tugged at his lips and he sat down on the settee.

"I don't want you lose'n your church because of me." She meant it. He cared about the community and needed to be here to help each and every one of them.

"Right now, I'm more concerned with you being harmed than I am about my church." He grasped her hand.

"You mustn't put anyth'n or anyone over your church." She believed that, but knowing he cared for her over his calling to the Lord, stirred her insides.

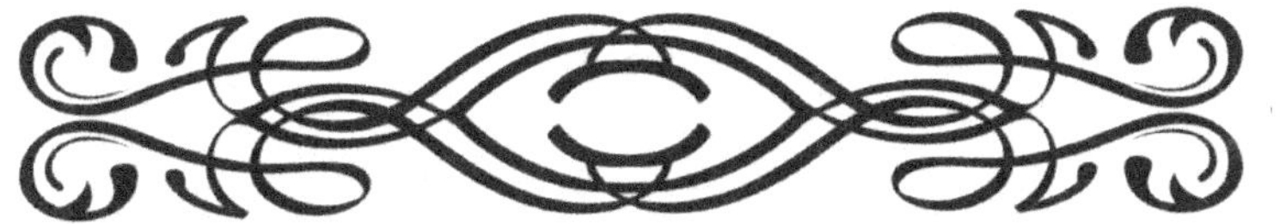

Chapter Fifteen

Lark stood, keeping hold of Savannah's hand. She was perfect in so many ways. He had to keep his past from tainting her.

"I'm going to tell the sheriff about the man. Maybe he can find out exactly who the outlaw is looking for."

"You're a man of the cloth. Perhaps this outlaw would talk to you. You would know everyone in the area."

Talking to Wild-Eye Ed would only make it easier for the man to discover the Topeka Kid was still alive. "I think this is a job for Ty." He pulled her to her feet. "Promise me you won't go anywhere outside this house alone."

Her lashes fluttered. "I promise. But I don't believe I'm in danger."

He wanted to kiss her lovely rose lips, but that would only make him want to linger, and he needed to talk with Ty and find out what Wild-Eye Ed was doing looking for Savannah.

"I'll check in with you tomorrow. We have a picnic to plan." He dropped a chaste kiss on her cheek and marched out of the room and the front door.

The evening hadn't cooled much. He strode past the saloon, across the street, and stepped through the open door of the Sheriff's Office. The deputy, Pete Reese, sat behind the desk, his feet propped up on an overturned pail.

"Reverend, it feels like summer is settin' in, don't it?" Pete didn't sit up, just pointed his chin to the other chair in the small office.

"It does. Where is the sheriff?" Lark didn't move toward the chair. He needed to see Ty.

"He's off-duty. What do you need?" Pete dropped his feet from the pail and leaned forward.

"I need to see Ty." Lark left the Sheriff's Office and headed to Mrs. Malley's boarding house. It was where Ty, Pete, and several other single men lived.

At the boarding house, the door was open and a screen door kept the insects out. Lark knocked and waited with his hat in his hands.

Mrs. Malley was a widow with two boys. Johnny was fifteen and Curtis thirteen. She was still a handsome woman and polite. He was surprised she hadn't found a husband yet.

"Reverend, come in. That was a nice pie social you and Miss Gentry provided after services today." Mrs. Malley drew him through the door and down the hall to the parlor.

Her boys, the attorney, William Conway, and the land grant officer, Abraham Howard, were sitting at a table playing the board game Fox and Geese. It appeared one boy and adult were playing against the other two.

"I'm looking for Sheriff Blake. Is he here?" Lark asked as none of the game players paid him any attention.

"He's up in his room. Would you like me to send Johnny up after him?" Mrs. Malley asked, stepping toward the game table.

"No. I'll talk to him there. Which room is he in?"

"The second door on the right." She walked over to a padded chair next to a sewing box and sat.

Lark headed to the stairs, took them two at a time, and rapped on Ty's door.

"Francine, I'm too tired to talk tonight," Ty said from inside the room.

Grasping the door knob, Lark twisted it and pushed the door in.

Ty sat in a chair, only in his drawers, sipping whiskey and looking relaxed.

"Lark, damn! What are you doin' here?" Ty swung the hand holding the jigger of whiskey toward the chair on the other side of the small round table. "Ignore that I called Mrs. Malley by her given name. We're all a little informal around here."

Lark lowered into the chair and grinned. "I see how informal. Do you always visit with Mrs. Malley in your long johns?"

The other man grinned. "If I'd been planning to talk to her, I would have put my pants on. Why are you here?" The merriment in his eyes changed to suspicion.

"I saw a man I believe is an outlaw at the Allman Hotel. Mr. Allman said he was asking about a woman who fit Miss Gentry's description. I told Beau and he suggested I come let you know." Lark wanted to stay as far away from Wild-Eye Ed and the whole situation as he could. He could live with losing his congregation if they didn't embrace Savannah, but he wouldn't be able to live with the shame if they learned about his life before becoming a preacher.

"You believe he's an outlaw. Any other proof than that? And what do we know about Miss Gentry? Could be she's running from an abusive husband or stole from a husband or someone else."

The sheriff didn't look like he was going to do a thing about Wild-Eye Ed.

"I think he's part of the Dellinger Gang."

"Dellinger? How would you know that gang?" Ty set his glass down and leaned forward, starring at him as if he could read his mind right through his skull.

"They hit a bank in the town I was living in about eight years back." He hoped that would be enough to appease Ty without giving more information.

"And you saw them? Or just this one guy in town on that day and think it's him?" Ty wasn't making this easy.

"I saw this man and several others ride out of town fast as someone else yelled the bank had been robbed." He was lying, just leaving out the part he was riding alongside Wild-Eye Ed. His hands were sweaty and he wiped them on his trousers. He'd stopped lying when he became a preacher, but just telling a half truth was churning his gut.

"Where was this?" Ty picked his glass back up and peered at him over the rim.

"Dickson, Tennessee." It had been the month before he'd had a talk with God in that outhouse in Kentucky and decided he was through with running with outlaws.

"Can you remember the date?" Ty continued to study him.

"Not exactly. I think it was in June, maybe July. I know it was summer." It had been a hot summer. One filled with ticks and skeeters and high tempers among the gang.

"You go down and ask Pete to give you the stack of wanted posters we have and see if you can find this man in them. If you can, I'll speak to him first thing in the morning." Ty poured more whiskey into his glass and raised it as if toasting his statement.

Lark nodded and stood. "I'll go look through the posters." He was pretty sure he'd find Ed in the posters. But would tomorrow morning be too late for Ty to do anything about the man?

Savannah walked into the kitchen the following morning and discovered Beau and the others with their heads together at the table.

"What's the secret?" she asked, trying to sound as if she wasn't put out that they were holding some kind of meeting without her.

"No secret," Beau said, straightening in his chair and staring at the ham and eggs on his plate.

The ladies all started dishing food into their mouths.

She hadn't slept well last night wondering about the man Lark had told her about. Had Mr. Cartwell sent someone to find her? If so, she had to leave. She wouldn't put Beau or Lark or any of these ladies in the middle of her struggle with the banker.

"Y'all most certainly were speak'n in hushed voices about someth'n. Someth'n you, perhaps didn't want me to hear?" She took her seat at the end of the table, facing her brother. Savannah picked up a biscuit and buttered it. "Did your conversation have anything to do with the man

Reverend Webster told you about last night?" She stared at Beau.

He stared back at her, barely flinching as she narrowed her eyes.

"I'm a big girl. I made it all the way from Georgia to here without hiccups, and I can take care of myself."

"Lark found a wanted poster of the man at the Sheriff's Office." Beau glanced around the table before resting his gaze on her. "You will be accompanied by someone everywhere you go." He cleared his throat. "Even the outhouse."

"Now see here. I'll not have one of these ladies stand'n around in the alley wait'n for me to do my business."

"You can take a chamber pot with you to the saloon," Mrs. Dearling piped up.

She scowled at the woman. "I'd rather take my chances walk'n to the outhouse in my nightdress."

Knocking at the back door, stopped the conversation.

Mrs. Dearling peeked out the curtained window before allowing the person entry.

Sheriff Blake walked in. His gaze landed on Savannah. "Miss Gentry, I'd like to have a word with you." He glanced around the room. "In private."

She shook her head. "I've noth'n to hide from anyone in this room. What did you come here to say?"

"The man, who was looking for a woman who fit your description, rode out of town sometime during the night." The sheriff glanced at Beau. "He told Orson that he'd found what he'd come looking for when Orson confronted him at eleven last night in the livery."

Savannah wasn't sure what to think of this information. He could have talked to the person he'd been inquiring about, in which case it wasn't her. She'd not set foot out of the house after Lark left. "Then he found the right person and left."

"From all I can find out talking to the people he talked with, he asked specific questions that only fit you. When someone mentioned your name, they said the man got a big grin on his face." Sheriff Blake took the coffee cup Mrs. Dearling placed in his hand. "You know who would send someone looking for you?"

Before she could answer, Beau said, "Winston Cartwell. He's a banker in Atlanta, Georgia."

Savannah couldn't stop her hands from shaking. How did Beau know Mr. Cartwell? And why would the man send an outlaw to find her?

Sheriff Blake motioned toward her with his cup. "Why is this banker looking for you?"

She glanced over at Beau. How much of their family's dirty laundry did he want her to air?

"She spurned his advances. It looks like the man can't take no for an answer," Beau said.

Nodding, she added, "He seemed more interested in my money than me." Which was true. He took everything that was hers except for the little she'd hid.

"Since you know who is looking for her—" the sheriff peered at Beau, "—you'll be taking precautions if this Cartwell fellow arrives in town?"

Beau nodded.

Sheriff Blake finished the coffee in his cup, handed it to Mrs. Dearling, and left through the back door.

Savannah didn't know if the tears trickling down her cheeks were of relief, knowing Beau planned to help her or from fear of what Mr. Cartwell might do to her new friends. The one thing she did know. She would not allow the vengeful banker to hurt anyone.

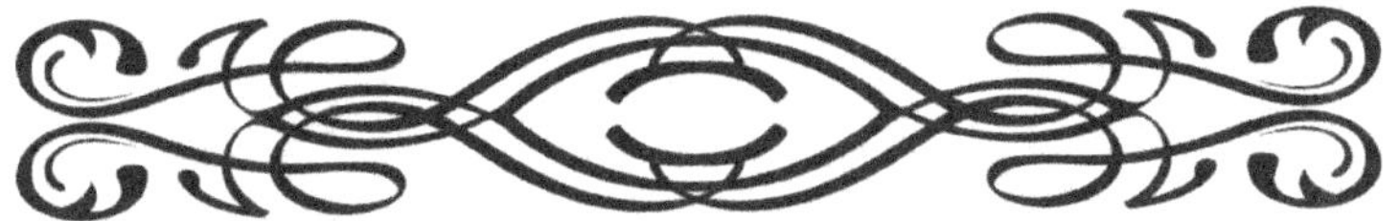

Chapter Sixteen

Because of what Miss Walker had said to Savannah, Lark made the decision to do the planning for the Fourth of July picnic at the boarding house. The threat of Wild-Eye Ed was gone, but he didn't want Savannah to fall victim to any vicious rumors the school teacher may have started around town.

Mrs. Dearling and the other ladies of the boarding house wandered in and out of the parlor as he and Savannah made posters, talked about the best way to run the auction, and everything but what he really wanted to ask her. Why was the banker so intent on finding her? She was a very desirable woman, but there were many women who would be happy to marry a wealthy man, no matter his looks or habits. It said a lot about Savannah that she wasn't willing to settle for a marriage based only on the man's wealth. Which led him to believe the man had another reason for wanting to find her.

"You're quiet today," Savannah said, glancing up from

the poster she'd carefully applied block lettering on.

"I'm concentrating on painting inside the lines you drew." He had to admit, she had a knack for drawing and printing up posters that were eye catching and came to the point.

"I'm glad you can paint. If I had to do all of this by my little ole self, the picnic would be over by the time I finished." She smiled and her eyes twinkled.

"Are you filling up a picnic basket?" That was a safe subject, given he wanted to pull her across the game table and kiss her.

"I've been think'n on that and I do believe I will." She propped her elbows on the table, put her chin in her hands, and leaned her face and lips closer to him. "What are your favorite things to eat on a picnic?"

He leaned across the table, bringing their faces only inches apart. "Anything you make will be my favorite."

She smiled. "Would it be too forward of me to ask why you haven't kissed me in days?"

He liked the playfulness and just a touch of naughtiness that made up Savannah. "We've rarely been alone, and I'm trying to make sure Miss Walker doesn't have any kindling for the fire she wants to start."

Her smile dimmed, and her gaze turned wary. "I see." She leaned away from him, her spine tight against the back of the chair.

"No, you don't see. I'm not worried about me." He reached across the table, grasping one of her hands and holding on tight, but gentle. "I want us both to be able to stay in this town. To do that, we have to meet like this, in places where no one would have reason to think anything other than work and a mutual desire to acquire an organ for the church is what we have."

"You feel that court'n me would put you in disfavor with your congregation?"

The tears glistening in her eyes was his undoing. Lark stood, pulling Savannah into his arms. He held her tight and kissed the top of her head. "No. I don't fear losing the congregation." He held her head and tipped her face up. "I fear you losing faith in me."

Her brow wrinkled and she studied him. "Why would you fear that?"

"It's complicated and something I'm working on." He knew before he could think about marrying Savannah, or any woman, he would have to tell them about his past life. If it came up before he could tell her, she'd not believe a thing he told her later.

They'd known one another barely a month, it was too soon to tell her his past and his dreams for a future with her. The only two things he knew were being a preacher and an outlaw. If he was run out of town as the preacher, he couldn't take her along. She deserved a respectable husband.

Savannah could feel Lark's attention going elsewhere. But she was in his arms, a place she enjoyed. And she knew how to bring his attention back to her. She tipped her chin and brushed her lips across his.

His arms tightened around her moments before his mouth captured hers in the type of kiss she'd dreamed about. His full warm mouth covered hers. His tongue traced the seam of her lips. The heat from this intimate touch caused her to gasp, and his tongue slipped inside her mouth. She froze.

His hands remained at her back, pressing her tight to

his strong lean body, his tongue touched hers and it was as if lightning struck her toes and radiated up her body and out her limbs.

"Reverend!"

Mrs. Dearling's voice shook her nearly as much as the kiss.

Lark set her away from him. "I'll return tomorrow to place the posters around town." He plucked his hat off the settee and strode out of the room.

Savannah sighed and spun toward the door where Mrs. Dearling stood, fanning her face with a dust cloth.

"It's a good thing you two are working here and not where others can see the goings on." The older woman stopped fanning and peered at her. "You are going to start rumors if this keeps up."

Savannah relayed what Miss Walker had said at the pie social.

"Well, I always knew that woman had a vicious side to her. I've heard some of the children complain about her high-handedness." Mrs. Dearling walked up to the table and peered down at the posters. "You are good at this."

"Reverend Webster helped me with the word'n." She didn't want to take all the credit. Lark had been a huge help.

"Have you talked to the newspaper yet?" Mrs. Dearling asked.

"No."

"Get your bonnet, and I'll walk you over there. I need a few items from the mercantile." Mrs. Dearling headed to the door.

"You don't have to watch over me anymore." It had been nearly a week since Lark had discovered the man looking for her. She picked up the paper she and Lark had used to write down the Fourth of July picnic information.

"Best you're seen around town with me, to keep rumors down about you wandering around alone and ending up at the church." The woman ducked out of the room, leaving Savannah to wonder if rumors were already flying.

Lark found four notes under the stone at his house. He'd come home every day this week from working on the posters with Savannah to find summons for his services. Wednesday was the only day there was none. The one day he wasn't with Savannah. He picked up the notes that were left today and placed them on the table as he poured a glass of water from a pitcher.

He sat down at the table, unfolded the papers, and read them as he drank. They were all from the families who had children in the lower grades. Upon closer inspection, the writing appeared to be the same on all of them. Of the notes he'd followed up on earlier in the week, several of the people were surprised to see him and said they hadn't left a message for him.

Grabbing today's notes and his hat, he set out in search of Miss Walker. He passed the Malley boarding house, waving at Mrs. Malley. She stood in the back yard beating rugs.

It was mid-afternoon, a warm time of the day for the woman to be working out in the sun. He changed his direction to make sure she wasn't overdoing.

"Reverend, what brings you by," Mrs. Malley asked, wiping the perspiration and wayward locks of hair from her brow.

"You shouldn't be beating rugs in this heat. That's a job for Johnny or Curtis." He walked over to the hand pump in the alley and filled the ladle hanging from a ring on the pipe.

"Johnny is working at the flour mill these days. He finished his schooling. Curtis. That boy. I'm not sure where he's off to. He's been coming home late from school every day this week." She took the ladle he offered and sipped.

"School is out for the day?" He'd hoped to catch Miss Walker with students around, so she couldn't misinterpret his visit.

Mrs. Malley nodded. "I saw the children walking home about thirty minutes ago."

"Do you know if the teachers remain for a time after the students leave?" The best place to confront Miss Walker with his suspicions would be the school.

"Yes. I don't generally see Miss Walker and Mrs. Beal headed home until around four-thirty or five." She handed the ladle back to him. "Thank you for the rest."

"You're welcome. If you feel tired or faint, go in the house out of the sun."

She laughed. "I'm not a wilting flower, Reverend. I helped my late husband plow fields and harvest the crops."

He nodded, smiled, and strode back to the street and down the road to the school house. Like the church, it had been built with the labor and money from the people of the town. It was a bit larger than they needed. All the citizens had hopes of their town growing and had provided for it with a good-sized school, which also doubled as a meeting hall, and when the judge was in town, as the court house.

He walked up the two steps to the threshold. The door stood open. Voices raised in anger and Curtis Malley rushed toward the door. Lark sidestepped to avoid being trampled.

The sound of pounding feet faded behind him as Lark entered the two-room school house. He walked through the cloak room and discovered Mrs. Beal and Miss Walker in a discussion in the room to the right.

He cleared his throat.

The heads of both women pivoted toward the door. Mrs. Beal's face was red. Miss Walker had the same expression on her face as he'd witnessed on Sunday when she'd spoken with Savannah.

"Excuse me. I didn't mean to interrupt." He took several more steps into the room. Mrs. Beal was upset. She turned from him as if trying to compose herself. Miss Walker smoothed her expression and a smile straightened her puckered lips.

"Reverend, it's so good to see you." Miss Walker walked toward him.

He peered beyond her to the other woman. "Mrs. Beal, are you all right?" he asked, ignoring the woman fawning in front of him.

"We- you caught us in the middle of a discussion." She had pulled out a handkerchief and dabbed at her eyes.

"Over Curtis Malley? His mother was wondering what was keeping him."

This caught the attention of Miss Walker. "His mother had you come looking for him?"

He decided to go with her question. It was obvious by her actions, she was worried what the woman would say. "Yes, she told me he had been coming home late from school with no reason why."

Mrs. Beal walked up behind Miss Walker. "Tell

Reverend Webster why you were keeping Curtis and his punishment. See if he agrees with me."

It appeared he was to be the mediator in an argument between the teachers.

Miss Walker's gaze darted about the room. Her hands wrung together.

"I am interested in what Curtis did that required punishment." He wasn't going to let the woman off the hook. It appeared she held her grudges with the children as well as with adults.

"He's been caught peeking in the outhouse when a girl is using it. Every day this week." She spit the words out in a disgusted tone.

"I see." It appeared he and the other men at the Malley boarding house needed to have a talk with the boy. Though it was nothing most boys his age hadn't done at one time or another. "And what has been his punishment?" He expected the boy to have to write one hundred sentences to the effect he would not peek in the outhouse.

Miss Walker glanced behind her at Mrs. Beal.

"Tell him what you picked as his punishment." Mrs. Beal glanced at Lark. "It is more like a reason for him to keep on peeking. It's unseemly."

This piqued his interest. "What is the punishment?"

"I-I had him looking at the pictures of women in the advertisements."

"Advertisements for unmentionables!" Mrs. Beal said, her revulsion evident by the way she blurted it out, her eyes wide, and lips down-turned.

Miss Walker stopped fidgeting, crossed her arms, and glared at him. "I thought if he saw what he wanted to know, he'd stop looking."

"Yet, this has happened how many times since you first showed him the advertisements?" Lark could see the woman thought she'd done the right thing. All she had done was ignite the boy's curiosity more. He knew what boys thought.

"All week, he's been caught."

"Do you know why he's been caught? Because he knew you would hand him the advertisements to look at after school." Lark shook his head. "I'll speak to him, and I'll instruct the men living at the boarding house about this and perhaps they can drop hints to the boy about what is proper and what is not when trying to appease his curiosity about women."

Mrs. Beal nodded. "Yes. That is what should have been done in the first place. Mrs. Malley should have been told and she could talk with her son." She tapped Miss Walker on the shoulder. "I want those advertisements out of this school room and if Curtis is found peeking again, he will be taken directly to his mother to tell her what he has done."

Miss Walker's eyes still held anger, but she did one bob of her head in agreement.

"What brought you to the school, Reverend?" Mrs. Beal asked.

He glanced at Miss Walker. The woman had been remanded already, he didn't like the idea of bringing up another poor choice she'd made. The scene of her threatening Savannah came to mind and his compassion turned to anger. He pulled today's notes from his pocket and held them up.

The color drained from the school teacher's face.

"I believe you have been leaving me notes every day

this week that caused me to visit people who had no idea I was coming."

Mrs. Beal reached out, taking the notes and examining them. "These do look like your writing, Miss Walker."

"I was only writing down what the children told me," the accused said.

"The children? Miss Walker, I have trouble enough finding time to do my duties when honest people request my visit. Adding visits that are not needed only shortens my time with those who do need me." He pivoted on his heel and walked to the door. With his hand on the door, he added. "You will go to Mrs. Malley and let her know what you have shown her son and why. It is the least you can do considering."

The woman gasped as he walked out the door, through the cloak room, and into the warm afternoon sun.

He had a feeling, given the outcome of this afternoon, Mrs. Beal would be more inclined to lean toward Savannah in any stories Miss Walker tried to spread.

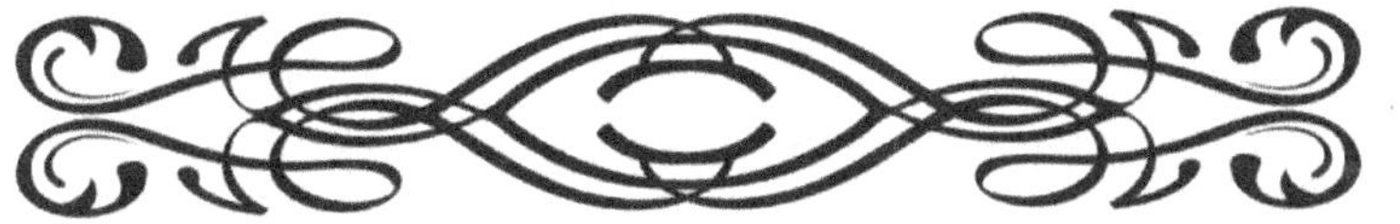

Chapter Seventeen

Savannah stepped out of the newspaper office in time to see Lark entering the Sheriff's Office. What could he need to say to the sheriff? She peered at the building, wondering if he would return to the street soon or linger.

Mrs. Dearling had left her at the newspaper office while she picked up items from the mercantile. A glance in the direction of the mercantile only found a couple of women chatting between the mercantile and the café and several men walking down that side of the street. Half a dozen horses were tied to the railing in front of the Silver Dollar.

A wagon drawn by two horses with a man, woman, and several children riding in it, spun dust into the air like a gray ground hovering cloud.

She placed a handkerchief over her mouth and closed her eyes. While she was beginning to like the quaint town, she did miss the cobbled streets and hustle and bustle of Atlanta. Back home she could walk the streets and only see a few people she knew directly. It was like being invisible while being in plain sight. Here, everyone nodded or said howdy. They all knew her name and everything about her life since moving here. That was a bit hard to get used to. Daddy had taught her to keep her family life and his business quiet.

Lark exited the Sheriff's Office as she removed the handkerchief from her face. Unsure whether to walk toward him or across the street to catch Mrs. Dearling, she stood still as an opossum. The boarding house owner's words rang in her head. *"Best to keep rumors down about you wandering around alone and ending up at the church."*

Mrs. Dearling liked to keep all the ladies in her house respectable in the eyes of the citizens of Shady Gulch.

Without another look toward Lark, Savannah stepped off the board walk and into the street. With both hands, she held up her skirt and trudged to the other side through the powdery dirt, avoiding a fresh pile of horse dung.

She stepped up onto the walkway as Mrs. Dearling exited the mercantile.

"Did you get things taken care of at the newspaper office?" the older woman asked.

"I did. As soon as we get home, I need to change and wander over to the Silver Dollar. It appears to be a good crowd already." She'd learned for every horse out front there were usually three times as many men inside. She didn't know where they all came from, but it was good for Beau and all of them.

Mrs. Dearling hooked an arm around Savannah's. They strolled down the walkway toward the Silver Dollar and the street to the boarding house.

"Mrs. Dearling!" Lark called.

She turned her attention to the man crossing the street. He might have called out the older woman's name, but his eyes were on her.

"Yes, Reverend?" Mrs. Dearling answered.

He stopped in front of them, his gaze glancing at the older woman before landing on Savannah's face. "I've learned some information that Beau and Miss Gentry might be interested in."

"What could you have found out of interest to my brother and me?" Savannah's eyes narrowed and her insides churned. What did he learn while at the Sheriff's Office?

"I'd prefer to discuss it at Mrs. Dearling's." He set his brown gaze on the older woman. "Are you two going back to the boarding house?"

"Yes. We've both finished our errands," Mrs. Dearling said.

"I'll get Beau, and we'll be there shortly," Lark said, touching his hat and walking into the saloon.

Savannah peered down at Mrs. Dearling. "What do you think that's about?"

"I have no idea, dear."

They continued to the boarding house and were taking their bonnets off when Lark and Beau entered through the kitchen door.

"What's so important you feel you can drag me out of my own saloon?" Beau asked, his face showing as much anger as his voice.

"Yes, why do you need to talk to us?" Savannah sat down at the table. Mrs. Dearling moved about putting her purchases away.

"After talking with you, Ty, Sheriff Blake, wasn't satisfied with your answer for this Cartwell looking for you."

Savannah grasped the edges of the table with her hands. What on earth did Mr. Cartwell make up about her?

"Ty discovered that Savannah came here because she is broke and looking for family to take care of her." Beau glanced her way and back at Lark.

"No. He discovered Mr. Cartwell claims Savannah ran off with jewelry that belonged to her father's estate and has charged her with theft."

Savannah couldn't breathe. Her chest sunk in, expelling all the air. Her fear and anger had dots floating in front of her eyes.

"Is this true?" Beau asked in a loud voice.

She tried to focus on him but her mind and body didn't want to cooperate. Gasping, she tried to gather air to speak.

Her body and chair jerked backwards. Lark pulled her to her feet and shook her gently.

"Breathe Savannah."

Lark's concerned voice caused the grip on her chest to release. She sucked in a huge breath and blew it out, drawing in another. He held her gently as she tried to regain her composure.

When she was breathing normal and didn't feel as if her whole body were frozen, she stepped away from Lark and stared at Beau. "I did keep four pieces of jewelry that were purchased by Daddy for me as gifts. They are worth next to noth'n in dollars, but mean a great deal to me." She narrowed her eyes. "The only way Mr. Cartwell would know of these is if my mother told him." The indifference she had felt toward her mother now turned to loathing.

"The pieces are up in my satchel. I'll get them and y'all can see they are worth noth'n. Least of all anyth'n that over-stuffed tyrant of a banker would want." She glanced at

Lark. He nodded and she left the room. What were Mr. Cartwell and her mother trying to do to her?

Lark faced Beau. "I haven't seen the jewelry, but I'd bet my Bible that what she says is true. Otherwise, she would have sold them to avoid working in the Silver Dollar and wouldn't have talked about working in Bismarck."

Beau sat down. "Mrs. Dearling, would you please bring me a pen and paper."

The woman did so and Beau began writing on the paper. He folded it and handed it to Lark. "When we finish here, take this to the telegraph office and have it sent." He dug in his pocket and held out a silver dollar.

Savannah walked through the door as Lark pocketed the note and coin.

"These are the pieces I kept from the men who came from the bank." She placed a brooch, necklace, and two pretty silver hair combs on the table. "Daddy gave me the hair combs on my sixteenth birthday." She touched the combs and then the brooch. "This when I turned eighteen." She cleared her throat, and he glanced at her face. Tears glistened in her eyes. "This necklace when he became ill. He said it would be someth'n to remember him by." Her voice cracked.

Lark put an arm around her shoulders. He wanted to take her into his arms and promise the man would never take away her gifts from her father.

"These aren't worth the wax it takes to seal an envelope." Beau's face was red and his eyes narrowed. "Why does this man think you have jewelry worth his time?"

Savannah shook her head. "I don't know." She stared at her brother. "How do we prove otherwise? I don't want to go to jail." She shuddered. "Or become that man's wife."

"You won't have to do either." Rage boiled inside Lark. He wanted to hop on the train and head southeast. He wanted to confront this man who was trying so hard to ruin Savannah.

His gaze latched with Beau's. Between them, they would do everything they could to keep her safe and with them.

"Go get dressed. I can use your help in the saloon," Beau said, standing and drawing her out of Lark's one-armed embrace.

"Don't make plans without me. This is my life. Y'all can't do things without me know'n." She bounced her gaze back and forth between he and Beau as she scooped her jewelry into her hands.

"We'll let you know what we plan," Beau said. "Go get changed."

One last glance between the two of them and she left the room. Her muffled footsteps on the carpeted stairs was the only sound in the room as he, Beau, and Mrs. Dearling all stared at one another.

"What are you going to do?" Mrs. Dearling broke the silence first.

"Wait for a response from that telegraph and make sure Ty knows the only jewelry Savannah has isn't worth the telegraph I'm sending." Beau walked to the kitchen door. "Have George send the answer to me as soon as he gets it."

"I will."

Beau left and Lark cast one last glance at the hallway leading to the stairs before making his exit. He wanted to get this telegraph sent out as soon as possible. He didn't know what was written down, but the answer would help them deal with this new problem for Savannah.

Hesitant steps carried Savannah into the Silver Dollar. She had become accustom to the ruckus and carrying on that was the atmosphere in the establishment. The locals knew she only worked behind the bar and played piano. Once in a while, a salesman or drifter would make advances and Beau always arrived at her side.

Tonight, with the threat of being thrown in jail and harboring the feelings she had for her mother, she wasn't feeling cheerful. When it was time to play the piano, she brought forth the memory of one of the saddest requiems she could remember.

As the last note faded into the quiet of the saloon, she heard sniffing and spun around to find half of the men present wiping at tears.

"You made every man in the place tear up," Lottie Mae said, walking up beside the piano and nodding toward the men standing at the bar. Even Beau had a sad expression on his face. He'd been so struck by the song, he hadn't walked over to escort her back.

She stood, held her head high, and strode to her place behind the bar.

"Come on, Jules, let's liven this place up!" Freedom hollered.

Jules shoved away from the end of the bar where he'd been standing and took the seat in front of the piano. A rollicking tune filled the room along with Freedom's playful, warm voice.

"A person can tell your mood by the music you play," Beau said, as he reached past her to grab a glass.

"Sorry. I can't help it. Playing the piano has always

been what I did when I was upset or happy."

Sheriff Blake entered the establishment. Unlike other visits, he didn't scan the room, he walked directly to the bar in front of her.

"Miss Gentry, we need to talk." There wasn't the glint of mischief or the spark of interest that usually lit his eyes. He was intent on something other than charming her.

"Now?" She knew what he wanted to ask her, but she was feeling puny about standing up to the lawman.

"I'd prefer now. I'd like to know if I need to get a cell ready for you." His gaze remained steady on her face.

She gulped and glanced toward Beau. He was handing a coin to a boy and taking a piece of paper from the young'n's other hand. "I'd like Beau to be there, and he's busier than a bee float'n in honey."

As if hearing his name, Beau walked over to them. "Ty. What are you doing in here bothering my help?"

"I have some questions for your sister." The sheriff didn't take his eyes off her as he answered Beau.

His intense stare was making her hot and causing her forehead to perspire. She'd never felt as cornered as she did at this moment.

"Can they wait until tomorrow morning when she isn't working?" Beau tucked the paper he'd received from the boy into his vest pocket. He waved toward the room. "As you can see, we have a full house."

The music became louder. Belle, Lottie Mae, and Liesa started doing the can-can on the stage. The crowd shouted, whistled, and carried on as if most of them had never watched the dance before.

"Come on!" Sheriff Blake said, reaching across the bar to grab her arm.

Savannah backed up, bumping the large mirror behind the bar. The huge mirror wobbled a bit before Beau managed to keep it from crashing to the floor.

"I'm not asking you, I'm telling you. Get out of here and stop bothering my help. We'll come by the Sheriff's Office tomorrow morning and speak with you," Beau hollered.

Sheriff Blake stared at Beau as the noise in the saloon started lowering. "You don't tell me, the lawman in this town, what to do."

"Then don't come in here bothering people when they are working." Beau glared back at the lawman.

"Stop, both of you." Savannah didn't want to see Beau getting in trouble over her. "If you need me to come by the office, I can be there in an hour. It's when I usually get done work'n."

Beau turned his glare on her. "You don't have to go tonight."

"I don't want you in trouble with the law. I can go tonight." She leveled a gaze on the sheriff. "I'll see you in an hour."

He nodded, scanned the room, and left.

"I don't want you going to talk to him without someone with you." Beau said, ignoring a man asking for a whiskey.

Savannah poured the man a jigger and huffed. "There's noth'n he can do to me but put me in jail until you come get me out."

Beau grabbed her shoulders. "You don't belong in jail. You've done nothing wrong."

She shrugged. "Maybe he just wants my side of the story."

"I don't like it." Beau released her and ran a hand through his hair. "Take care of things while I read the telegraph that came."

She nodded, wondering why he needed to read a telegraph when she could be in danger of going to jail.

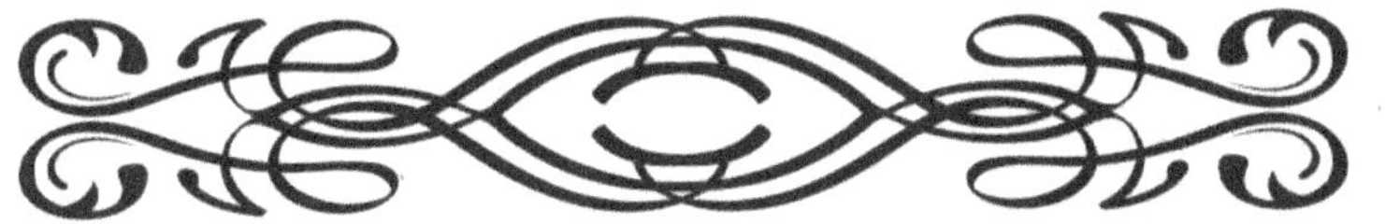

Chapter Eighteen

Lark sat at the table, trying to work on Sunday's sermon but his mind kept running the conversation he'd had with Beau and Savannah over and over in his head. It was late. He should have gone to bed an hour earlier.

Pounding on his door shot him to his feet. Who needed him at this time of the night?

"Reverend Webster. Wake up!" slurred a voice on the other side of the door.

He pulled on the latch and Dewey Dunston, a young man who worked at the flourmill, nearly fell into his arms.

"Are you all right, Dewey?" He glanced over the man's body, looking for a sign he'd come to harm.

"I'm good. Real good." The young man straightened and held out a piece of paper clutched in his hand. "Beau said to give this to you on my way home."

Ty wants Savannah at the jail tonight. Meet her there.

"When did he give you this note?" He knew Savannah left the saloon by ten every night. It was close to midnight now.

"When I left the Silver Dollar." Dewey leaned against the door frame.

"Just now?"

"Naw, I stopped off at Mad Dog."

Lark grabbed his hat, shoved the drunk man outside, and pulled the door shut before he headed at a run toward the Sheriff's Office. What had Ty discovered that had him questioning Savannah at this late hour?

He turned the corner of the street as several men exited the Silver Dollar.

"Reverend, where are you headed in such a hurry!" one shouted.

He ignored them, not stopping until his feet hit the wood planking in front of the jail. Without preamble, he shoved the door open and scanned the room.

"Where's Miss Gentry?" he asked Pete.

The deputy waved his hand toward the backroom, where the jail cells were.

"What is she doing in a jail cell?" Lark strode across the room and flung the door to the backroom open.

Savannah sat rigid as a pole on the edge of the cot in the first barred area.

"Savannah," he said her name gently, hoping to ease the fear marring her pretty face.

"Lark!" She shot off the cot and pressed against the bars.

He wanted to put his arms around her and tell her everything would be fine but the dang bars were between them. "What happened?"

"Sheriff Blake came to the Silver Dollar. He wanted me to come over straight away, but Beau told him I would come see him in the mawnin', I offered to come on over when I finished work'n.'"

He put his hands on top of hers, offering all the support he could. "Why did he want you over here?"

"He received a list of the items I'd supposedly stolen." The fear in her eyes smoldered into anger. "The list has all items I know my mother took with her. She cleared out her jewelry box and the safe when she left. Daddy didn't have the money to pay people because she took it."

"How would Mr. Cartwell get a list of the jewelry?" Lark was trying to figure out if Mrs. Gentry had a hand in this harassment of her daughter or if it was just the banker.

"I would guess Daddy's Will would have listed all the jewelry." She peered into his eyes. "I don't like bein' in here," she whispered and her lips trembled.

"I'm staying here until Beau comes to get you."

"Thank you."

"Pete, what the hell is that door doing open?" Ty's voice bellowed.

"Reverend Webster is in with the prisoner," the deputy replied.

Ty appeared in the doorway. "Well, if this ain't convenient. How did you know Miss Gentry was staying the night?"

"Beau sent me a note to be here when she came over. However, the person delivering the note made a stop at the Mad Dog." Lark kept one hand on Savannah's as he faced the sheriff. "Why did you lock her up?"

"I learned she had stolen a considerable amount of jewelry. I don't take kindly to thieves in my town."

"I told you. I didn't steal any jewelry. My mother took it when she left Daddy." Savannah's voice sounded stronger, more confident.

Knowing his presence did this for her, made him proud.

"Where have you been?" Lark asked.

"Searching the boarding house."

"You had no right to disturb Mrs. Dearlin'," Savannah said. "She has noth'n to do with Mr. Cartwell's grudge against me."

"You locked Savannah up so she couldn't tell the others you were rummaging through their things." The other women would have still been at work. "Did Beau know you searched his house?" Lark asked, knowing full well, Beau would have thrown the man out, lawman or not.

Ty tapped the star on his chest. "I'm the law. I can do what I want to discover the truth."

"And did you discover any jewelry?" Lark hoped the other women in the house didn't have expensive items.

The sheriff lost his steam. "All I found were a few pieces of cheap jewelry in Miss Gentry's, Liesa's, and Mrs. Dearling's rooms. Nothing that was described in the theft report."

"Then you can let Miss Gentry go." Lark stepped away from the bars to allow the man access to the lock on the door.

Ty picked up the keys hanging on a nail by the door and walked over to the jail cell. He inserted the key into the metal lock and swung the bars open.

Savannah flew out and stood close to Lark as if she feared the sheriff would change his mind.

"Why would this man think you stole jewelry?" Ty asked Savannah.

She shook her head. "I don't know. Because I didn't

come crawl'n to him when he took everything. Because I refused to marry him. Because he had always been jealous of Daddy. I don't know. I thought leav'n Georgia and start'n over here with Beau would be a new life far from the society that scorned me when my mother took everyth'n and left Daddy and I penniless."

To his benefit, Ty appeared to have sympathy for Savannah.

"Come on. I'll walk you to the boarding house," Lark said, putting an arm around her shoulders. He didn't care what people thought. The woman needed a shoulder to lean on after her ordeal tonight.

Savannah was in shock that the sheriff had actually locked her up, and then searched, not only her belongings, but those of the women she lived with. Her mind was flashing back and forth between guilt that she'd brought all this trouble to her new friends and anger that a man so far away could cause her so much torment.

Larks' strong arm around her shoulders led her down the street and up the front porch of the boarding house. "Do you want me to come in until the others get off work?"

She nodded. Knowing Sheriff Blake had been in here, and that Mrs. Dearling must be angry with her, she didn't want to face any of the other boarders alone.

Lark opened the front door. A light was on in the kitchen. She assumed Mrs. Dearling left it on for the women to see by when they came in from working in the saloon.

They walked down the hall and discovered Mrs. Dearling mixing something in a bowl. She dropped the spoon and bustled over to Savannah.

"You poor dear! I've been worried sick about you."

The older woman drew her to a chair and sat her in it. "How about a nice cup of warm milk to help you sleep?"

Savannah was grateful Lark sat in the chair beside her. "I'm so sorry," she said.

"Sorry?" The woman faced her. "Sorry for what? You're the poor dear who was left in a jail cell so that pushy sheriff could search your things."

"But he searched your things as well. And-and all the other's rooms. I've brought nothin' but trouble to y'all."

"That's not true." Lark grasped her hand closest to him. "You have brought culture to the saloon with your piano playing. You've brought vitality to the church with your pie social. And you've been a friend to many people since you arrived."

She peered into his eyes. He meant every word he said, but her guilt still ate at her. What other trouble might Mr. Cartwell bring to these wonderful people because of her?

Mrs. Dearling set the steaming cup of milk in front of Savannah. "You're one of us. We take care of one another. I checked the rooms after the sheriff left. He was tidy with his searching. No one was hurt and he discovered that you're not a thief, which I could have told him if he'd took the time to listen."

Savannah picked up the cup of milk and sipped. It gave her time to think and not have to talk. Larks' warm hand continued to hold hers.

"Does Beau know Sheriff Blake searched the house?" Lark asked.

"Lordy no!" Mrs. Dearling exclaimed. "To avoid him going to jail it would be a good thing not to tell him."

Lark shook his head. "I can't do that. I have to be honest and tell him I was late meeting Savannah at the

Sheriff's Office and didn't keep her out of jail."

"But you came as soon as you knew." Savannah peered into his eyes. "That is what matters. You were there when I needed you."

"Not soon enough to keep you out of jail."

The regret in his eyes, started her heart pattering. The depth of his caring for her became even more clear tonight. She had to do something to either put distance between them or to find a way to appease Mr. Cartwell so he wouldn't torment her anymore.

Chapter Nineteen

Savannah and the other women jumped as Beau banged the kitchen door open and stormed into the room. They all sat at the table eating breakfast after having discussed Sheriff Blake searching the house the night before.

"Why didn't you come get me when Ty searched the house?" he hollered at Mrs. Dearling.

Savannah charged out of her chair, placing her body between her brother and the older woman. "Because she knew this was how you would behave." She glared at him. "We didn't need us both in jail."

His angry gaze landed on her. "What do you mean both of us? I sent a note to Lark to be there when the sheriff talked to you."

"He received the note late, but arrived as soon as he knew what was happen'n." She grabbed his arm and led him over to the table. She'd already filled the ladies in and apologized for their things being rummaged through by the sheriff. They had all been sympathetic and not bothered by the intrusion.

"Damn Dewey! He was to take the note straight to Lark." Beau grabbed her hand. "I'm sorry for the trouble this man Cartwell and your mother are putting you through."

She stared at his face. What was he saying? "You know my mother has someth'n to do with all of this?"

All expression smoothed off his face. It was obvious he'd said something he hadn't planned to say.

"What do you know about my mother?" She pulled her hand from his grasp and planted both hands on her hips, glaring at him.

"Only from what you've said, she sounds like a woman who likes to stir the pot." He reached out to put hotcakes on his plate.

"You know someth'n. I'm tetchy that you think I don't know when you're keep'n things from me." She knew her brother wouldn't spill anything, but Lark wouldn't be able to keep something he knew from her. He was too honest and honorable.

"I have posters to finish." She walked out of the kitchen and into the parlor to think on her own a bit and wait for Lark to come by and get the posters he said he'd put around town today.

Savannah and Liesa had all the posters finished and waiting for Lark when he arrived close to dinner time. She'd expected him sooner but from the grave expression on his face, something had happened this morning that had nothing to do with her and her troubles.

She led him into the parlor where they could be alone and peered into his eyes. "What's wrong?"

"There was an accident at the grain elevator. Bjorn Olafsen isn't going to make it. Doc Nolan is doing everything he can to make the man comfortable, but…"

"Did you know him?"

"His wife, Rona, just had a baby. We were going to christen the boy this coming Sunday." Tears glistened in Lark's eyes. "They were a happy couple. I married them two years ago."

No words could help his suffering. She put her arms around him and held him, trying to take away his sorrow. His compassion for his congregation made him a wonderful preacher. And this compassion had been one of the things she'd witnessed in him from their first meeting.

He eased out of her embrace. "I came to tell you, I won't be able to put up the posters. I need to be there for Bjorn and Rona." He smiled. "Thank you for being here to lean on."

Her heart flipped at the genuine gratitude she witnessed in his eyes. "You can lean on me any time. It's a tough life be'n a preacher and fix'n everyone's troubles."

"I like knowing I have someone I can lean on." He kissed her cheek. "I don't know when I'll be able to see you. I'll- I'll have to stay with Bjorn until…"

"I understand. I can ask one of the ladies to help me put up the posters before she goes to the saloon." She put a hand on his cheek. "I'll stop by Dr. Nolan's later and see if I can do anyth'n for Rona."

His eyes lit up. "I'm sure she would appreciate that. Her family is in Duluth."

He lingered even though she knew he should leave. The burden of knowing how much people needed him, had to weigh heavy. Even with the Lord on his side, he couldn't do anything but help the ones left behind grieve, and give comfort to those who were dying.

Mrs. Dearling entered the room, "Oh! I didn't know you were here, Reverend. Would you like to stay for dinner?"

"I can't. I have to go." He smiled at Mrs. Dearling and grasped Savannah's hand, squeezing it gently and releasing. "It would be nice if you stop by later." He placed his hat on his head and left the room.

She heard the front door close and faced Mrs. Dearling. "Bjorn Olafsen had an accident at the grain elevator." She shook her head. "He isn't go'n to make it."

"Oh my! And his young wife and child. Oh my!" Mrs. Dearling dabbed at her eyes with a handkerchief. "I'll go around and check on them after dinner."

"I'm sure she would find that comfort'n. I believe they are at the doctor's house from what Reverend Webster said." Savannah didn't feel much like eating knowing a young woman's life had been altered today. But she did need to ask if one of the ladies would help her hang up the posters.

The four women were chatting and putting food on their plates when she and Mrs. Dearling entered the kitchen.

"Reverend Webster won't be able to help place the posters around town. Would one of you like to help me?" She took her seat beside Belle and stared at her empty plate.

"I won't be as good looking as the reverend but I can help," Lottie Mae said.

Savannah glanced at the woman. She was the most outspoken of the four and tended to dress to show off her ample curves. If they happened to run into Miss Walker, having Lottie Mae at her side would be good.

"We'll start after dinner. Thank you." She chose a slice of bread and picked at it.

"You need to eat if we're going to walk all over town," Lottie Mae said.

"I'm not very hungry." She put a small piece of the bread in her mouth to appease not only Lottie Mae but the concerned expression on Mrs. Dearling's face.

"Did Reverend Webster say more than he couldn't put up posters?" Freedom asked, studying Savannah.

"Yes."

"He didn't tell you he didn't want to be seen with you, did he?" asked Belle. Her distrust in men soured her perception of everyone in trousers but Beau.

"No. He…" She glanced at Mrs. Dearling. The woman nodded. Savannah told the others about the accident and young family.

"That is very sad." Liesa said, dabbing at her eyes. The sorrow in their pale blue depths was more than for the young couple and baby. She'd yet to learn this woman's past. From her reaction, it was a good bet she'd lost her young family.

Lottie Mae stood. "If that's all you're going to eat, we might as well get started."

Savannah agreed and stood. She pointed to Mrs. Dearling's basket. "May I use your shop'n basket to carry the posters, hammer, and tacks?"

"That's an excellent idea. Yes, you may." Mrs. Dearling hurried over to the shelf where she kept the basket and pulled out the cloth with the weeks eggs nestled within.

Savannah hurried up the stairs to her room to grab her

hat and gloves. While she would have rather had Lark along, she was happy to have something to do outside. They would have to hurry. Beau would expect Lottie Mae at the saloon no later than two.

Back downstairs, Lottie Mae had already placed everything they needed in the shopping basket. She had it over her arm and waited at the front door for Savannah.

"Thank you for help'n me," she said as they stepped out the door.

"I like being outside this time of year." Lottie Mae drew in a deep breath, expanding her amble bosom. "I don't like being inside all the time." She headed left toward the bakery.

"There is someth'n about the sun on your face, the fresh air, and hear'n the sounds of life." Savannah had always enjoyed horse rides and walks about their small estate in Atlanta.

At the bakery, Savannah entered the establishment and asked the owner, Mrs. Hansson, if they could tack up a poster.

"Ja. Ve are excited to be part of the picnic." She wiped her hands on her apron. "I vill also have a basket." Her face reddened. "My Knut vill buy it."

"Thank you. The picnic will be fun." Savannah turned to head back out the door.

"Vait!" Mrs. Hansson hurried forward with two cookies. "One for you and one for your friend."

"Thank you."

Outside, Savannah handed both cookies to Lottie Mae. Then she grabbed the hammer, a tack, and a poster out of the basket and fastened the announcement to the front of the building at eye level.

"This is a good cookie," Lottie Mae said, as they nibbled the cookies and walked over to the hardware store.

Every business they asked allowed them to put up a poster. By the time they finished, every business had a poster, except the Mad Dog Saloon. Savannah didn't want to enter the establishment to ask. Lottie Mae offered to go in, but Savannah didn't want something bad to happen to her new friend.

"Anyone go'n in there will see the posters on all the other businesses along this street." Savannah had one poster left. It was for the church. "Do you think we should put this up at the church or leave it for Reverend Webster to put where he sees fit?"

Lottie Mae smiled. "We can go see if he's there."

"He isn't." Her glance darted back toward the end of town where the doctor lived.

"We can place it on the first pew in the church. He'll find it there." Lottie Mae walked briskly down the street toward the church and cemetery.

"You're go'n to be late. I can put it in the church if you want to head back to the board'n house to change." Savannah had kept Lottie Mae longer than she'd planned. Many of the business owners had been talkative.

"I should get dressed." Lottie Mae scanned the street. "Are you going to be all right alone?"

Savannah laughed. "There's no reason to worry yourself about me. I'm fine. Go change." She took the basket from the other woman and they parted ways. Lottie Mae headed east toward Mrs. Dearling's and Savannah went west toward the church.

As she passed Lark's house, something or someone darted behind the building. She stared as she walked but didn't catch sight of anyone. At the church, she unlatched the door and walked in.

The afternoon sun through the stained-glass windows scattered colors about the room like looking through a fractured rainbow. The beauty and peace drew her to a pew. She sat for several moments, reflecting on her life, and how, while her mother's actions had lost her her home and father, she'd gained a new town, family, friends, and a gentleman in her life who was becoming the most important person to her.

The sound of the door opening spun her in the seat.

A young woman, clutching a baby, stumbled up the aisle and collapsed in a pew.

Instinct told her it was Mrs. Olafsen. She left the basket and moved down the aisle toward the woman.

Her shoulders shook and mournful moans filled the building. The baby started crying, adding wails to the heart wrenching sobs.

Savannah put a hand on the woman's shoulder as she asked, "Mrs. Olafsen?"

The woman peered up at her through red, swollen eyes, filled with tears. "Ya?"

"Would you like me to hold your baby?" She held out her hands.

Mrs. Olafsen glanced down at her wailing child as if she'd forgotten she held him. "My…his.." She burst into tears.

Savannah sat on the pew next to the woman and placed her arms around her. She knew grief. It wasn't that long ago it had been the only emotion she knew. To lose a parent who was elderly and ailing was different than losing a husband who was just starting his life.

Mrs. Olafsen cried, clinging to her, and the baby wailed between them.

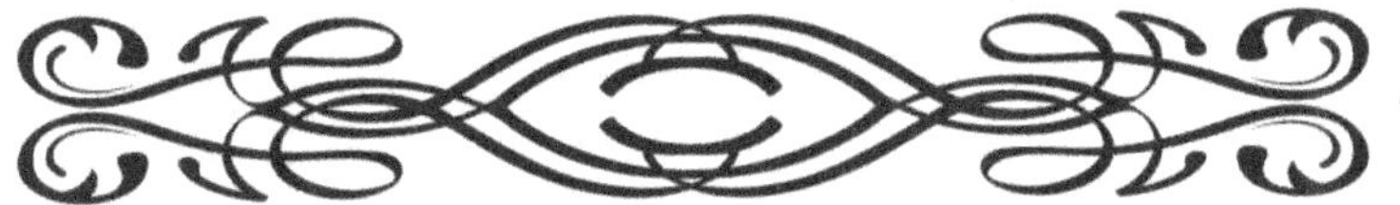

Chapter Twenty

Lark had exited Dr. Nolan's house in time to see Mrs. Olafsen running down the street toward the church. He didn't completely understand the grief she must be going through, but since Savannah came into his life, he understood it better than when he'd consoled a grieving wife or husband in the past.

The church door stood open. He walked up the two steps and into the building. His heart lodged in his throat, hearing the woman and child crying. But the sight of Savannah holding them both, spun his heart. He'd never met a more caring and giving individual.

He approached the women quietly. Savannah spotted him first. The sadness in her eyes nearly took him to the ground.

"Mrs. Olafsen?" He waited until the woman contained her tears and peered at him. "Mrs. Dearling has offered to put you up at her boarding house until you decide what you want to do."

The young woman continued to stare at him as if she didn't know what to say. He glanced at Savannah.

"That's a wonderful idea. I live there." She released the woman, but continued to hold the child. "Would you like me to take you over to the board'n house? Everyone else will be at work. You and Mrs. Dearlin' can get acquainted." She beamed down at the child in her arms. "She'll love hav'n this little young'n around."

Lark's gut felt as if someone had punched him. He wanted to see this woman holding a child they had made together.

"Y-yes. I need to go somewhere. I-I can't go to the house. Not without…" Tears started sliding down her cheeks.

Savannah stood, still holding the baby. "Come on. We'll get you tucked in with Mrs. Dearlin'." She nodded for Lark to help the woman to her feet.

He stepped beside Mrs. Olafsen, grasping her arm and helping her to stand. With an arm around her shoulders, he walked her to the door. Savannah walked just behind them.

"Don't you worry little one, this town will take care of you and your mama," Savannah said as they walked down the street toward the boarding house.

Mrs. Dearling stood on the threshold watching for them. She'd told Lark when she'd visited the doctor's earlier she would take the mother and child in until Mrs. Olafsen made a decision of what she wanted to do. As soon as the woman had dashed out the door after watching her husband take his last breath, he'd asked the doc to let Mrs. Dearling know he would be bringing the woman to her.

"There, there dear. A nice cup of tea for you and a bottle for the baby. That's what you need to get your bearings." Mrs. Dearling took the baby from Savannah and put an arm around the mother, leading them both into the boarding house.

Lark took hold of Savannah's hand, keeping her from entering the house. Her gaze latched onto his. "What you did for that woman…" He didn't know how to put it into words.

"I would hope if I were in the same situation someone would comfort me." The sadness lingered in her eyes.

"Did you get the posters put up?" he asked to change the subject.

"Yes. Oh! I left the last poster in the church and Mrs. Dearlin's basket." Her hand slipped from his as she walked down the steps.

"I'll come with you." He wanted to hold her in his arms. In the sanctuary of the church, he could without worrying about being seen.

They walked back to the church, not saying a word. Just walking beside her was all he needed.

Inside, she ambled down the aisle and picked up the basket and the poster as he made sure the door was closed tight.

He strode toward her, taking the items from her and pulling Savannah into an embrace.

Her arms wrapped around him, her head rested on his shoulder.

He breathed in her sweet floral scent. His heart danced in his chest holding her, feeling her life and vitality. "I needed this."

"Me, too." She snuggled her face into his neck. Her hot breath and lips touching the delicate skin brought his body to life.

"Savannah." He grasped her chin, tilted her face up to his, and captured her mouth. His body hummed. This was the first time today his world felt whole.

She pressed against him, opening her lips to allow him entry.

He groaned and entered, brushing his tongue over hers, and eliciting soft mewing sounds from her. His hand slid down her neck, cupping a breast. His mind told him this wasn't proper actions for a man of the cloth in a house of worship but his body needed to feel alive. To know the touch of another.

Savannah pulled out of the kiss and took a step back. "We can't. Not here." Her lips were puffy, wet, and the most desirable he'd ever laid his eyes on. Her chest heaved and her eyes sparkled with desire.

"There is nowhere in this town we can be together without someone noticing." He ran a hand across his face, hoping to still the need coursing through his body and fueling the length of his shaft. An idea came to him.

"I think you need to go to Bismarck and look at organs to give the congregation an idea of the price." He liked this idea, they could take a trip to Bismarck on Wednesday. He could dress as he did when being a courier for the bank. No one would know he was a preacher. They could spend the day together as normal people, without the eyes of the congregation on them.

"I can look up organs in the catalogue at the mercantile." Her smile grew. "But I would rather try the organ to make sure it has a nice sound."

"Then it's settled. You can mention you want to check out organs in Bismarck and I can escort you on Wednesday when I make my usual trip for the bank." Elation filled his heart.

"You don't think anyone will wonder that I picked the same day?" Her eyes sparkled but her lips didn't tip into a smile.

"It would make sense to have someone escort you. And since I'll already be headed that direction, I don't think anyone will say a thing. Especially given the information about Mr. Cartwell. I'm sure Beau wouldn't want you traveling alone."

Her eyes widened. "I'd plumb forgot about that conniving man." Savannah's lashes lowered, hiding her eyes. "Do you think he'll come after me?"

"I don't know what to think." He put a hand on her arm. "But your brother and I won't let him harm you."

The door opened.

Lark dropped his hand and faced Harold Smith, the undertaker and cabinet maker.

"Heard about Bjorn. Doc Nolan told me to speak to you and Mrs. Olafsen about the coffin." The man's gaze shifted from him to Savannah and back to him.

"Miss Gentry, I'll find a spot for the poster." He picked up the poster and handed the basket to Savannah.

"Thank you." She slipped her arm through the handle and smiled at Harold. "I'll let Mrs. Olafsen know y'all are com'n." She walked down the aisle and out of the church.

Harold watched until she was gone then swung back around. "People have been saying you could use a wife."

Lark stared at the man. What had he surmised from what he'd witnessed? "I've been thinking about it myself." He waved for the man to walk to the door. "Mrs. Olafsen is at Mrs. Dearling's boarding house."

Harold exited the church and faced him. "Miss Gentry

sure has took up raising money for the church."

A grin spread on Lark's face. "That she has. And she has been helping people."

They sauntered down the dusty street toward the boarding house.

"Someone has been spreading rumors you and Miss Gentry have been inappropriate." Harold didn't look at him and said the words almost as if talking to himself.

"Miss Gentry's arrival in town has brought out jealousy in a few of the women." He wasn't going to name anyone, even though he had a pretty good idea who was saying such things.

"And giving some of us a better chance at turning a head or two."

Lark studied the man walking beside him. He didn't have any flaws in his person or, as far as Lark knew, in his manners. Any woman who became Mrs. Smith would be well cared for. "Not every woman is capable of being a preacher's wife."

The man nodded.

They walked up to the front door of the boarding house and knocked.

Savannah opened the door. She'd hurried back to the boarding house to tell Mrs. Dearling what was about to happen. From her brief encounter with Rona, she didn't think the young woman would be ready to deal with this just yet.

"Come in," she said, making sure she didn't give Lark any more eye contact than the man with him. "Mrs. Dearlin' just managed to get Mrs. Olafsen to lie down. I don't know if we'll be much help to you, Mr—"

"Smith. I'm Harold Smith, the town's undertaker and

cabinet maker." The man had a pleasant face, red hair, and a few freckles. She remembered seeing him at the pie social.

"I'm pleased to meet you." She led the men into the parlor.

Mrs. Dearling bustled in. "I'm so sorry Mr. Smith, I don't know what the poor thing will want to do." She shifted her gaze to Lark. "Do you know anything about their finances? Mrs. Olafsen told me all her family is in Duluth. I encouraged her to send a telegraph, but she said she'd write a letter tomorrow."

"I'm sure Judd Campbell will help pay for the coffin," Lark said.

"The whole town will help," offered Mrs. Dearling.

Mr. Smith nodded. "I'll get started on the box." He studied Lark. "You'll let me know when he'll be buried?"

"Yes. With this heat, I'm sure it will be within a day or two," Lark said.

"I'll get busy then." Mr. Smith left the room, escorted by Mrs. Dearling.

Savannah took the limited time they had together to study Lark. There were so many things about this man that she liked. One of them being he wasn't a typical preacher.

"I'll mention to Beau I'll be go'n to Bismarck on Wednesday. Give him time to think about it."

Lark stepped closer to her and in a quiet voice said, "Good idea. He'll think about it and come up with asking me to escort you on his own."

The door closed and Lark stepped away from her.

Mrs. Dearling entered the room. "As soon as Mrs. Olafsen wakens, I'll ask her about the clothes to use to lay her husband out. I'll get Mrs. Cleary to help me."

Lark nodded. "With Mrs. Olafsen's permission, we'll bury him day after tomorrow. No sense in him laying around if she's sending a letter. It will take a week for a response from her family."

"I agree." Mrs. Dearling turned to Savannah. "You need to change and get over to the saloon."

Savannah glanced at the mantle clock. She would be late. Not a good way to start the day if she wanted to ask Beau's permission to take a trip to Bismarck.

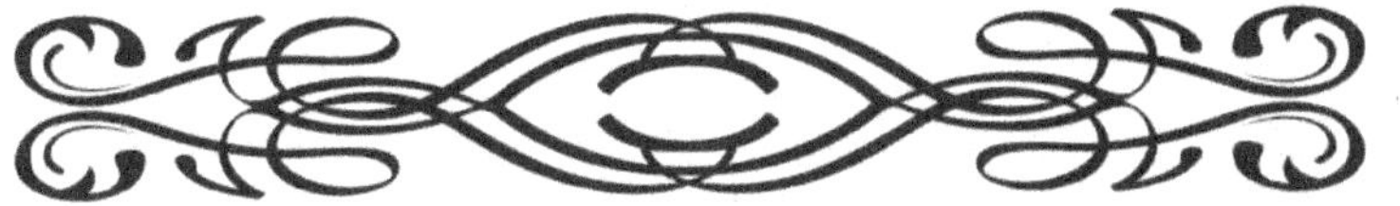

Chapter Twenty-one

Savannah waited until after she'd played the piano to talk with Beau. She had two things on her mind. One had to do with her trip to Bismarck and the other about the Fourth of July Picnic.

Lottie Mae patted her arm. "That was a stirring song. I like the ones that get soft and loud and soft again. Makes them feel like a story of sorts."

She smiled at the woman. "They are a story. A story the composer tells with the notes and chords he chooses."

The other woman smiled. "I like that." She moved out from behind the bar, making room for Savannah.

While it was a busy night, there weren't nearly as many men packed into the establishment as on other nights.

As Lottie Mae, Freedom, and Belle were getting ready to dance, Savannah stepped up beside Beau. "I would like to go to Bismarck on Wednesday to look at organs and get an idea of how much money the church needs to raise."

His attention swung to her in a heartbeat. "Don't you

already know how much one costs?"

"Back in Atlanta, yes. Here, no. I've discovered many things cost a pile more here." She was glad he asked that first instead of questioning the day of the week she'd picked.

He studied her. "Why do you have to go? Couldn't Lark check when he goes there as a courier for the bank?"

"He could. But I can try them out and know exactly how much money we'll need, because I'll know which organ sounds the best." She breathed in slow and easy. Which was hard to do with his steady gaze peering at her as if she were up to something.

"I'll have to think about it." He shifted his attention to a man at the end of the bar.

"That's fair," she said, taking empty glasses from a tray Liesa set on the bar.

"Six more beers."

Savannah glanced at Liesa, then stopped what she was doing and studied her. "What's wrong?"

Liesa shook her head, but Savannah saw the glimmer of tears in her eyes. She grasped the woman's arm, leading her into the back room.

"What's wrong? I see the tears in your eyes." Savannah plopped the woman on one of the chairs she and Beau sat on when they came in here to talk.

"The man. Gambler. He pinch me." Her lips trembled.

"Where?" Savannah found it hard to believe a man would go against Beau's rules of not touching.

"Here." Liesa pointed to her upper leg. "Hard." She raised her skirt and her short drawers, exposing a small round purple blemish on her thigh, close to her backside.

"How did he pinch you there?"

"I lean over table by his, picking up empty glasses." Her face puckered. "I do not want to go near him."

Savannah understood Liesa wasn't just scared of the man, he had humiliated her by touching her in an intimate area.

"Stay here." She strode out to the bar.

"Where have you been? And where is Liesa?" Beau confronted her.

"In the back. Get Jules over here. You need to see someth'n."

Beau didn't argue. He whistled, catching Jules attention and half of the patrons. He waved the man over to the bar.

"What do you need?" Jules asked when he stepped up to the bar.

"Take over a minute." Beau turned Savannah to the back room, and they both stepped behind the blanket.

Liesa spotted Beau and her face puckered up again.

"Shh. It's go'n to be all right. Show Beau what you showed me," Savannah said, stepping up to Liesa and putting a hand on her shoulder.

"What happened, Liesa?" Beau asked, crouching in front of her and speaking so soft, Savannah wouldn't have known it was her gruff brother if not for seeing him.

"Gambler. Pinch me." She slowly drew her skirt up her leg and stopped just shy of her small drawers. She peered at Beau as her shaking fingers pulled the hem of her drawers up several inches, exposing the growing purple bruise.

"Holy hell!" Beau said, on a rush of breath.

Liesa leaned back. Beau put a hand on her cheek. "Did he hurt you anywhere else?"

She shook her head.

"Put your skirt down and come to the blanket and point him out."

She dropped her skirt, and he held a hand out to her, helping her stand. He stood behind her as she peeked out from behind the blanket.

Savannah knew by Beau's curse that the man had broken the rules of the Silver Dollar Saloon before.

"You stay here until I get him out of my saloon," Beau told Liesa. He motioned to Savannah. "Take over the bar. I'll need Jules' help."

She nodded and walked out behind the bar. "Beau needs your help," she told Jules.

He stepped out from behind the bar and followed Beau to a table where there had been card games going on all night. She wasn't surprised when Beau walked up, grabbed a fancy dressed man by the back of his jacket, and lifted him out of the chair.

"This is what happens when you touch one of my girls," Beau boomed. He dragged the man by the back of his coat to the entrance.

She had expected Jules to open the door and Beau to throw the man out. But they both went out, Beau still dragging the man. Half the men in the room jumped up and ran to watch.

Lottie Mae, Belle, and Freedom hurried over to the bar. "What happened?" they all asked in unison.

"That man put a bruise on Liesa." Savannah could tell by the shouting and cheering, Beau and Jules were doing more than showing the man out of the establishment. "Will they get in trouble for beatin' the man?"

Lottie Mae shook her head. "Anyone who comes in here knows how Beau feels about us. And he told the sheriff, anyone who touches us will be taught not to touch another woman again.”

Freedom went into the back room and came out with Liesa. “Don’t you worry. That man won’t be back.”

The men moved away from the door and returned to their seats. Their voices were loud and raucous. Within minutes, Beau and Jules returned. Jules strode over to the piano and played a rollicking tune.

The ladies filled up trays with mugs of beer and began passing them out.

Beau stepped behind the bar. His knuckles were bleeding. He wrapped them in a towel and poured a jigger of whiskey, downing it in one swallow.

“He won’t be back to bother anyone.” Beau glared out at the men sitting around the room. “I don’t like anyone hurting any woman.”

Savannah wished they weren’t in the saloon so she could ask him why. It was plain to see something in his past had compelled him to help women. Was it because of his mother or someone else?

To take his mind off what had just happened, she decided to ask her other favor. “I’ve been thinkin’,” she started.

“We all think,” he quipped, pouring a jigger of whiskey and sliding it down the bar to a man about three feet away.

“Is there a way we could move the piano out to the walkway on the Fourth of July? I could play for the whole town. I would love to have the women and children hear classical music.” She’d been thinking about this for some time. It wasn’t fair that only the men were allowed to hear her music.

Beau stopped and stared at her. "That's a good idea. I'm sure the women and children would enjoy hearing you play. And if you did it in the morning, before the picnic baskets are auctioned, prices might go higher."

Savannah was pleased Beau thought it was a good idea. "I know several patriotic songs as well."

"Good. Good." Beau smiled and went back to filling glasses.

Finally, she would play for a crowd that wasn't all men drinking liquor.

Lark had been busy consoling Mrs. Olafsen and preparing for the burial of her husband. The warm summer sun made having the burial services at the cemetery and church the best place. They had the coffin setting under the largest tree and tables of food under the two smaller ones. The whole town had turned out to pay their respects and support the widow.

He'd wanted to talk to Savannah, but it seemed every time he'd visited Mrs. Olafsen at the boarding house, she was out. Now she stood behind one of the tables laden with food, helping serve.

To walk over and single her out would draw attention. He'd have to wait until a moment arose that he could talk with her. Perhaps, he would be invited to dinner tomorrow after the Sunday Service.

Mrs. Cleary walked up to him. "Reverend, we're ready for you to speak over Mr. Olafsen."

He nodded and walked over to the coffin. Everyone gathered around. Mrs. Dearling and Savannah stood on either side of the widow. Mrs. Olafsen clutched her child so tight he cried. Savannah eased the child from the mother and jostled the baby up and down, soothing him.

She would make a wonderful mother.

"Reverend?" Mrs. Cleary said.

Lark ripped his gaze from Savannah and began.

At the last prayer, he finally allowed himself a glance at Savannah. The child slept in her arms.

The pallbearers packed the coffin over to the freshly dug hole and using ropes, lowered it into the ground.

A wail pierced the silent graveyard.

He turned and watched Mrs. Dearling and Savannah leading Mrs. Olafsen away. The poor woman had confided in him that her family had not been happy with her choice of husband and she feared they would not allow her to come home. This town would rally around her and help her and her child survive.

A smile twitched his lips. The town had to see how hard Savannah worked to get an organ for the church and her compassion for others as she took care of Mrs. Olafsen and the baby.

As the pallbearers shoveled dirt into the hole, Lark returned to his house to finish tomorrow's sermon.

Chapter Twenty-two

Savannah was the first one ready to go to church. She'd received her answer from Beau the night before about going to Bismarck and couldn't wait to tell Lark she would see him on the train.

"You're in a hurry to go to church this morning," Lottie Mae said, walking into the parlor in her Sunday dress. "Could it be because of the way a certain preacher was drinking you up as you held that child yesterday?"

"What are you talk'n about?" She hadn't noticed Lark watching her. In fact, she'd felt as if he'd kept his distance.

Lottie Mae grinned. "Don't act like you didn't see him. Mrs. Cleary had to pull his mind off you and back to his job."

She shook her head. "I didn't see him watch'n me." She lowered her voice. "I thought it felt like he was avoid'n me."

"Oh no. When he wasn't speaking, his eyes were on you."

That wasn't good. Especially if everyone else saw the same thing. "Oh my! Did anyone else notice?"

"A person would have to be blind to have missed it." Lottie Mae patted her arm. "Don't worry. From what I've heard, the town is happy for the reverend."

"Happy? In what way?"

"They like the idea of him having a wife. It makes him more likely to stay here."

Savannah studied the woman. The town was hoping he'd get a wife and settle down? "He's not likely to go anywhere. His brother set roots here."

The rest of the women, including Rona and the baby, walked into the parlor.

"Is everyone ready?" Mrs. Dearling asked, leading them out of the room and the house.

As one procession, they walked down the street to the church. Many horses and wagons were already lined up under the trees. People walked down the streets toward the white building with colorful stained-glass windows.

Savannah's heart filled with joy. The church was beautiful, the congregation welcoming, and the preacher…her heart stuttered, taking in the handsome man in the black suit standing at the door to the church, shaking hands and welcoming his congregation.

When it was their turn to enter, he grasped each woman's hand, holding hers a few seconds longer. "It's good to see all of you here this morning."

"We wouldn't miss it," Mrs. Dearling said, shooing them all through the door like a covey of quail.

Savannah wanted to stay on the step by his side, but propriety didn't allow such a gesture. Instead, she followed the group down the aisle. Mrs. Dearling shuffled into a pew with the other women following. They all sat down. Being last, she ended up without a seat. She glanced around and spotted Beau and Jules. She walked over and made the two scoot over to allow her to sit.

The sermon was wonderful. The best part being she could stare at Lark for an hour without worrying someone might come to the wrong conclusions.

At the end, he held up the picnic poster. "Don't forget the Fourth of July Picnic and basket auction to raise proceeds for a church organ will be a week from Tuesday. Ladies put together your best foods in a pretty basket and we'll make money for the church and allow some of these bachelors a chance to eat with a pretty lady." Lark's gaze rested on her for a brief moment as the congregation laughed at his comment. When the voices died down, he announced all of the other things happening on the fourth.

Beau stood up.

"Mr. Gentry, do you have something to say?" Lark asked.

"On the fourth, we're going to pull the piano out onto the walkway in front of the Silver Dollar and my sister, Miss Gentry, will play for the town."

Murmurs and clapping surprised her. The town was willing to hear her play and accept she had a talent other than working at the saloon.

"That is wonderful news," Lark said. "It will give everyone a chance to hear Miss Gentry's talent and see what getting an organ for the church would mean to this town." His smile lit up his face and his eyes twinkled.

Her idea had made so many people happy, tears trickled down her cheeks.

"Why are you crying?" Beau asked quietly as the

congregation started flowing out of the building.

"It's happiness. I can't believe so many people want to hear me play the piano." She sniffed and dabbed at her eyes with a handkerchief.

"Women," Beau huffed and moved her out of his way so he could exit the pew and the church.

Jules followed behind him but not before putting a hand on her shoulder. "It is a good thing, *ma chérie*. You will see."

She nodded. The building quieted, and she realized she was the only person still in the church. Even Lark had left. A last dab at her eyes, and she strolled out.

Many people still lingered in the church yard.

Several women she didn't know by name came over to her.

"We're so glad you will play for us. Our husbands come home from the saloon and tell us how your music moved them," one of the older women said.

She didn't know what to say. "I enjoy play'n. I've wanted to share my music with the whole town."

"Thank you," said another woman.

"We've all been itching to hear you," said another.

Soon they all wandered off and she was left scanning the yard for anyone from the boarding house.

"Looking for someone?"

She spun toward the voice that always warmed her. "The ladies from the board'n house, but you will do," she teased.

Lark's grin grew. "I've been wanting to talk to you for days. We never seemed to meet up."

"I had hoped we'd get a chance to talk today." She glanced around, didn't see anyone, and leaned closer.

"Beau agreed to let me go to Bismarck on Wednesday."

Lark's smile spread, popping out his dimples and adding a sparkle to his eyes. "That is good news." He glanced around. "Any chance you could invite me to dinner at the boarding house?"

"You know, you're always welcome there." She wanted to wrap her arm around his and be escorted properly, but refrained. Instead, she strolled toward the street, and he fell into step beside her.

"Were you really caught stare'n at me yesterday?" She still couldn't fathom how she'd not seen it.

"I'm afraid I was. Mrs. Cleary about pulled my ear off afterwards telling me I had 'to keep me mind on me work,'" he said, pitching his voice higher and speaking like Mrs. Cleary.

They both laughed.

He sobered. "You looked so right holding that child and soothing it."

His soft warm tone sent heat swirling in her center. "I didn't know how I felt about children until this whole ordeal." She smiled. "Turns out, I like them more than I thought."

Lark wanted to put a hand on her arm and escort her proper, but after the chastising he received from Mrs. Cleary yesterday, he wanted to make sure his courtship with Savannah, as seen through the eyes of his congregation, was slow and steady. Nothing that would put either of them in disfavor with this town.

Her acknowledging her love of children only made him want her in his life more.

At the boarding house, he opened the front door, allowing her to enter and announce she'd brought him home for dinner.

"We were expecting you," Beau said, as he stepped out of the parlor and walked toward the door.

"You were?" Lark closed the door and faced Savannah's brother.

"Yes. When Savannah stayed behind, we figured she was inviting you." He motioned for Lark to step back out onto the porch.

Lark glanced over the other man's shoulder and spotted Savannah standing in the hallway. Fear had frozen her features.

He nodded and opened the door, walking back out into the summer sun and heat. "What did we need to step out here and talk about?" Had the man figured out he and Savannah had planned a clandestine trip?

"What do you know of Rona Olafsen's family?"

This wasn't what he'd expected. But he understood Beau's concerns. The large man championed all women in trouble.

"She and her family aren't on speaking terms since she married Bjorn. She's waiting to hear back from a letter she sent. I believe she hopes they will ask her to return and live with them." He'd had several long conversations with Rona. She believed her husband was killed because she'd betrayed her family by marrying Bjorn. That God had punished her in this way for her betrayal. He'd tried to make her see that wasn't true, however, her feelings were her way of coping with her loss.

"And if they don't take her in? Has anyone stepped forward to say they would help her if she stayed?" Beau asked.

"There have been some who are willing to help out.

Judd said he'd give the house to her, and Mrs. Polzin said she could give her some work. I think if she stays she will be taken care of." He knew the gruff saloon owner with the soft heart would make sure the woman didn't want for anything.

"Good." Beau reached for the door knob then spun around. "Are you going to Bismarck this Wednesday?"

This was what he'd expected when they'd first stepped out on the porch. "You know I am. I go every Wednesday for Owen."

Beau studied him. "This may be letting the fox in the hen house, but would you keep an eye on Savannah? She's got it in her head she needs to go play organs to find the right one for the church." His eyes narrowed. "I blame you for this."

Lark gulped. "Why do you blame me?"

"You put the notion of her playing for the church in her head."

He released the tension that had tightened his shoulders and smiled. "You know having her play the organ at services would bring the congregation closer to God."

Beau grunted and entered the house.

Lark let out a whoosh of air. Either the man hadn't figured it out, or he was silently giving his approval for Lark to court his sister.

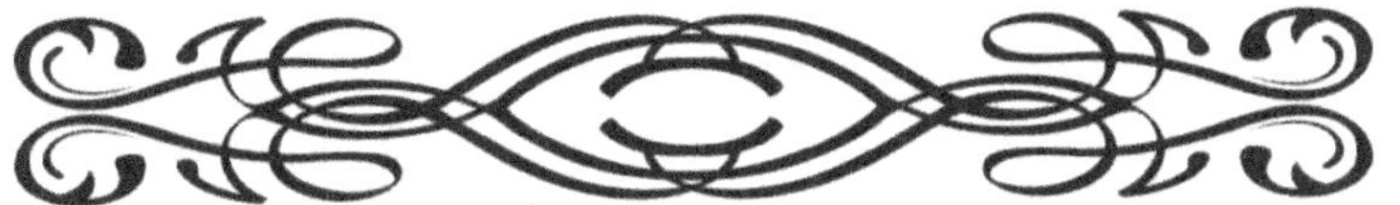

Chapter Twenty-three

Savannah's stomach was fluttering so much she couldn't eat a morsel for breakfast. And now, as she sat on the train, waiting for Lark, she wished she'd taken the biscuits Mrs. Dearling had offered her for the trip.

The older woman had raised an eyebrow when Savannah told everyone at the breakfast table she would be late getting to work because she was traveling to Bismarck to research which organ would be best for the church. Lottie Mae had winked at her. Liesa had blushed. Belle had frowned, and Freedom told her to enjoy her day.

From all their reactions, they knew she was meeting Lark. Would the whole town figure it out as well?

The train whistle blew and still no sign of Lark. Her stomach lurched along with the train car as the engine chuffed smoke and pulled out of the depot.

Had he missed the train? Something must have come up that he couldn't leave. She didn't worry about finding the music store in Bismarck by herself, but she would have to spend several hours alone, waiting for the return trip.

The train picked up speed and she peered around the car. She'd opted to only purchase the cheapest fare. Sitting on the hard wood seat would be bearable for the three hours to Bismarck.

The door at the front of the car opened. Her heart raced. Lark walked toward her dressed in boots, wool britches, chambray shirt, red bandana, and wide-brimmed hat. He wore the holster and gun she'd noticed the first day they met and carried the valise.

He stopped beside her seat, touched the brim of his hat, and grinned. "Mind if I sit next to you, Ma'am?"

She pinched her lips together to keep from laughing. "I reckon, you could keep the seat warm." She slid over, allowing him plenty of room.

"You don't have to scoot away like I have fleas," he said, quietly.

Savannah settled her skirts and slid a tiny bit back toward him, so their arms would touch. Feeling the heat of his arm against hers sent her insides fluttering.

"I thought someth'n came up to keep you," she said softly. There were few passengers on the train and none that she knew, but she felt the need to talk softly and not let anyone know their meeting was planned.

"No. I waited until the last minute, like I always do, and boarded a couple cars up. If Joe glanced out and saw my change of routine, he might be curious, knowing you had boarded the train." He peered at her from under the brim of his hat.

She liked that she was just the right height to study him without him having to take his hat off. "That was smart. Although when I told everybody at the board'n house I was headed to Bismarck today, they all looked like the cat that got into the chicken pen. I think they knew I would be do'n more than look'n at organs."

"Tickets! Tickets!" hollered the conductor as he came through the front door.

She dug her ticket out of her purse and held it up. Lark held his up. Once the man took their tickets, Lark grasped her hand in his and settled them between their thighs. The valise on his lap and her skirts hid the fact they held hands.

His hand clasped hers with gentleness. His thumb stroked softly across hers. Her heart ached with happiness.

They talked of her life in Atlanta and his life growing up the son of a wheat farmer.

"Neither you or Owen wanted to continue your daddy's wheat farm?" she asked.

"Our older brother, Frank, took over. He was always more interested in helping Pa than we were."

She could tell by his closed down features, he didn't like to talk about his oldest brother. But she had one more question. "Did y'all get along?"

His face became stormy, and his grip tightened on her hand. "No. Once Pa started ailing, Frank thought he could force me to help him." His gaze landed on her face. "I'm not proud of how I behaved for a long time. But when I vowed to God I'd become a servant for him, I turned things around."

She saw the conviction in his face and heard it in his voice. One day, she hoped he would tell her what had caused him to change his ways. "Does he know you're a preacher with a congregation that loves you?"

He shook his head. "If he does, he didn't hear it from me."

She squeezed his hand. Her stomach grumbled loudly. "Did you eat anything this morning?"

"I was too excited and nervous." She glanced at him. The concern in his eyes started her heart flopping around, giving her grumbling stomach competition.

"Here." He pulled a brown paper wrapped package out of his valise. "I didn't want to change my routine so I stopped in at the bakery to pick up a roll for my lunch."

She released his hand and took the roll, breaking it in two and handing him one half. "Mrs. Dearlin' tried to send me with biscuits, but I didn't think I'd be able to eat them." She bit into the roll, enjoying the yeasty, buttery taste.

"I plan to take you to a nice café for lunch after we look at organs." He didn't bite into his half of the roll.

His gaze leveled on her mouth, making it hard for her to swallow. She plucked a crumb from her lips with her tongue and watched a spark light in his eyes before he shuttered them with his lashes.

"I should have brought someth'n to drink. This roll is go'n down like a burr in a sock." She choked the words out.

He reached into his valise and pulled out a flask. "Don't worry, it's only water. But to anyone watching, it looks like whiskey. It makes me look tougher than I am."

She laughed and took the flask. Opening the lid, she sniffed, found no alcohol, and took a swallow. After rinsing the roll down, she replaced the lid and handed the flask back.

"Is that why you wear a holster and gun, to make anyone think'n to steal the valise that you're a lawman?"

"Something like that. I carry important papers and bank drafts and don't want them to get into the wrong hands." He studied the passing scenery. "We're getting close. The first thing we'll do is drop this off at the bank."

She nodded, tucked her hand down beside her, and smiled when he folded his hand around hers.

Lark couldn't stop smiling. This day had been one of the best in his life. After dropping off the valise at the bank, they strolled to the music store. He listened to Savannah play hymns on four different organs before she'd determined which one would be best for the church. The salesman said it would cost them fifty-six dollars. It would take more than the pie social and the picnic basket raffle to raise that much money. But Savannah gave the man the six dollars and seven cents from the pie social and asked him to hold it for her. "We'll continue paying toward this beautiful organ," she told the man.

After the music store, they had lunch at a café he'd walked by many times and never went in. The best part was walking arm in arm through the town and the city park, enjoying the summer day. He wanted to kiss her, but even though they were away from prying eyes, to kiss her in public the way he wanted to kiss her, it was best to refrain.

"That bench looks invit'n. Could we sit a spell?" Savannah asked, pointing to a long wooden seat partially hidden behind a large elm tree.

He led her to the bench, waited for her to get settled, and sat beside her, his arm stretched behind her across the back of the bench. "Have I been walking you too much?"

"No. Walk'n is good. I stand too much work'n at the saloon." She leaned closer to him. Her eyes gazing into his. "Would I be too forward to ask you for a kiss?"

He grinned. "I've been wanting to kiss you since sitting beside you on the train." Lark leaned closer, keeping his hands away from her body to keep the kiss light.

Their lips touched and sparks spread throughout his body. This woman did things to him, he'd never experienced before with only a chaste kiss. What would it be like to love her fully? His shaft hardened and throbbed as the thought circled in his head. He fisted his hands to keep from touching her as she deepened the kiss and placed her palms on his chest.

Her hands trembled and her fingers clutched at his vest. It was humbling to know he affected Savannah the same as she affected him.

He leaned back, drawing away from her and the kiss. It was the hardest thing he'd ever had to do. His body fought against his better sense. But this was not the time or place to show her how much she meant to him.

Her eyelashes fluttered up and she gazed into his eyes. "Don't you like kiss'n me?"

"There is nothing I want to do more, but we're out here where anyone walking by could see." He glanced around and didn't see another soul.

"Can we go somewhere that no one will see us?" Her hands rubbed back and forth across his chest. "I want to kiss you more."

Her plea shot him to his feet.

"There's one way we can have privacy." He escorted her back to the bank where he picked up the valise, and they walked back to the railroad station.

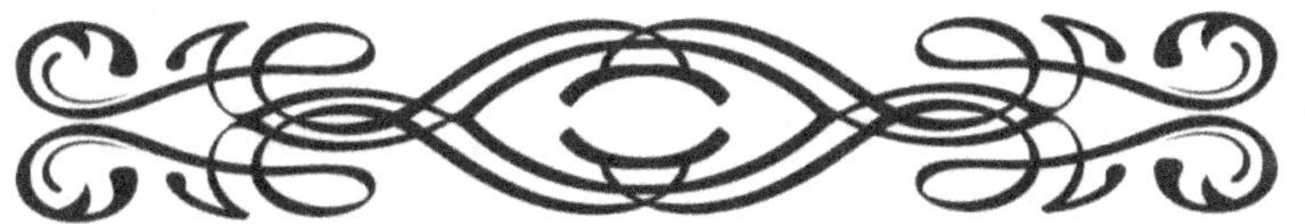

Chapter Twenty-four

Savannah stood inside the drawing room of the palace train car with her eyes taking in the opulence.

"You shouldn't have spent this much money," she said, facing Lark.

He stood inside the door grinning. "Seeing the look on your face and knowing we'll have three hours of uninterrupted time, it's worth every dollar." He hung his hat and holster on a hook by the door and tossed the valise in a chair by a small table.

The small room was the width of the car except for the narrow passage they'd walked down to enter the room. Along with the door opening to the passageway, there was a door that opened to a tiny closet with a washstand basin. The door on the other side of this room opened into another drawing room. The furniture consisted of a long sofa on one side of the room and two large arm-chairs on the other side, facing the sofa. Two brass spittoons sat by the chairs. Mirrored glass everywhere made the room sparkle and appear larger. The hooks and rods for the curtains were silver plated.

"Take off your hat and gloves. Get comfortable."

A knock on the door and the words "Conductor" had Lark reaching for the door. He opened it, handed the man the tickets, and closed the door. "Now, no more interruptions."

Savannah liked the sound of that. She removed her gloves and unpinned her hat, placing it on the chair with the valise. She sat on the couch, relieving her aching feet. Her new boots weren't broken in yet. She wiggled her feet.

"Are your feet sore?" Lark asked, sitting on the couch next to her.

"I'm afraid I've not been walk'n enough to wear in my new boots."

"Here." He picked up the foot closest to him and unlaced her boot. With slow easy movements, Lark pulled the boot off her hot, sweaty foot.

"Oh! That feels wonderful." She wanted to cry feeling the cool air and release of her foot.

He left her foot resting on his legs and picked up her other foot. Soon she sat on the couch, her stocking feet in Lark's lap.

She wiggled her toes. "That feels refresh'n as a spring shower. I didn't realize how much they hurt until you released them."

"I can do more than save them from your boots." He began gently massaging her foot.

She'd never had anyone treat her with such care. Her heart nearly burst out of her chest at the gentle ministrations and deep concentration he had on her foot. He gave both feet the same attention.

When her body had heated to the boiling point from his touches and caresses, she leaned over and kissed his cheek. "I think it's time you gave my lips some shugah."

He laughed and moved his hands up her legs, stroking the calves and teasing the soft flesh behind her knees. "I think that is a good idea." Lark reached over with the hand not on her legs and cupped the back of her head, drawing her lips to his.

She gasped at the sensations swirling and sparking in her body from his touch and the deep tongue tangling kiss. Her body was on fire. With their lips still connected in the kiss, she unbuttoned her walking coat. Lark's hands slid under the coat and together they slid it off her body. She knew to be alone with him like this and craving his kisses was improper, but they had so little time alone, she wanted to experience all she could while with him. Perhaps, by sating her hunger for his kisses, she'd be able to look at him without wondering when they would kiss again.

Her body arched toward him when his hands slid up her sides, resting against her breasts. There was a bodice, chemise, corset, and shift between their skins, but the pressure and knowledge his hands rested so intimately sent her senses spinning. She knew this was wanton behavior, but the idea of not allowing him to touch her made her heart ache.

Lark's lips moved down her chin and neck, leaving a wet trail of kisses. She sighed and dropped her head backwards, offering him the soft, sensitive skin.

Shivers of delight converged with the heat building low in her body.

His mouth came back to hers, drugging her with another mating of their tongues. One hand had returned to her legs. He trailed his fingers up and down her calf. Her legs quivered. His other hand held her close, continuing the kiss.

When she couldn't catch her breath, she pulled away from his lips, placing her head on his shoulder.

"Lord a mercy! I didn't know kiss'n a man could start a fire in my body." She continued to breathe heavy as his hand on her leg moved up to her thigh.

"Not every man will do that to you." Lark peered into Savannah's shining eyes. "Only you make my body heat and have me wishing I hadn't put a white collar around my neck." Right now, he wanted to be the Topeka Kid. Lay her out on the couch and make love to her. But given his new life, he would have to settle with touching and kissing Savannah until they were properly married.

She studied him. "What do you mean about the white collar?"

"If I hadn't taken up the calling of a preacher, we could be married now, without having to prove to a congregation you're worthy of being a preacher's wife." He wanted her to know how much he cared and wanted her.

Her eyes widened. He could see her mind working behind her brown-rimmed irises.

"You desire me so much you wish you weren't a preacher?" The question sounded more like she was taking in the meaning.

"Yes. Savannah, I have never wanted a woman as deeply as I want to cherish you." He didn't have to fake emotion. It was the solid truth. He wanted to cherish this woman the rest of his life.

Tears glistened in her eyes and her lips tipped up into a smile. "I feel the same way. You care so much for the people in your congregation, and they respect you not only as a preacher but as a man." She dropped her gaze then raised it slowly. The love shining in her eyes spun his heart. "I would be pleased to have you take me as your wife and take me to bed."

"Savannah," he groaned and captured her lips, kissing her with the pent-up emotions he wanted to share with her whole body.

The conductor strode down the passageway calling, "Next stop, Shady Gulch."

Lark drew out of the kiss. "You need to get dressed and I need to move to one of the other cars."

She nodded, but her arms didn't unwrap from around his neck. "Can we do this again soon?"

He dropped a soft kiss on her lips. "We'll have to do something or I won't be fit to preach."

She laughed and released him. He put her boots on her feet as she pulled on her jacket and pinned on her hat.

When she was dressed, all but her gloves, he grasped her hands. "I promise to start courting you proper soon."

"I hope so. The sooner you court me, the sooner we can marry and you can ease this fire." She stepped closer to him and whispered. "I don't believe God would think unkindly of you if you put me out of my misery by bedd'n me."

He laughed, strapped on his holster, plopped his hat on his head, and picked up the valise. "I'll see you tomorrow."

She nodded, her eyes shining.

Lark couldn't help but feel he'd just become the luckiest man alive. He walked down the passageway and through the cars until he came to the last one. He sat in the last bench by the door and couldn't wipe the smile from his face. He'd best stay away from Beau tonight or until this smile went away. He'd put two and two together and realize he and Savannah had done more than organ shop.

Savannah stepped off the train, hoping for a glimpse of Lark, but she didn't see him anywhere on the platform. It was nearly supper time. She hurried down the street past the Allman Hotel, mercantile, café, bootmaker, and the Silver Dollar. At the corner by the Silver Dollar, she glanced over her shoulder and spotted Lark entering the bank. She smiled and continued to the boarding house.

"How was your trip?" Mrs. Dearling asked when Savannah walked into the kitchen.

"Good. I put the pie social money down on an organ that has the most beautiful sound. It will make the hymns sound twice as wonderful." She picked up a glass and poured water. It wasn't as fun as drinking from Lark's flask, but it quenched her thirst. Who knew kissing so much could make a person parched?

"What did you do when you weren't looking at organs?" The older woman handed her plates of food to put on the table.

"W- I walked through the park and saw a bit of Bismarck." She'd almost slipped up. The raised eyebrows and pinched lips on Mrs. Dearling showed she had.

"I'll flit on upstairs and change so I can go to the Silver Dollar as soon as I eat." She hurried out of the kitchen and up to her room. Standing in front of the mirror, repining her hair, she noticed how red and swollen her lips appeared. Had Mrs. Dearling noticed? Upon a stricter inspection of herself, she noted pinker cheeks and shinier eyes. Would Beau notice? The other ladies?

Her heart pattered in her chest. Happiness, an emotion she had thought she'd lost, filled her. She didn't care if anyone discovered she and Lark had spent the day together in Bismarck. He made her happy. Something she hadn't thought would come to her after losing Daddy and the home she knew.

She finished her hair, shook out the skirt of her fancy dress she only wore while at work in the saloon, and headed down to the kitchen.

Freedom and Belle were already seated and eating. They both looked up. Belle frowned, but Freedom's smile spread across her face.

"Did you find an organ?" she asked.

"Yes. It's beautiful. I can't wait until it's paid for and we bring it to the church." Savannah picked up her fork.

"Mr. Montgomery said he seen you and Reverend Webster both get on the train this morning," Freedom said.

"I'm sure he did. Today is Wednesday. The day the reverend makes his bank courier run to Bismarck." Savannah put food in her mouth to avoid saying anything more.

"He said you two were going off together," Belle said.

Savannah took a sip of water and said, "I don't know how he could jump to that idea. I didn't see Reverend Webster until the train had pulled out of the station."

"But you did see him?" Belle insisted.

She studied the other woman. Why was she so insistent? What did it matter to Belle if she and Lark had met up in Bismarck?

"Yes, I did see him. We went to the music store together. We both picked out the organ and we had lunch together." She glanced around the room. "There was noth'n wrong with us both pick'n out the organ. I'll be play'n it and the instrument will be in Reverend Webster's church."

Freedom nodded. "Sounds reasonable to me."

Belle narrowed her eyes. "Did you tell Beau you and the reverend were meeting in Bismarck?"

"Not that it's any of your concern, I did not. We decided the arrangement when we met on the train." Savannah stood. Even though she hadn't finished her meal, she was tired of the questions. "I'm go'n on over to the saloon." She glanced over at Mrs. Dearling. The woman hadn't said a word during the conversation. Right now, she appeared to be thinking on something real hard.

Savannah ducked out the door, across the alley, and into the backroom of the Silver Dollar. She hoped Beau didn't question her like Belle.

Pushing the blanket to the side, she was met by the usual ruckus, smoke, and yeasty scent of spilled beer and sickening sweet stench of the spittoons. Even though Beau and Jules dumped the spittoons every morning, they only washed them out once a month. By the end of a month, the smell became almost nauseating to Savannah.

She stepped up to the bar.

Beau caught sight of her and marched over. "What the hell were you thinking sneaking off to Bismarck with Lark?"

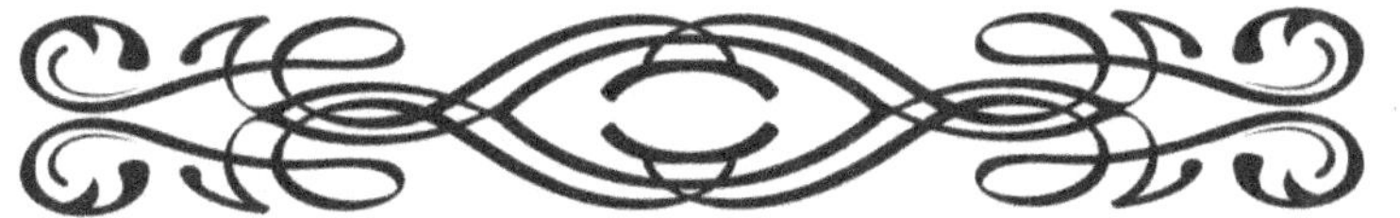

Chapter Twenty-five

Savannah took a step back before her spine straightened and her anger came to a boil. She pointed a finger at Beau, poking him in the chest. "I've had enough of everyone accus'n me and Lark of do'n someth'n wrong. All we did was ride the same train to Bismarck, check out organs, have lunch, go for a walk in the park, and ride the train back here. If someone says different, they are spitt'n false words."

She glared at her hulking brother and saw the surprise in his eyes and disbelief on his face. It was evident he'd expected her to try and hide the facts. Well, he didn't know her very well if he thought she'd lie. The more she thought about it, she didn't understand why Lark was being so secretive about their attraction.

He grabbed her hand. "Don't ever point your finger at me." He released her hand. "If you say that's all that happened, then the stories the men have been coming in here with all day don't mean spit."

Her heart slammed against her ribs. "Stories? What stories?"

"That you two secretly boarded the train for Bismarck this morning. Speculations on what you two might have been up to is not for a woman's ears." He nodded as her face heated and her insides tied in knots.

"They…" she stared at the men sitting at the tables in the saloon, "think Lark and I…" She knew what the men thought. It was what she'd practically begged Lark to do. Savannah stepped closer to Beau and whispered. "We didn't do anyth'n other than what I said. How do I make the town believe that?"

"Tell everyone the truth and don't act ashamed." He picked up a towel and started wiping out the dirty glasses on a tray.

Liesa and Lottie Mae both walked up to the bar with trays of dirty glasses.

"How was the trip?" Lottie Mae asked.

"Good. We picked out an organ for the church. Wait until y'all hear it, you'll think we're in heaven." She smiled and unloaded the trays.

"We? As in you and Reverend Webster?" Lottie Mae asked.

"Who else would need a say in the purchas'n of an organ for the church?" She stared the other woman in the eyes.

"I guess that's true," she said as Freedom and Belle returned from dinner.

"Our turn to eat. Come on, Liesa," Lottie Mae said, smiling and herding the smaller woman out through the back room.

Belle picked up a tray of full glasses of beer and

headed out through the tables.

Freedom picked up her tray but peered at Savannah. "Some of these men have been saying mean things about you and the reverend."

"If anyone makes a comment, just tell them we picked out an organ for the church." Savannah hoped the women of the community weren't as sour-minded as the men seemed to be.

Lark dropped the valise off at the bank and had a short discussion with Owen about the rumors spreading about he and Savannah sneaking off to Bismarck together. This was exactly what he'd feared. The congregation getting the wrong idea. They had to see Savannah was of a pure heart. And had a lusty nature. He grinned as he walked up to his house. He had no doubt that if they were married, every night would be an adventure with Savannah.

There were three notes fluttering under the rock by his door. He picked them up and read the first one. Rage reddened his mind and blurred his vision. Someone had left a note suggesting he not allow the women of the Silver Dollar in the church anymore, for it seemed they were distracting him from his duties.

He shoved his door open and read the next two. Both similar to the first. No one had minded the Silver Dollar women coming to church before. Everyone knew that they were just women down on their luck and Beau helped them out. Who was spreading all these vicious rumors?

While he hadn't planned on seeing Savannah again today, he needed to warn her about the comments being made. He took off his holster and headed back out the door. He'd check at the boarding house before talking to her at the saloon, considering the rumors being spread.

He strode down the street and up to the kitchen door of the boarding house. Lark knocked on the back door and waited for Mrs. Dearling to answer.

She didn't greet him with the usual good humor. It was obvious she wasn't happy with him.

"Mrs. Dearling, is Miss Gentry here?" He took off his hat, holding it in his hands as he nodded to Lottie Mae and Liesa.

"She's at work. You spent the day with her, why are you looking for her now?" The woman crossed her arms and stared at him.

He held out the notes he'd picked up under the rock.

She uncrossed her arms and read them. "Oh my! These are nasty!" She glanced over at the two women eating. "And so untrue." She shook the notes. "How could someone jump from you and Savannah traveling to Bismarck to look at an organ, to this?"

He shook his head. "I don't know, but I wanted to warn her about the rumors."

Lottie Mae stood up. "She's already figured that out. The men have been talking about the two of you leaving on the train together, all day."

Lark slapped his hat against his thigh. "Would it have been any different if we had told the whole town we were going to put money down on an organ?"

Mrs. Dearling nodded. "It wouldn't have looked like you were sneaking around."

The tips of his ears felt as if they'd caught on fire. "I just thought it would be easier to not make a big deal out of the two of us going to Bismarck on the same day."

"Now, you'll have to figure out how to fix this." The

older woman wagged her finger. "Running into the saloon right now isn't the way."

He agreed. The best way to nip this problem would be to tell everyone about the organ. He'd change into his preacher clothes and visit all the eateries that were still open. And tomorrow, he'd visit all the businesses. And maybe, while he visited with people he'd discover who had left the notes.

Savannah hadn't set foot around town since the trip to Bismarck. Mrs. Dearling told her about the notes, as did Lark when he visited her Thursday morning to pick up the receipt and brochure on the organ. He said he wanted to show the people around town the instrument they'd picked out for the church.

She knew he was spreading honey around to make their friendship less vile to the people who were writing notes and spreading rumors.

Today she couldn't avoid the townsfolk. It was Sunday and in only two days it would be the Fourth of July Picnic. She'd donned her best dress, made sure not a hair was out of place and pulled on her gloves.

In the parlor, everyone was dressed in their Sunday best waiting for her. They had all been told about the notes and not a one of them was going to be kept from attending the Sunday Service.

Mrs. Dearling opened the door, and they all filed out, their heads high and their backs straight. They proceeded this way down the street and up to the church. A few women stared, but most acted the same as usual. Mrs. Dearling called good morning to her friends, and they all walked up to the door and Lark.

"Good morning, Ladies. I'm glad you could all make it." He squeezed each one's hand and made eye contact.

When Savannah stepped up to him, he took her hand. "I'm glad you're here. We can tell the congregation about the organ we picked out."

She smiled. "Yes, we can."

He released her hand, and she moved on into the church, once again, taking a seat next to Beau and Jules.

She heard whispering behind her, but ignored it.

The sermon started, and she was pleased Lark had picked the topic of not judging a person by the clothes they wore. At the end, he held up the poster again.

"This Tuesday is the Fourth of July. Ladies, don't forget to put together a mouth-watering picnic basket to be auctioned to the highest bidder. The bidder of your basket and you, will then share the contents. As you all know, the money from the sale of the baskets will go toward an organ for this church. This past Wednesday Miss Gentry and I went to Bismarck and put the money from the pie social down on this organ." He held up the flyer with a picture of the organ. "Miss Gentry played every organ in the store, and I have to agree with her choice. This instrument had the most heavenly tone. And while the price may take us some time before we can purchase the instrument in full, it will be worth the time and effort to get."

He stepped down to the pews and handed the flyer to the deacon in the front row. "Pass this around and see what will one day sit in our church and lead the hymns."

He glanced her way. She smiled and tipped her head.

Beau jabbed an elbow in her arm.

"Ow, what was that for?" she whispered.

"Don't send him secretive smiles in church if you

don't want rumors flying," he whispered back.

"It wasn't secretive. I was just support'n the way he handled tell'n the congregation."

Many had started to leave the church, including Mrs. Dearling and the other ladies. She stepped into the aisle and as much as she wanted to glance over her shoulder for a glimpse of Lark, she walked toward the door.

Mrs. Cleary put a hand out, stopping her. "Do yer think we'll be able to raise the kind o' money I seen on that organ?"

Savannah smiled at the woman. "Yes. I believe we can. Not only can we have events like pie socials and picnic basket auctions, we'll also see if the businesses can give a little." She put a hand on the woman's arm. "Don't worry. We won't be ask'n for any more than y'all are will'n and able to give."

The woman smiled. "I told those gossipy gooses you and the reverend wouldn't do anything wrong. You both are too good-hearted."

"Thank you, Mrs. Cleary. I wish more people saw us for what we are instead of mak'n things up."

The older woman leaned close. "I think yer'd make a right good preacher's wife." She winked and moved down the aisle ahead of Savannah.

The woman's words put a smile on her face and lightened her steps. Not everyone thought the worst of her. If Mrs. Dearling and Mrs. Cleary could sway the others, she and Lark might have a chance to court without censure.

Outside, she walked over to where the ladies of the boarding house were in a discussion with Mrs. Polzin, Mrs. Beal, and Mrs. Flanagan.

"Miss Gentry, we were just asking the ladies if we

could tie a ribbon or do something to our baskets so our husbands would know which basket to bid on," Mrs. Flanagan asked.

"Oh, you will stand up with your basket. We don't want anyone mistak'n a married woman's basket for a single woman's. We'd have fist fights gon' on." She laughed and the others laughed along with her.

"We are much pleased you will play the piano for everyone," Mrs. Polzin said. "I have not heard classical music since leaving my home in Russia."

"Do you have a favorite?" Savannah asked.

"Peter Ilyich Tchaikovsky." Mrs. Polzin closed her eyes and hummed a stanza of one of the pieces Savannah knew.

"I know that concerto. I'll play it on Tuesday."

"That would be wonderful," Mrs. Polzin said and called to her children. The small family headed across the street toward her store and home.

"That was nice of you," Mrs. Dearling said.

"It is a beautiful piece. Everyone will enjoy hear'n it." She turned to the other women. "Do y'all have any favorites?"

They acknowledged they knew very little about music. Only that they enjoyed hearing it.

Beau and Jules walked up to them.

"Ladies, we're getting hungry, how about I treat today and we all go to the Allman Hotel for dinner?" Beau said, touching the brim of his hat to the two married women.

"My, that is kind of you, Mr. Gentry, to take this many to dinner at the hotel," Mrs. Flanagan said.

"I happen to know they will all be fighting over the kitchen at the boarding house later today and tomorrow making treats to put in their picnic baskets for Tuesday. This way Jules and I will get to eat." Beau grasped Mrs. Dearling's arm.

"See y'all Tuesday," Savannah said to the women as Beau led his ladies down the street toward the Allman Hotel.

Chapter Twenty-six

Lark watched Beau escort the women who lived at the boarding house down main street as he finished talking with the last of the congregation to leave.

"Larkin!"

He spun toward his name. Owen trotted down the road from his house.

"Good, I caught you. Elsa isn't feeling well. She suggested you and I eat dinner together. How about the Allman?" Owen stopped a few feet from him. "That is if you haven't received an invitation already."

Lark glanced the direction his brother indicated and discovered Miss Walker standing back, waiting to talk with him. He groaned inwardly but pasted a smile on his face. "I'll accept your invitation, no matter what that woman says."

Owen raised an eyebrow, but nodded as Miss Walker walked up to them.

"Reverend, that was an interesting sermon. I'd like to

invite you to dinner and we could discuss it more," Miss Walker gave a brief nod and made eye contact with his brother.

"I already have plans for dinner, but thank you." Lark motioned for Owen to start walking.

"We're going to the Allman, Miss Walker. Would you care to join us?"

Lark glared at his brother. What in blazes was he trying to do?

"That would be wonderful. I don't believe we've chatted very much, Mr. Webster." Miss Walker wrapped her arm around Lark's and the three walked down the street to the Allman Hotel.

It took all his control to not pull his arm from the clinging woman. He tossed a glare at his brother every time Owen looked his way.

He didn't want to walk into the hotel with the woman hanging on his arm, nor did he like walking down the street with her being so familiar. It would give the wrong impression to anyone watching.

"Miss Walker. Please, release my arm. This is most improper." He finally shook her loose.

She stopped and glared at him. "You can travel with that strumpet to Bismarck and pretend it was only to purchase an organ but I know better. You should be ashamed that you refuse to walk the street with a proper woman and go on clandestine meetings with a saloon girl." Her voice grew in volume.

He grabbed her arm. "Miss Walker. I don't know why you refuse to see the caring, giving woman that Miss Gentry is, but I'll not have you shout to the world that she is anything else." He shook her. "Control yourself if you want to eat with my brother and I."

She ripped her arm from his grip. "I'll not break bread with a preacher who has no morals." She spun on her heel and marched down the street.

"You handled that well," Owen said, with laughter in his tone.

"I'm positive she's the one starting all the rumors about Savannah and me." He ran a hand over his face and stared at the woman stomping down the board walkway, her steps echoed along the quiet street.

Owen put a hand on his shoulder. "You can't change her opinion. She believes she is the better woman to be your wife."

Lark stared at his brother. "How do you know that?"

"She's told Elsa that a time or two."

"But I've never…" He had treated her the same as all the other women in his congregation whether they were married or single. No one, until Savannah arrived, had attracted him enough to want to court or think about marriage.

"Come on, let's eat. I'm sure the other women know she is just being mean to get back at you liking someone else." Owen led him into the hotel.

"Ah, the Misters Webster. Welcome to the Allman. Are you here for dinner?" Mr. Allman came out from behind the hotel registration desk.

"Yes, we are," Owen said, following the owner into the restaurant.

Lark's mood perked up at the sight of Savannah.

Beau raised his hand. "Mr. Allman, they may sit with us."

He mentally thanked his friend and wasn't surprised

when the extra chairs were placed between Beau and Savannah.

Owen started to sit next to Savannah then grinned at him and sat next to Beau.

"I didn't know you were eating here," he said, knowing they didn't have to watch what they said in front of these people.

"Beau invited us. He seems to think the house will be a battleground when we all start mak'n food for our picnic baskets." Her smile filled him with joy.

"Are you making a picnic basket?" He sat back as Mrs. Allman began placing plates of roast beef, potatoes, carrots, bread, and applesauce in front of them.

When the plates were all delivered, Savannah picked up her fork. "I am. I hope a certain preacher will be able to afford it."

He laughed. "I have a feeling I will be outbid. I'm but a humble servant of my congregation and the only money I have is what I get for playing courier on Wednesdays."

Owen butted in. "He gets paid well, he knows the bank manager."

The whole table laughed.

The conversation during the meal ranged from what music Savannah would play on Tuesday, to who was spreading the rumors about the women of the Silver Dollar Saloon.

Lark was glad when Owen picked up the conversation.

"I'd say from the spectacle Miss Walker just made outside when my brother asked her to release his arm, that all your problems are coming from that woman." Owen glanced around the table and settled his gaze on Savannah.

Her eyes narrowed. "Why won't that woman leave me

alone. I've done noth'n to her."

"You've moved here and stolen her hopes of becoming the preacher's wife," Mrs. Dearling stated.

Savannah glanced at Lark. Had he made overtures to Miss Walker that had her thinking she would be his wife? He'd cringed when Owen commented about their encounter with the woman.

"Did you give the woman reason to believe she would become your wife?"

"No." He spit the word out with such anger, she was sure he meant it.

"I haven't given her any more attention than I have the women sitting here or anyone else in the congregation." He grasped Savannah's hand. "I hadn't even had thoughts of marrying until you fell off the train."

She stared into his eyes and saw the truth as everyone at the table laughed.

"Tell us what happened." Lottie Mae said.

Savannah let Lark tell his version of their first meeting while she reckoned on the honesty of his words. Was she ready to marry? She didn't come here to find a husband. She came here to live her life as she saw fit. But remembering the kisses she'd shared with Lark, she couldn't think of another she'd care to be so intimate with. And the way his touch, voice, and kisses made her heart race, she had a feeling she was falling in love with him.

"And then Sheriff Blake saw me holding her skirt as she crossed the street," Lark said, causing the table to break into laughter again.

Savannah smiled. This was what she'd missed growing up. A table full of family and friends to enjoy the good times with. Her mother's parties had always catered to the people with money who thought it improper to laugh and have a good time.

"How long do you think it will take to purchase the organ?" Mrs. Dearling asked.

Savannah shrugged. "It'll depend on people who come to the picnic and if businesses or people are will'n to give money for the purchase."

"I'd sure like to have it by Christmas," the older woman said.

"I'm not sure that is doable, but if you say a few prayers and talk to the community, maybe we can get a donation that would bring the organ to Shady Gulch for Christmas," Lark said.

A brief look between Jules and Beau had Savannah wondering if the two would make it happen.

"Thank you for dinner, Beau," Mrs. Dearling said, standing. "Come along, Ladies. We all have some baking and cooking to do for Tuesday."

Savannah stood, but not before Lark stood and pulled her chair back for her.

"Thank you," she said, her arm brushing his as she stared up into his eyes. What she wouldn't give to walk down to the station with him in the morning and get on the train for another day of being themselves without eyes watching. One of these days, she hoped they could walk around Shady Gulch without feeling as if everyone was waiting for them to do something improper.

"I could walk with you to the boarding house," Lark said. She could tell he wished for more time together as well.

"Why don't you come over to my house," Owen said. "Erik hasn't played with you in a while."

"Go play with your nephew." Savannah put a hand on Lark's arm. "I'll see you Tuesday."

"I'll stop by tomorrow." Lark patted the hand on his arm and followed his brother out of the restaurant.

Beau walked up beside her. "You two either need to announce you're courting or you need to stay away from one another."

Her gaze shot to her brother's face. "What do you mean?"

"You two can't look at one another without everyone seeing how you feel." He grasped her hand, tucking it in the crook of his arm. "My suggestion is to announce Lark is courting you at the picnic. Maybe after the two of you share your basket. Especially, if you stay where everyone can see you when you eat and you both act respectable."

She glared at her brother. "Why would we act any other way when we're in public?"

Beau laughed, catching the attention of the others walking ahead of them down the street. He caught his breath and said, "Because you two spark like flint and a knife when you're together." He waved the arm she wasn't hanging onto. "The whole town can see it. Why do you think when someone started the rumors they were so quick to believe it?"

That was the reason so many thought the worst? Because she and Lark couldn't hide their attraction?

Savannah released Beau at the end of the street. "Thank you for your concern big brother. I'll ponder on your words."

She hurried to catch up with the others and entered the front door in time to hear Freedom proclaim she already had her basket planned and was getting started. Savannah took off her hat and gloves and walked up to her room. She not only needed to figure out what she would put in her basket and what ingredients she might need, she also needed to think about Beau's comments.

Chapter Twenty-seven

Savannah sat at the piano. Jules and Beau had carefully moved it out onto the walkway in front of the saloon. All the buildings with second story balconies had red, white, and blue swathing hanging from the balconies.

She'd never been so nervous about playing. Men, women, and children stood in the street, their attention on her as Beau stepped forward.

"Happy Fourth of July, everyone! We'd like to start the festivities off today with some music by my sister, Savannah Gentry."

She stood, smiled, and said, "Good mawnin' everyone. I'm so happy to see y'all here. I'll start with a couple of classic concertos and then play some patriotic songs for you." She sat back down, locked gazes with Lark, and set her fingers to the keys.

Once she started, she forgot the people, and that she sat on a walkway in front of a saloon. As always, she became caught up in the music. When she finished the first song, she took a breath, brought the other song to the front of her memory, and started.

At the end of the second concerto, she raised her hands and her head, peering into the proud eyes of Lark.

The crowd clapped and cheered.

She stood, bowed, and returned to her seat. Her fingers danced across the keys as she began the first patriotic song.

After four songs, she stopped and stood.

The crowd cheered.

Beau stepped up to her side. "That was wonderful," he said.

"Thank you. Play'n the piano is the one thing my mother did for me that I'll forever be grateful." She glanced around and spotted Lark talking with the sheriff.

"Shall we go watch the kid's sack race?" Beau asked.

"That sounds like fun." She put her hand on Beau's crooked arm, and they walked over to the school yard where the volunteers were arranging children by age for the race.

She stood under one of the few trees in the school yard watching the sack races and an egg race.

Lark walked over to her. "Do you need to do anything to prepare for the auction?"

"I can't think of a thing." She glanced at the pin watch on her bodice. "I should go to the board'n house and get my basket afore the auction starts."

"Would you like me to come with you?" The hope in Lark's voice made her smile.

"I would like that, but I believe you win'n my basket and eat'n with me is enough for the congregation to handle in one day."

He laughed. "You're probably right."

Savannah walked out of the shade of the tree and

headed down the street toward the boarding house.

Lottie Mae caught up to her. "I think you played even better today than you have at the saloon."

"Thank you. I was inspired by all the people want'n to hear someth'n special." She glanced at her friend. "Are you go'n to get your basket, too?"

"I am." Her face deepened in color.

"And do you have a certain person in mind who will be purchas'n your bak'n?" Savannah asked.

"I may." Lottie Mae blushed and opened the kitchen door, allowing Savannah to go first.

Their baskets were the only two left in the pantry. It appeared the other women were eager to be part of the auction.

They carried their food back to the church where everyone had gathered for the auction. Lark and Owen stood at the steps of the church.

"Remember, the proceeds for this auction go toward the purchase of a church organ. You just heard Miss Gentry play the piano. Can you imagine what she could do with an organ?" Owen asked.

Her cheeks heated at his compliment and the people in the crowd agreeing.

"How are we doing this?" Owen asked Lark.

"These are the rules as set on paper by myself, Mrs. Dearling, and Miss Gentry." Lark held up a piece of paper. "Any woman sixteen or older may offer a basket for auction. The person bidding and purchasing the basket will also have the pleasure of eating with the woman who put the basket together. In the event a married woman's basket is purchased by someone outbidding the woman's husband, the husband is allowed to also partake of the food and company."

The crowd laughed.

"And Owen Webster, as banker of this town, is the man you give the money to when you are the winning bidder." Lark folded the paper back up and put it in a pocket inside his suit coat.

"Who goes first?" someone in the crowd asked.

"Women with baskets, line up to the left of Mr. Owen Webster," Lark said.

Some rushed forward to be the first in line. Savannah wasn't in any hurry. Lark would be busy helping watch the bidders. She took a spot at the end of the line and listened to the good-natured banter and bidding. This was a good place to live. All the citizens were genial. Her gaze roamed over the crowd and her heart stopped.

She blinked, gulped, and stared where she thought she'd seen a blemish from her past. He wasn't there. She was almost certain she'd caught a glimpse of Winston Cartwell's black top hat. A shudder down her spine added to her certainty it had been the troublesome banker.

Trying to keep her mind on the bidding as the line slowly moved her closer to the Webster brothers, she also scanned the crowd for another glimpse of Mr. Cartwell. She hoped her mind had been playing tricks on her. Now was a bad time for him to show up and cause her trouble.

The women and their bidders had paired up and stood to the side, watching the rest of the baskets being auctioned.

"And now we have the last basket. It appears to belong to Miss Savannah Gentry," Owen said, motioning for her to hold up her basket.

She forced a smile, but sought Beau. Please have him

step in if anything happens, she prayed.

"Who will start the bidding on this basket and lunch with the talented Miss Gentry?" Owen asked.

Beau raised his hand. "Ten cents."

"Fifteen," said Lark.

"Twenty," added Jules.

"Twenty-five," said Sheriff Blake.

She couldn't believe so many people were bidding. Beau and Jules stopped bidding when it was up to seventy-five cents. She'd only paid slight attention to the other bids and knew a couple had gone for a dollar but that was the highest.

"One dollar," Lark said, and held up a shiny silver dollar.

Sheriff Blake shook his head and backed up.

"Five dollars!" shouted a voice she'd dreaded hearing.

A round belly covered in a jacquard vest appeared out of the crowd followed by the rest of the tailored gray suit and Winston Cartwell's white, puffy face and tall black hat.

Shock appeared on Lark's face. He didn't know this man, and he didn't have that much money.

Beau stepped forward. "Six dollars!"

The rage on her brother's face told her he knew who he was bidding against. And he knew Lark could never afford what it would take to outbid the man.

"Seven!" shouted Mr. Cartwell. He wasn't accustomed to not getting what he wanted.

She knew he would make her pay for slipping away from him.

"Eight!" countered Beau.

The crowd gasped and watched the two volley numbers back and forth until they were up to fifteen dollars.

If Beau won the bid, she would owe him more hours in the saloon and a lot of gratitude.

"You want this whore that bad you can have her!" shouted Mr. Cartwell.

Savannah couldn't believe his accusations and the whole crowd gasped and took a step back.

Beau and Lark launched themselves at the outsider.

"Don't you talk about my sister that way," Beau growled and grabbed Mr. Cartwell by the front of his suit.

"The illegitimate heir to the diminished Gentry fortune," Mr. Cartwell said, rubbing salt into Beau's wounds.

"Don't you say such filth about my brother," Savannah said, throwing herself into the fray.

"Who are you and what gives you the right to interrupt our basket auction?" Lark demanded.

"I'm Winston Cartwell. This woman stole from me before leav'n Atlanta. It took time and money to find her. While I was will'n to pay to get her, I'll not allow her to go anywhere other than the jail or back to Atlanta with me."

"Sir." Sheriff Blake stepped up to the man Beau still had a grip on. "I've searched Miss Gentry's belongings. She has nothing of value. I reported my findings to the Atlanta Police."

Mr. Cartwell sneered. "I'm sure she sold them while hunt'n down her bastard brother."

Beau punched the man in the face.

Mr. Cartwell's head lolled to the side and his body slumped.

Fear for Beau squeezed her chest. "You can't do that. He'll ruin you," she said, prying her brother's grip from the man's clothing.

Lark and Sheriff Blake each grabbed one of the man's arms and dragged him toward the church.

Beau's eyes were dark and angry.

Jules stood beside him. "Do not let that man stir you up, *frè*."

The bystanders all watched with varying degrees of interest and disdain.

Savannah looped her arm through Beau's. "Come on, you won my basket." She led him over to the shady side of the church. Her mind bounced around like bubbles in a boiling pot. Would Mr. Cartwell be able to take her back to Atlanta?

"I never expected to see that man here," Beau said. He peered into her eyes. "Did you tell me the truth about you and him?"

Her own brother didn't believe her. How was she to convince anyone else she had done nothing more than elude the man's advances? "He's never had a body tell him no or not do his bidd'n. I'm sure his only reason for com'n is to get revenge. I avoided him at parties and never did I ever say I would marry him. Daddy and I always told him 'no.'"

He studied her.

"And I didn't take anyth'n more than what I showed y'all."

"I know. I asked a Pinkerton to discreetly find out where your mother was and how she was living. It appears when she is in between men, she sells expensive pieces of jewelry. I believe the pieces Mr. Cartwell thinks you stole."

Her heart started beating again. He did believe her, and he'd been checking up on her mother. "Is there a way we can prove it?"

"The Pinkerton is working on it." Beau held out half of a roast beef sandwich to her. "Eat. Lark and Ty will keep Cartwell busy and find out why he's really here."

She took the sandwich from Beau, wishing it was Lark who sat with her, but she'd rather have him deal with Cartwell. She feared Beau would end up in jail for killing a man if he were in the church.

Lark stared down at the flabby, older man who still hadn't come around. How he ever thought a strong-minded woman like Savannah would marry him made no sense.

"Think we should bring him around?" Ty asked, standing over the man with a disgusted expression on his face.

"The longer he's out, the longer Savannah will have some peace to enjoy the event she put together." He should be the one outside enjoying her cooking, but he'd rather be in here waiting for the disgusting man to wake. They had to discover why Cartwell felt the need to come all the way here for trinkets worth less than his train ticket.

Ty's right hand rested on his holstered gun. His fingers tapped against the leather. "I'd rather wake him and go find something to eat."

"Yeah, maybe we should get him awake and get him on the next train out of here." The longer Lark studied the man there was something familiar about him. He didn't like the niggling feeling that came with that recognition.

Ty leaned over and slapped the man's face. Not hard enough to make a mark but enough to try and rouse the man. It took several smacks before the man started to come around.

"What?" Mr. Cartwell's eyes opened. He peered around, then narrowed his gaze on Ty. "What is gon' on here?"

"You blacked out," Ty said, not elaborating.

The man studied Ty before he settled his gaze on Lark. "You and I were bidd'n on Miss Gentry's basket. Then her brother—That bastard hit me!" Cartwell sat up. "I want that man hauled to jail."

"I do believe you provoked Beau," Ty said. It was clear he wasn't going to let this man badmouth his friend. "You called his sister a whore and him a bastard. I believe I'd hit a man who did the same to me."

Cartwell frowned. "What kind of lawman are you? You have to take my account and throw the man in jail."

"No, I don't. I was there. I saw the provocation." Ty crossed his arms. "How about telling me why you came to my town and caused trouble?"

"Your town?" Cartwell sputtered.

Ty nodded. "Why are you here?"

"I came to get the jewelry Miss Gentry stole before run'n away." Cartwell shoved to his feet.

"What was she running away from?" Lark asked, wanting to see if this man acknowledged his interest in her.

"The law of course, because she stole the jewelry." Cartwell glared at him.

"According to her, she ran away because you were pushing advances on her and she wasn't interested." Lark returned the glare.

Ty snickered, which made Cartwell furious. His puffy face reddened and his nostrils flared.

"That woman stole from me. I want her arrested!" Cartwell bellowed.

"There is no proof she did. You'd best get on the next train leaving here and not come back," Ty said. "And in the meantime, find a place to cool off that isn't here upsetting the community festivities." He spun on his heel. "Let's get back out there."

Lark was in agreement, however, he had a notion Cartwell wouldn't leave that easy. He and the sheriff walked out of the church and stood outside the door.

"He's not leaving, is he?" Ty asked.

"Not until he's made Savannah and Beau's life hell." Lark spotted the two sitting at the corner of the church.

Ty nodded that way. "Tell Beau if he hits Cartwell again, I'll have to take the man's charges and throw him in jail."

Lark nodded and walked over to where the brother and sister sat along with Jules and Mrs. Dearling.

"Is he going to leave?" Savannah asked, her voice shakier than he'd ever heard it.

"I don't think so. He's filled with anger and revenge." He didn't like to bring her bad news but he couldn't hide the man's actions.

She ducked her head, then peered at Beau. "Don't hit him again. He has lots of power and can cause you trouble."

Lark didn't like seeing Savannah appear so defeated. "We won't let him take you back or throw you in jail. Sheriff Blake told him you don't have the jewelry and to leave."

A spark of hope lit her eyes.

The church door opened and Cartwell stepped out, he scanned the people milling about and sitting in pairs eating. His gaze stopped on them. He spun their direction and stomped over.

"What did you do with the jewelry?" he demanded.

"I told you. I did not take any jewelry worth any money. Mother toted it all out when she left." Savannah shoved to her feet and stood with her hands on her hips.

"When I spoke to Varicella, she told me it was all still at the house." He glared back at her.

"She's ly'n. If there had been jewelry to sell, I can darn sure tell you, I would have stayed in Atlanta, not made my way to people I didn't know and have to be at their mercy." She crossed her arms and glared at him.

It was wrong, but Lark thanked her mother for taking the jewelry, otherwise, Savannah would not have come into his life.

Cartwell studied her. He snorted. "You still owe me five hundred dollars."

"Whatever for?" Savannah's eyes widened. "You took everyth'n that wasn't nailed to the house."

He narrowed his eyes. "Your father mortgaged all his assets to pay off his debts afore he died." The man's gaze ran the length of her. "I believe you to be one of his assets."

Savannah gasped and stepped backwards. Beau roared to his feet, and Lark stepped between the man and Savannah.

"Now see here. A person isn't an asset." Lark wasn't going to let this man take Savannah no matter what he said.

"Mr. Gentry owed me five hundred more dollars. All that is left of his estate is his daughter." Mr. Cartwell stared at Savannah. "She won't want to tarnish her daddy's name."

Lark put his arm out when he felt Savannah moving forward. "She is not a commodity to be bought, sold, or used as a mortgage." Without dropping his gaze from the man, he said, "Mrs. Dearling, would you please bring my brother over here?"

The older woman stood and hurried toward Owen and his family sitting with the Allmans.

"My brother is a banker. He can clear this matter up," Lark said it as much for Cartwell, as to hopefully, soothe Savannah's fears.

Owen walked up behind Mr. Cartwell. "Mrs. Dearling said you wanted to see me?"

Cartwell spun toward Owen. "You were the auctioneer."

"Yes, I'm also the owner of the bank. What can I do for you?"

Lark nodded toward Cartwell. "Mr. Cartwell believes that because Mr. Gentry, Savannah's father, didn't leave enough assets upon his death to clear the mortgage he had with the bank, Savannah is part of the assets."

"I know you are from the south and you believe people are commodities, but they are not. You cannot force Miss Gentry to go with you as a part of her father's assets." Owen scowled at the other banker. "I feel sorry for the people who bank with you if that is how you have treated all of them."

Cartwell huffed, glared at Lark, and pointed his finger at Savannah. "No one puts one over on me." He pivoted and walked away from the church.

Lark released a breath and spun around, gathering Savannah in his arms. "Are you all right?"

Her body trembled. "Yes. But he'll find another way. I know he will." Savannah snuggled into his embrace and his heart raced with happiness.

"We won't let him cause you any harm," Beau said.

"He'd never win in a court of law," Owen added.

Lark glanced over his shoulder at the man walking down the street who could take all his happiness away.

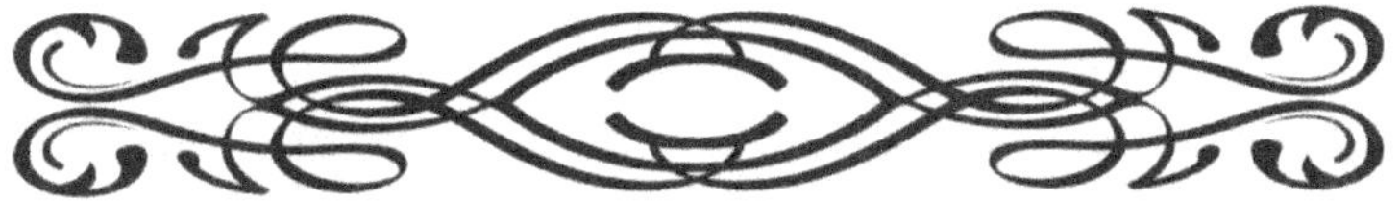

Chapter Twenty-eight

Savannah held onto Lark's solid frame and prayed that Mr. Cartwell would give up on getting her as a wife. But with his last threat, she had a feeling he'd come back with lawmen he could control.

"People are watching you two," Beau said.

"Let them watch. They all know that man said awful things to you and Savannah. There's nothing wrong with me comforting her." Lark's voice came out as a snarl.

She leaned away from him. He'd gone from calmly outwitting Mr. Cartwell, to her protector in the blink of an eye. "You don't need to upset the congregation any more than Mr. Cartwell's name call'n most certainly did."

Lark peered into her eyes. "I know he only said that to rile us up. And I'm sure with all you have done for this community, there isn't a soul here who would believe the names."

She glanced over Lark's shoulder and felt the anger of one person's gaze. Miss Walker. "There's one person in this town who, bless her heart, would love to use Mr.

Cartwell's words against me."

Lark spun and she knew the minute he spotted the woman. His hands balled into fists. He released them just as quickly as they'd clenched.

"There are few who believe what she says." He tucked her hand in the crook of his arm. "Let's mingle and see how everyone enjoyed the auction."

She was hesitant to walk up to these people after what they'd heard Mr. Cartwell call her. But after the third encounter, she relaxed. Everyone seemed to be leery of the strange man who'd barged into their festivities.

They stopped to visit with the Beals and Miss Walker joined them. She saw the woman's anger burning in her eyes.

"Thank you for planning a wonderful event," Mrs. Beal said.

"We're glad everyone can enjoy themselves while helping pay for a church organ," Lark said.

"It will be a pleasure to hear you play in church," Mr. Beal said. "Your talent on the piano is something I've never heard."

"Thank you," Savannah said.

"I can't believe everyone thinks this woman should play an organ in our church." Miss Walker raised her voice. "You heard what that man, who clearly knows her better than us, called her."

"Agnes, that is uncalled for," Mrs. Beal reprimanded.

"Miss Walker, that man has as much anger in him as you do and all for the wrong reasons," Lark said.

Savannah didn't know what to say. With so many people standing up for her, she didn't understand Miss Walker's deep need to tear her down. "Mr. Cartwell is a wealthy man who has used that money to get everyth'n he wants." Savannah shuddered. "Except me. I ran away to keep from be'n in his debt." She peered into Mrs. Beal's eyes. "I did not steal jewelry. I left with two sets of cloth'n and trinkets my daddy gave me, noth'n more."

"Miss Gentry, we have all seen your generosity and caring for our community. We believe you over that stranger." Mrs. Beal nodded to her husband.

Miss Walker stomped off.

"I'm sorry Miss Walker finds it hard to see the real you." Mrs. Beal's gaze landed on Lark. "She believes you are in her way for happiness."

"I have never said anything to make her think—"

"Reverend Webster, I know you haven't. Some women believe what they imagine." Mrs. Beal settled a sad smile on them both.

"Thank you for participating in the basket auction," Lark said, leading Savannah toward the school yard where she saw more games getting underway.

"Do you think Mr. Cartwell will get on the next train?" she asked.

His hesitation told her what she feared.

"I hope he does, but he has a strong need for vengeance on you. Did your father ever do anything to cross the man?" Lark asked, as they drew closer to the games.

"Only when it came to ask'n to marry me. Daddy always told him 'no'. That who I married was my decision and I didn't wish to marry him." She stopped and studied Lark's face. "Do you think all of this is him be'n as blind to my desires as Miss Walker is to yours?"

He scanned the people behind her. "I don't know. He

seems more vindictive."

"Savannah! Over here!" Belle called.

She waved at the woman. "Best we all don't spend too much time together." Savannah walked over to where half a dozen women, including Belle and Liesa, stood talking.

Mrs. Polzin was among the group. She stepped forward. "It was beautiful. Your music."

"That's because you asked for such a beautiful song to be played."

The small women's eyes glistened. "It reminded me of home."

Belle turned to Savannah. "We were wondering if you could play for us to practice singing carols? You know, like a choir, but for Christmas."

"That would be wonderful, but the only piano I know of is the one at the saloon." She studied the faces of the women. "Y'all'd have to come into the saloon, and we'd have to get Beau to agree."

"No one is in saloon Sunday afternoons," Liesa said.

"Can everyone be at the saloon next Sunday at two?" Savannah asked.

All the women nodded.

"I'll ask Beau and let y'all know what he says."

"Thank you!" the women chorused. The four besides Liesa and Belle wandered off talking amongst themselves.

"This will be fun," Belle said. "I remember Christmas chorales as a child. If we can get the organ by December this will be the best Christmas Shady Gulch ever had."

Savannah picked up on the woman's excitement. It would be wonderful to have the organ by Christmas and to have a choir.

Lark strode over to Beau, Jules, and Ty. He didn't even wait for them to finish their conversation before getting his thoughts out in the open. "I don't think we should let Savannah wander around town by herself."

Beau crossed his arms. "Do you think she's going to like that any better than when that man was here asking about her?"

He knew she would hate having someone with her at all times. But he didn't want anything happening to her. "She may not like it, but she knows Mr. Cartwell isn't giving up on taking her back to Atlanta with him."

"That's what I don't understand." Ty pushed his hat back on his head. "Why does he want her in jail or heading down south with him?"

Lark shook his head. "All I know is Savannah's father has been telling the man he can't marry her for years, and he thought once Mr. Gentry owed him, he'd get her for his wife." Just saying it put a knot in Lark's guts. There was no way he'd allow that man to marry or harm Savannah.

Beau nodded toward where Savannah talked with Belle and the other women. "She came here hoping I could help her." He scanned the men around him. "That's what I intend to do. If that man sets foot in my saloon, I'll throw him out." He glared at Ty as if daring him to say anything about it.

"I'll see what I can find out about the man." Ty settled his hat down on his head and walked toward the street.

"We can watch Savannah and have the other ladies stay close to her," Jules said.

"I'd appreciate that." Lark nodded toward the men in the open area between the church and the school, setting up the wood boards for the fireworks display. "I need to make sure everyone knows what they are doing."

He strode over and helped set up the four boards. One had the flag outlined with the tubes holding a mixture of gun powder, sulfur, saltpeter, charcoal, and a metal for color. Another board had an eagle, the largest was an outline of Abraham Lincoln, and the last was of George Washington. They also had a board on a perch with tubes of various concoctions ready to light for the end of the evening's fireworks display.

The suns heat and glow dimmed as the townsfolks started to gather in the school and church yard.

Manfred, the blacksmith, was in charge of lighting the fireworks. He stood by a small fire far enough from the set-up boards that sparks wouldn't carry.

Lark scanned the darkening landscape for Savanah. She and the other women from the boarding house stood in the church yard. He sauntered over, visiting with people along the way. The sun had vanished. The small fire cast a circle of light about five feet from the flames. The stars sparkled in the sky. Lark kept his sight on the silhouetted group he'd last seen Savannah standing beside.

At the group, he could see enough of each person to find Savannah. Grateful for the dark, he grasped her hand and held it as they stood side-by-side waiting for the fireworks.

She leaned against his shoulder. He released her hand and put his arm around her shoulders. After the day she'd had, he didn't care what the congregation thought. He wanted her to know he was here for support any time.

Manfred stabbed a long stick into the fire, twirled it, and walked over to the first board. He touched the fire to the bottom of the design and soon the eagle flared into view in white sparkling lines.

Ooos and ahhs filled the night air along with the crackling of the fireworks. When that design went out, Manfred lit the next board, Abraham Lincoln, and then Washington. The flares dimmed and he lit the flag. The sparking blue, red, and white lines brought the image to full glory. Clapping started with a few and grew to a roar.

Lark's heart filled with pride that this small community in a territory of the United States had such strong feelings toward the country. He squeezed Savannah's shoulders.

Manfred walked over and lit the combination on the raised platform. The boom of several rifles charged the air as white, blue, and green sparks blew into the air about ten feet and fluttered down.

Using the hand not already holding Savannah, Lark captured her chin and kissed her on the lips. Long and slow. He wanted her to know, he would be here for her no matter what happened and he felt blessed to have witnessed this evening with her. She didn't pull back. She fell into the kiss and pressed closer to his body.

They broke apart as the crowd started moving.

"I'll see you tomorrow," he said, releasing her as she moved into the group from the boarding house.

He watched the dark moving mass, until it turned down their street.

Not ready to retire, he remained to help Manfred clean up the mess and make sure all flames and sparks were doused.

"See you later, Reverend," Manfred said, when they were both satisfied everything had been wet down.

"Thank you for taking care of the fireworks," Lark

replied.

The man waved and Lark walked through the cemetery behind the church and over to his house. As he stepped to the front of his home, he caught motion in the street alongside Mrs. Polzin's home. Worrying about her and the children being alone, he hurried across the street and stood at the corner of her building.

Recognition struck him like a bolt of lightning when he spotted Wild-Eye Ed and Cartwell talking in the light of the Mad Dog Saloon. When he'd rode with the Dellinger Gang, they had stolen money from a bank and given it to Cartwell. How did he get this information to Ty without him discovering his past? And how was he to keep Savannah safe knowing Wild-Eye Ed was in town and could ruin his life?

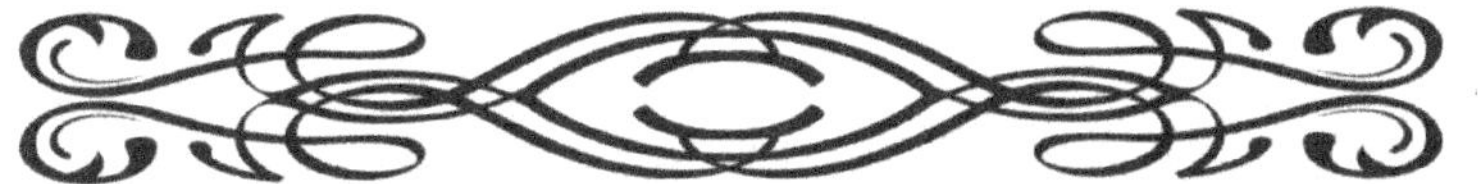

Chapter Twenty-nine

Savannah had a feeling Beau or Lark, or both, had asked the ladies of the boarding house to never let her be alone. The past week, she'd had someone offering to walk with her everywhere and 'Oh, they needed to use the privy, too, and would wait.' In the bar, she'd noticed Beau scrutinizing every stranger who walked through the door.

It was coming on the weekend and she'd yet to ask Beau about using the saloon and piano for the Christmas choir, as she'd come to think of them. She decided she'd better ask before women showed up here on Sunday and found the doors locked.

"Beau, could I talk with you?" She put down the glass she was wiping clean and moved toward the back room.

He raised an eyebrow, scanned the establishment, and followed. "What do you want?"

She didn't settle on the chair as they had in the first weeks of her working in the saloon, when they'd spent quiet moments to catch up and learn about one another. She remained standing. They had to get back out to the bar, it was a boisterous group tonight.

"Some of the women asked me if I would play piano for them to start a Christmas choir."

He studied her, his brow wrinkling. "There's only one piano in town."

"I know. The one here. We wondered if maybe on Sunday afternoons, we-all could use the piano and saloon?" She smiled and gave him her best innocent expression.

"Jules and I clean the saloon on Sunday." He shook his head as if he planned to say no.

"We all won't be in your way. The ladies can stand on the stage and I'll be at the piano. You can go about clean'n. We'll just work on the music." She added. "The ladies want to have a Christmas program filled with carols and music. They're hope'n we'll have the organ by then."

"If you keep having tyrants like that Cartwell bidding on your baskets and pies, I'm going to be broke and you'll have that organ in no time." He narrowed his eyes. "I'm going to expect you to pick up the slack around here, now that I paid fifteen dollars for your picnic basket."

"I wouldn't expect anyth'n else." She'd known this talk would be coming, but had expected it on Wednesday, the day after he'd spent so much money, not Friday.

"I'll allow you to use the saloon Sunday afternoon, but you have to clean up any mess you make and come in every morning before we open and wash the glasses." He raised one eyebrow. She knew that was a sign he was ready for a fight if she disagreed.

"I can live with that." She stood up on her tiptoes and kissed his cheek. "I'm so glad I found you." Without another word, she returned to the bar.

When Belle and Liesa walked up with trays laden with

empty glasses, she told them they would be singing in here on Sunday. That brightened both of their smiles. "We'll need to let the others know to come at two on Sunday."

"I can go around to their houses tomorrow morning and tell them," Belle said.

"Good. I'll be in here wash'n glasses." While she didn't mind, and knew she owed it to Beau for all he had done for her so far, the idea of getting up earlier than the others to come in here and wash glasses felt as if a boulder had been tied around her neck. It would also mean less time to bump into Lark.

The last few days, they'd managed to run into one another and sit somewhere in the open and talk. While she would have rather they could hide away somewhere and share more kisses, she was happy to see him every day.

Wednesday, they had met in the evening while she ate her dinner. He'd gone to Bismarck on his courier run. But Mrs. Dearling hadn't left them alone for a minute. He'd taken the money from the basket auction, all twenty-two dollars and fifteen cents, to the man holding the organ.

Tonight was so busy, Beau asked her to stay until they closed. The men had been rowdier during her performance. Jules threw two men out for trying to grab Lottie Mae by the legs while she was dancing.

"What is wrong with these men tonight?" she asked Beau.

"They get like this sometimes. That bunch over there are traveling through on their way to either find gold in Deadwood or work for the Homestake Mine." He pointed to the group that had been the loudest all evening. "Those cowboys are hoping to join the new cattle ranches that have started on the west side of the territory. If we're lucky, they'll all be moving on tomorrow."

"I hope so, while it's good business for you, the girls and I are get'n tired."

As if to prove her point, Liesa walked over slowly, her face a study in weariness.

Savannah spun to Beau. "Let Liesa go on home. She was the first one here this mawnin'."

He studied the smaller woman and nodded. "Liesa, go to bed. Savannah will take over for you."

"Is not time," she said, her back becoming straight and her eyes pinning her boss's.

"You're tired. Go on. You were here hours afore I was." Savannah put her arm around the smaller woman's shoulders and led her to the back room. "Get some rest."

Liesa didn't resist. She nodded and slowly walked out of the back room.

Savannah was glad she dressed more modestly. She wouldn't have to worry about anyone trying to peek down her bodice or stare at her legs.

Beau had the tray Liesa had carried to the bar cleared of the dirty glasses and filled with full ones. She picked up the tray and headed out among the tables and men.

A man with one eye looking out to the side, pointed for her to place a glass down in front of him. As she did, he said, "About time they let you out from behind that bar."

She peered into his eye that peered at her. "No one lets me do anyth'n. I do what I wish." She straightened, but not before she caught sight of the man's grin. It wasn't the normal leer she'd become accustom to ignoring. It was more a smirk. As if he were mocking her in some way.

By the end of the night, she held even more respect for the women who served beer, danced and sang, and remained on their feet for ten to twelve hours.

Beau and Jules ran the last of the men out the door at two in the morning.

She and the other women waited in line to use the privy before heading into the boarding house. Savannah sat on the backdoor step waiting her turn.

Freedom exited the privy. "You want me to wait for you?"

The woman could barely stand, she was so tired.

"No. You need to get off your feet. I'll be right in." Savannah stood, eased her sore feet over to the outbuilding and did her business.

Her mind was on dropping into her bed as she opened the door to the privy and stepped out. An arm circled her waist and a dirty glove covered her mouth. She fought but was too weary to break away from the strong arms banded around her. Her heel connected with the man's shin.

He cussed and the hand clamped over her mouth swung out and back, hitting her alongside the head and turning her world to black.

Lark knocked on the back door of the boarding house and waited for Mrs. Dearling to answer. He wanted to tell Savannah that he'd learned Mr. Cartwell had left last night. He found it odd the man hadn't left by train, the way he came in, but was happy he'd gone.

"Reverend, I'm surprised to see you this early. Come in," Mrs. Dearling held the door open.

The scents of sweet rolls and frying ham started his stomach growling. He'd also forgone breakfast at home, knowing he would be asked to join the women and Beau for breakfast.

"What are you doing here, Lark?" Beau asked, at the same time Lark noticed Savannah wasn't at the table.

"Where's Savannah?"

"She worked late last night, I imagine she is sleeping," Beau said.

"She told me she was going to wash the glasses early this morning," Belle said.

Beau shook his head. "She wasn't when I came over here." He stood. "Anyone look in on her this morning?"

"Her bed was made. I figured she'd gone over to the saloon." Belle put down her coffee cup.

The other women stared wide-eyed at him and Beau as Mrs. Dearling hustled out of the room.

"Who saw her last?" Lark asked.

The heavy hurried footsteps of Mrs. Dearling upstairs echoed in the room.

"I saw her at the privy after work last night." Freedom said. "She was the last one and told me to go on in."

"That's why he left in the night!" Lark couldn't shake the fear and rage that vibrated in his body.

"Who?" Beau asked.

"Cartwell. I told Werner to let me know when Cartwell left town. He sent Otto over first thing this morning to tell me that Cartwell left during the night." He stared at Beau. "The only reason he would leave during the night would be because he had Savannah."

Mrs. Dearling huffed into the room. "I don't think she slept in that bed. I put stockings I'd mended on the end of her bed yesterday and they are still there."

Liesa jumped up. "I tell sheriff."

Beau put a hand on her shoulder. "We'll get Ty and anyone else we can to go after her. Ladies, I'll need you to help Jules run the saloon."

Jules stood up. "I will go. Miss Savannah is like a sister to me."

Beau studied the man longer than Lark's nerves could take.

"I'm going to tell Ty. You two decide what you're doing and meet me there." Lark stepped out of the boarding house and took off at a run for the Sheriff's Office. He hit the door hard, banging it open.

"Damn Lark!" Ty snapped. He stood up, rubbing his knees. "Your banging through the door made me smack my knees into the desk."

"Cartwell has Savannah," Lark said, heading for the cabinet housing several rifles.

"Now, wait a minute." Ty placed his body between Lark and the guns. "How do you know?"

"Werner said he left in the middle of the night and no one has seen Savannah since last night after they finished working in the saloon." He put his hand on Ty's shoulder to move him out of the way.

"How do you know she didn't go with him?"

Lark glared into his friend's eyes. "Because she was scared of him and loathed him."

Beau and Jules stepped through the door.

"What's taking you so long?" Beau asked, shoving Ty aside and grabbing a rifle. He tossed one to Jules and handed one to Lark. Beau took one himself. "Are you rounding up a posse or are we doing this ourselves?"

Ty shook his head. "Why are you so sure your sister didn't run off with this fellow?"

"Because she came here, to me, for protection from him." Beau spun on his heel and walked out the door.

Jules and Lark followed.

"All right. If you're right, where do you think they are going?" Ty had a rifle in his hand as the four strode down the street.

"My guess is along the tracks to Duluth to catch a train to Atlanta," Lark said, trying to remember if Wild-Eye Ed had any friends in the Dakota Territory.

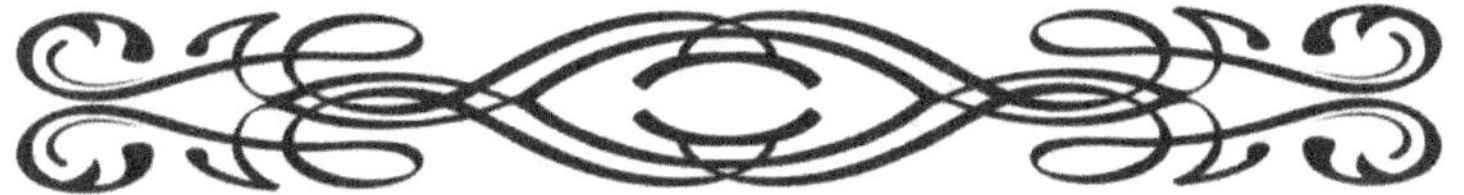

Chapter Thirty

Savannah awoke with a pounding head and a jabbing pain in her back. A horse snorted and stomped. She eased her eyes open and looked up at blue sky between cottonwood limbs with only a smattering of yellow leaves. What was she doing outside? She'd left the saloon, used the privy…The hand over her mouth and arm around her middle came back to her.

Fear and anger collided. Anger at someone grabbing her and fear that she knew who it was. Barely moving her head, she looked toward the sound of the horse. Three saddled horses were tied to a line between two trees. Beside one of the trees stood two men.

Her heart squeezed with panic as she recognized the back of Mr. Cartwell. He couldn't have grabbed her with such strength. She peered at his accomplice. There was something familiar about him. He shifted and she caught sight of his face. It was the man from the saloon. The one who'd grinned as if he knew something.

Lark! He'd be beside himself when he discovered she

was missing. How in the world would she get back to Shady Gulch? No one would know she'd been taken or even where these two were taking her.

The jabbing in her back became more than she could bear. She rolled to her side, hoping they would think she was still asleep. She needed time to think and come up with a plan.

The wild-eyed one spotted her moving and hurried over. "Don't get comfortable, Missy. We need to get mov'n." He reached down, grabbed her by the arm, and hauled her to her feet.

"Ow!" She yanked her arm out of his grasp and glared at him.

"There now, that's no way to handle my future wife," Mr. Cartwell said, walking over and holding out a cup of steaming liquid. "I saved you a cup of coffee, my darl'n."

She knocked the cup from his hand. "I'm not your darl'n. I loathe you and will never marry the likes of you."

"I like a challenge." Mr. Cartwell pointed to the horses. "Ed, put her on a horse and let's get go'n."

When Ed reached for her, she ducked and took off running as fast as she could, holding up her skirts. The yards of fabric caught on a bush and she fell, face first to the ground. She'd flung her hands out to stop the fall and was rewarded with a pain shooting up her arm and a wrist that ached. Before she could push to her knees, hands grabbed her ankles and dragged her along the ground.

Rocks, sticks, and other objects poked, scratched, and tore at her body and clothing. "Stop! Stop!" she shouted, trying to hold her skirt around her legs to keep from revealing too much and to protect her body.

The pulling stopped, and she scrambled to get covered.

"You gonna do as you're told?" Mr. Cartwell asked, a nasty grin on his face.

"Yes." She stood, brushed the debris from her tattered clothing, and marched over to a horse.

Ed grabbed her around the waist, shoving her up onto the saddle. Once she was astride, her skirt riding a bit higher on her legs than she cared for, he tied her feet to her stirrups. "That'll keep ya from slippin' off the horse."

Savannah had never felt the level of hatred for anyone, as she did now for the banker and the man doing his bidding.

The man, Ed, led her horse. Mr. Cartwell rode behind her as they left the area that appeared to have been a camp. How far had they traveled before stopping? Were they near enough to Shady Gulch that she could make her way back if she were able to get away?

She rubbed her scratched palms, wiggled her aching wrist, and took satisfaction in the fact her dress had torn and a piece of the cloth was missing. If Lark came looking for her, he would see the cloth and know he was on the right path.

After a short prayer, asking God to show Lark the way to her, she set her mind to coming up with a plan to get away from these men. Hopefully, before they were too far from Shady Gulch.

Lark asked Orson Montgomery, the livery owner, when Cartwell had left and which way he went as the posse grabbed horses and saddled up.

"You mean that man who called Miss Gentry and Beau names at the picnic?" Orson asked, grinning at Beau.

"Yes, that man." Lark wanted to get the conversation

over and be riding out of here.

"He didn't come get any horses."

"Did anyone get horses last night? Maybe two or three?" He'd always found the livery man difficult to deal with. Montgomery always tried to find a way to make an extra penny but didn't spend it on his family as he should. His nature was one to cause aggravation.

"There was a fella came in and purchased three horses. It was early this morning. About three. He pounded on the door until I woke up."

"What did he look like?" Lark's chest squeezed. He had a notion who the man could be. And the thought he'd have to confront him had his guts churning. But he'd rather lose his congregation and Savannah than have her married to a man she hated.

"He had one eye looking off that way while the other one seemed to stare a hole in you."

"He was in the saloon last night." Beau said. "He was one of the last to leave."

Lark knew he had to tell them some of what he knew. "I saw that man talking with Cartwell after the fireworks on Tuesday."

"So Cartwell and this man have Miss Gentry?" Ty asked, walking up with his horse saddled. "Did you see which way they went, Orson?"

"All I saw was the man leading the horses down the street."

Beau, Jules, Ty, and Lark mounted their horses.

"If we're lucky, they're headed to the next train station," Ty said, kicking his horse into a trot. The other three kicked their horses into the same pace and followed.

Lark prayed harder than he'd prayed in his life, that

they would find Savannah safe.

The heat of the sun scorched Savannah's face. Never had she gone outside without a bonnet or hat to shield her face from the sun. The hotter and tenderer her skin became, the angrier she became with Mr. Cartwell. Even though her feet were tied to the stirrups, she was willing to see if she could get her horse to take off at a run and pull the rope from Ed's hands. She'd stared longingly at groves of trees as they continued at a fast walk across the prairie. They had passed one watering stop for the railroad. The water tower had been easy to see. Where were they taking her?

The sun was now at her back, beating down on her dark green dress, causing her to perspire even more than the sun on her front. At least the sun no longer scorched her face.

Ed stopped, reached in his saddlebag, and pulled out a paper wrapped parcel.

Mr. Cartwell rode up beside her, holding out a similar package. "Care to have a sandwich?"

She didn't want to take anything from the man, but her stomach had been grumbling and she would need strength when she found her chance to run. Savannah took the offered food, but glared at the man, making sure he knew her displeasure.

Lark dismounted along with the others, but followed Ty to the residence of the man in charge of watering the locomotives at that stop. He couldn't see Cartwell riding a horse all the way back to Atlanta.

Ty knocked on the door. "Sheriff Blake from Shady

Gulch," he called.

The door opened. The man was of average build with shaggy blond hair. "Ja?"

"Did two men and woman ride through here or wait to get on a train?" Ty asked.

The man shook his head. "I have not seen anyone other than train going vest."

They thanked the man.

"We need to get going," Lark said, swinging up on his horse.

"The only thing in our favor is the train heading east won't be through here until tonight." Ty set his horse into a trot. "That is if they are trying to catch a train."

The knot in Lark's stomach tightened. He didn't think he'd read Cartwell wrong, but he was friends with Wild-Eye Ed, which means he could ride for days without stopping.

Savannah watched as they walked right on past a small town with a train depot.

"I won't be able to ride all the way to Atlanta," she said, hoping one or the other of the men would hear it. Her backside was already feeling bruised.

"We'll be off these horses tonight," Cartwell said.

That was a bit of a relief. But where would they get off? And would there be anyone around she could ask for help?

Lark knew they couldn't keep up the pace they'd been pushing on the horses. The small settlement of Eldridge was a few glowing dots in the distance. They could get a meal and a bed and head out first thing in the morning.

Beau rode up alongside Lark. "Plan to stop here tonight?"

"Yeah. The horses have been pushed hard today. We'll check with the depot and see if Cartwell happened to stop here to catch the train."

At the outskirts of the small community, they dismounted. Beau and Jules took the horses to the livery. Ty and Lark walked to the train depot to ask about Cartwell.

The building was dark. They walked around to the back side and knocked on the door to the living quarters.

"Coming. No trains until—" A tall thin man opened the door. His gaze fell on Ty's silver star. "What can I do for you, Sheriff?"

"Did anyone ask about a train heading east today or tonight?"

"Yes. There was a man older than us, tall top hat, and a belly." He made a rounded motion in front of his body.

Lark's heart picked up the pace. "Did he purchase tickets?"

"For the midnight stop." The man peered at them with interest. "He do something wrong?"

"How many tickets did he purchase?" Lark asked.

"Three."

"Did he say where he would be until it was time to board the train?"

"Only one place they could be. The Trenton's boarding house. Can't miss it, it's the biggest house in town."

"Thank you." Lark spun from the stoop and headed toward the collection of buildings that made up the town.

"You can't go barging into someone's house," Ty said,

catching up to him.

"I don't intend to. We'll wait for them to come out to board the train. It's after nine now." Lark spotted the largest residence. "Over there. I'll keep an eye on it while you and the others get something to eat."

"It's after nine. The only place we might get fed bread and butter is the boarding house," Ty said. "I'm going to see if there is a lawman in this town. I'll meet you back here."

Lark stood across the street from the boarding house, wondering if Savannah was behind one of the lit-up curtains on the second floor. He wasn't even sure if the three were in the boarding house.

He heard the muffled footsteps of someone approaching. It was a moonless night, making it hard to see the person, no persons. There was more than one person walking his way.

Two dark figures walked up to the boarding house door. Before the door opened he made out the figures of Beau and Jules. Did they think he and Ty had already settled into rooms?

He started across the street to warn them he thought Cartwell was in the house. Jules backed away from Beau and started around the side of the house. Lark changed his direction and followed the man.

He caught up and Jules turned, his fist ready to punch him in the face.

"It's me, Lark."

Jules dropped his hand. "Thought you was someone coming to cause me grief." He pointed to the back of the house. "Livery man said two men and a woman rode in and sold their horses to him. He sent them over here to wait for the midnight train."

"We learned Cartwell bought three tickets for the train." Lark eased by Jules. He'd entered several places like this in his days as an outlaw. He knew how to get in and out of buildings without being seen.

At the back door, he stopped. "You wait here. I'll bring Savannah down."

"You sure you want to go in there alone?"

"Yes. Easier for one man to go unnoticed than two." Lark slowly eased the door open and slipped into the dark kitchen. A light shone from the parlor down the hall. He heard Beau speaking to someone. He knew it wasn't Savannah, the female voice that replied was too old.

He picked his way up the stairs, a step at a time. One creaked and he held still. He listened for anyone coming out of the parlor to check on the sound. Nothing.

Lark made it to the top and peeked down the hall. His eyes adjusted to the blackness, revealing the darker outline of a person sitting on the floor in front of a door. It had to be Ed, and Savannah would be in the room.

Chapter Thirty-one

Savannah paced the room. The woman who ran the boarding house had expressed concern for her injuries and torn dress. Mr. Cartwell had told the woman his wife had fallen from her horse, and they were going to continue their journey by train. Could she find his wife a suitable dress to change into and some food?

The insufferable man had stayed with her and was now sleeping on the bed while she paced the floor in her tattered clothes. She would not take the woman's dress nor try to cover up the treatment she'd received. Savannah had used the excuse of needing to use the privy to try and talk with the woman only to discover Ed stood outside the room.

She glanced out the window for the tenth time. If the banker wasn't asleep on the bed, she could use the sheets to climb out the window. The porcelain pitcher and bowl came into her view every time she walked by the washstand. Could she bash the man over the head? If she did, she could quickly tie the sheets together and get out the window.

Her conscience played war with her desire to be free of this man. Her anger and self-preservation overruled her conscience.

She crept over to the washstand, grabbed the pitcher, and tiptoed to the bed. The man made a snoring sound that startled her. She about dropped the pitcher on his head.

Steeling her nerves, she prayed for forgiveness and smashed the pitcher on the man's head. His head lolled to the side and the snoring stopped. She rolled his body off the bed and onto the floor. The two sounds resounded twice as loud as she'd expected. The door knob wiggled. She froze in the motion of grabbing the sheet.

Banging, cursing, and a struggle ensued in the hallway. She didn't know whether to open the door or continue with her plan. Had Lark found her?

Unable to believe he had, she tied the sheets together, knotted one end to the bed, and tossed it out the window. She put a leg over the window sill and the door burst open.

Lark stood in the dim light of the lantern.

"You came," she whispered, as he pulled her out of the window.

"Of course. Come on. We need to get out of here before Ed wakes up."

She took his offered hand and followed him down the stairs.

Beau stood at the door.

Jules came down the hall from the kitchen.

They had all come for her.

"This way," Beau said, directing them all out the front door. They hurried into the street.

"What are we go'n to do? When they all wake up, they'll come look'n for us?" Savannah asked.

"Where's Ty?" Beau asked.

"He went to see if there was a lawman in this town," Lark said, pulling Savannah into his arms. She hugged him tight. Her faith in him had been founded.

"We must find a place to hide and hope they get on that midnight train or get out of here," Jules said.

Beau strode down the street. "I say we get fresh horses and get out of here."

On the way to the livery, they found Ty walking out of the saloon. "You found her. I didn't find a lawman."

"Cartwell and Ed are both knocked out, but we don't know for how long," Lark said.

Savannah stopped. That was the second time he'd called the wild-eyed man by his name. "How do you know that man's name?" Her heart twisted at the realization, Lark knew the man who had helped Mr. Cartwell abduct her. A man who was obviously of poor character.

"Didn't you say his name?"

How quickly he tried to make it seem as if she had told him, added to her distress. "No. I most certainly did not tell you that man's name." She jammed her fists on her hips. "How do you know his name?"

"Now isn't the time to talk about it. We need to get out of here." Lark hadn't realized he'd slipped up. He could have made it in and out and no one would have known of his association with the Dellinger Gang if he hadn't called Ed by his name. Once he told everyone the truth, he'd have to reinvent himself again. That didn't hurt as badly as knowing he'd lose Savannah. She'd never want to be tied to a man with his past.

Beau grabbed his sister, forcing her to walk down the road. At the livery, they roused the owner out of his home to purchase horses.

"I only have three that haven't been ridden today. We don't have much call for horses."

"We'll trade the three we rode in on for the three fresh horses you have," Beau said.

Ty was already leading his horse out of the corral. "Sorry boy, looks like you'll have a long day."

The man agreed to the trade. Lark put his saddle on the strongest looking of the three, planning to carry Savannah on the horse with him.

They led the horses out of the stable. Lark held out a hand to Savannah to help her onto his horse. She turned to Beau. Her brother swung up into the saddle and offered her a hand. She settled onto the back of his horse.

Lark swung up into his saddle and followed Beau, Savannah, and Jules out of town at a trot.

Ty rode up beside him. "How is it you did know that man helping Cartwell?"

The way this day had gone, it was only fitting a lawman would ask him that question. But he felt he owed Savannah the explanation before his friend. "I'll tell you after I've told Savannah."

Ty snorted. "I don't think she's going to give you the time of day. You knew one of the men who abducted her. From the look of her clothing, they weren't gentle with her."

He'd noticed the torn dress and scratches as well as how she'd favored one of her hands. His gut tightened. His first instinct was to spin around and do more damage to Ed and Cartwell. That would only bring more harm to both he and Savannah.

"I wish she would have rode with me. I wanted to ask

her about her injuries and tell her about my past." Dread seeped into his heart. Would she see him for the man he had become or only think of him as the young man who had thought being an outlaw was adventurous?

"I'll go talk to her and see if she might want to ride a bit with you."

"Thank you," Lark said.

"I'm not doing it for you, I want to find out about your past. If you won't tell me until you tell her, I'll get her to listen." Ty urged his horse faster and moved through the darkness.

Lark shook his head. That was what made Ty a good lawman. He dug for the facts. He stared hard at the backs of the horses and riders ahead of him. He had to keep close to see them. How was Beau sure they were headed in the direction of Shady Gulch?

Savannah tried not to kick the horse in the flanks as she rode behind her brother. But she felt awkward leaning against him to put her arms around his waist, which left her body and legs flopping more than she liked.

The trotting made it even harder to keep hold of the back of the saddle.

A horse moved up alongside of them. She stiffened thinking it was Lark. As much as she would relish being in his arms, her pride would not allow her to give in. He had known the beastly man who dragged her across the ground and treated her worse than a dog. How could he know such a cruel person? He spoke of him as if they were quite familiar.

"Miss Gentry."

She relaxed hearing the sheriff's voice. "Yes, Sheriff

Blake?"

"I was wondering if you'd take it upon yourself to ride a bit with the reverend."

She glared at him, even though in the dark he wouldn't be able to tell. "Lord a mercy, did he send you here to ask me that?"

"He didn't. He told me he wouldn't tell me how he knew the man who kidnapped you until he'd told you first. I'm just trying to get to the truth behind everything." The sheriff sounded sincere and determined.

"Beau, what do you think? Do you know why Lark didn't tell us about that man?" She hoped her brother had the answer so she wouldn't feel compelled to ride with Lark.

"I know his past. He told me one night, kind of feeling me out for how I thought others would act when they knew." Beau heaved a sigh. "He knew it would catch up to him someday, but I'm pretty sure, he didn't know you would be caught in the middle of it."

His answer only made her more curious than angry. What about Lark's past would have him, a reverend, confiding in a saloon owner? She contemplated whether she could ride with Lark and not allow her heart to soften.

"Well, Miss Gentry?" Sheriff Blake asked.

"Fine, but I'll only ride with him long enough for him to tell me."

"I'm not stopping again in five minutes," Beau growled. "If you keep changing horses, we'll never get far enough away."

She didn't like the idea of having to ride for any distance with Lark, but she realized they couldn't stop and have a discussion. The more distance between them and

Mr. Cartwell, the better she'd feel.

"I'll ride with Lark until you stop," she said, heaving a deep sigh. If her brother knew the man's past and hadn't tried to stop their attraction, it couldn't be that bad, could it?

Beau stopped. The other hoofbeats behind them stopped.

"Slide off," Beau said, putting his arm out for her to grasped as she slid her off side leg over the horse's rump.

Her feet hit the ground and she wobbled a bit. The last day and night, she'd ridden more than she did in a month at home.

"Savannah is coming back to ride with Lark," Beau said loudly.

"I'm right here," Jules said, helping her navigate past his horse.

"Back here, Savannah," Lark's voice penetrated the dark and guided her to his horse.

She touched the animal's neck and bumped into Lark. He had dismounted.

"I'll ride behind you," he said, putting his hands on her waist and placing her in the saddle.

She stood in the stirrups to smooth her skirt out under her and try to cover her legs as much as she could, even though in the darkness no one would be able to see her stockings. Once she was settled, she removed her foot from the stirrup closest to Lark.

Within seconds, she felt his hands grip the front of the saddle. She and the saddle tilted to the left and his body settled on the horse behind her.

"Ready," he called out.

The three darker images ahead moved out. Savannah

urged her horse forward. Lark's arms settled around her waist. While it was comforting, the brazenness also irritated. He knew she was unhappy with him and still he put his arms around her.

She cleared her throat. "I'm not of a mind to have you touch'n me so familiarly."

His arms disappeared.

They rode on for what seemed like an hour or more without him saying a thing.

"I'm here so you can tell me how you come to know the man that dragged me across the ground, tied me to a saddle, and took liberties of touch'n me."

Lark's body vibrated. "I'll kill him," he whispered.

"That's not very preacherly talk," she said, wondering how a man of the cloth could speak of breaking a commandment.

"I'm not sure any preacher would be able to keep from feeling the rage I feel when someone they care about has been handled the way you were." Lark's tone held the same menacing tone she'd heard once before.

"Why don't you tell me your recollection of the man, Ed?"

He cleared his throat, but only the sound of his breathing followed for several minutes.

She started to say something and he began, "I'm not proud of my past. I left home at the age of fifteen, following a friend who was several years older. We fell in with a gang of outlaws."

She gasped and quickly staunched her words when she felt more space grow between she and Lark. "Go on." Her heart raced. He had been an outlaw! Killing, thieving, and who knew what else.

"Wild-Eye Ed was the leader of the Dellinger Gang. I was known as the Topeka Kid." He blew out air and continued. "I did kill two people, but they were other gang members who had drawn on me. It was shoot them or die. I'm not proud of taking their lives." He sighed heavily. "It was shortly after killing the second man that we had planned to rob a bank. Things went wrong. There were lawmen everywhere and the brother of one of the men I'd shot wanted revenge. I hid in an outhouse, prayed no one would find me, and told God I would become a preacher if I made it out of that town alive.

"After dark, I slipped out of the outhouse, rode to the next town, and took a train back home. From there I entered a seminary school and when I finished my schooling, Owen suggested I come to Shady Gulch. The town had just started up and there wasn't a preacher or church. The first year we had services in your brother's saloon. Seeing how I was connected to the community and willing to stay, the townsfolk pooled their money and talents to build the church and Owen paid for the house I live in."

Savannah's chest constricted. He'd killed two men, robbed banks, and… "Does anyone besides my brother know about your past?"

"Owen knows."

"And he allows you to carry bank business?" Had Lark changed or was he that good of a liar?

"He understands I left home to find adventure and became caught up in a life I didn't truly want to be in. I got out the first chance I could without someone trying to put a bullet in my back. The only name the gang knew me as was Topeka Kid. It was the only right thing I did when I joined them. I didn't give them my real name."

Her mind ran in circles trying to understand how a bank manager could give an important job to an outlaw and how that outlaw could become a preacher and fool a whole congregation. She'd lived with a liar and thief her whole life. Her mother had told stories to her father to keep him from kicking her out. She'd lied to other men telling them she wasn't married. And she'd stolen the jewelry that Mr. Cartwell accused Savannah of stealing. She didn't want another liar and thief in her life.

"Savannah, believe me when I say, I have changed. I was never a real outlaw. I was a young man caught up in the adventure." He put a hand on her shoulder.

She shook it off. The women at the boarding house had hard lives, but they didn't lie or steal. They were her new family, and she wasn't going to pin her heart to a man who lied and stole.

"I'm glad we found you and you're safe." Lark said, and that was the last of their conversation as she waited for Beau to stop and let her change horses.

Feeling the heat of Lark's body behind her as the air grew colder and the sun started a glow across the prairie, she struggled with keeping her body erect and not lean into his warmth. She knew he would keep her warm and allow her to sleep in his arms. Her body craved both, but her mind couldn't forget the pain of being a victim of another's bad choices.

Beau finally stopped. She walked her horse up beside him as he dismounted.

Lark slipped off the back and raised his hands to help her. She ignored his offer and slid off the other side, bumping into Beau.

He glanced over at Lark. She saw his head give a negative shake.

Her heart cracked from the betrayal and the realization she'd fallen in love with an outlaw.

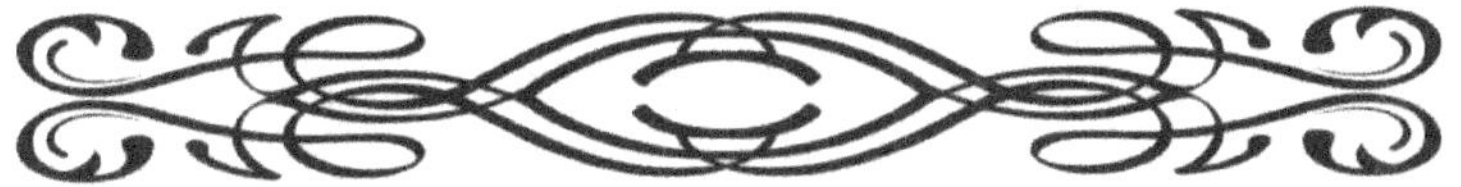

Chapter Thirty-two

The sun heated their backs as they rode up to the small depot in Crystal Spring, two stops before Shady Gulch. Ever since the sun rose, Lark had stared at Savannah as he rode, willing her to forgive him.

Ty had ridden beside him, listening to his tale of a young boy hooking up with the wrong people. He'd nodded and glanced at Savannah as well.

"I don't know what to tell you about Savannah. Seems she takes your association with the outlaws a mite harder than I do. I understand a young man seeking adventure. Heck, I did almost the same thing before getting wise." Ty reached over, slapped him on the back, and rode up beside Beau.

Everyone dismounted at the depot.

"You know, if Cartwell and Ed get on the train headed this way, they'll already be on when we get on," he said to Beau. Savannah didn't even look at him. His heart couldn't be crushed any more. The fact she couldn't see the man he'd changed into, hurt.

Beau clamped a hand on Ty's shoulder. "We have the law on our side. Ty can arrest them for kidnapping Savannah."

There was little to say against that line of thinking. They did have the law on their side.

Beau purchased tickets. Ty tied his horse to a hitching rail and led the other three to the livery. Jules went in search of food. Lark and Savannah sat on opposite ends of the station bench.

"You're holding your wrist. Do you need a doctor?" he asked.

"It doesn't hurt that bad." She turned her head to stare away from him.

"You have to know I've changed. I'm not the same person I was when I was fifteen." He had to make her see.

"I lived with a liar and a thief. I know how well you can twist words to cover your actions and make others think they are wrong."

Not only had her mother caused her to be kidnapped but now she was harming his chances with Savannah.

"Your mother is a grown woman who has made the choice to use others. I grew up, learned that wasn't the life for me, and I've become a preacher to help others. Can't you see the difference between us?"

Beau walked over, sat down next to Savannah, and took her hand. "We'll get you back home."

"Thank you," she muttered.

Lark stood. "I'm going for a walk. How long until the train gets here?"

"Thirty minutes," Beau answered.

He nodded and strode down the street. He was tired. More tired than when he'd sat up with someone all night.

He was weary to the bone, heart-broken, and miserable. A small building with a cross on the roof drew him.

Inside the small church, that appeared to only be used when a traveling preacher came through, he removed his hat and knelt at the altar.

"Dear Lord, forgive me for the actions I have taken to save the woman I love. Help her to forgive me for the sins of my past. Show her the man I have become. I ask this not just for myself but for the people of my congregation. She is the perfect woman to help me guide the town and keep me on the path you have provided. Amen."

His heart felt a bit lighter for having placed the outcome of his affection for Savannah in God's hands.

The train whistle shrieking through the still air brought him to his feet. Outside the building, he plopped his hat on his head and strode to the depot. If Cartwell and Ed were on the train, the others would need all the help they could get.

Savannah wrung her hands as the train pulled up to the platform. She believed Beau's words that having Sheriff Blake with them would keep Mr. Cartwell from taking her again, but fear was a hard emotion to ignore. She scanned the area looking for Lark. Then scoffed at herself for wanting comfort from a former outlaw.

The train chuffed and blew steam and soot as it stopped. She turned from the debris floating in the air.

Jules had returned ten minutes after Lark left with rolls he'd purchased at the boarding house. She'd eaten hers and drank from the jar of water he'd also managed to scrounge up.

As Lark returned, Jules handed him a roll. "This is the

last one."

"Obliged." Lark bit into the roll and gazed into her eyes.

She witnessed hurt and something almost akin to a glow of resolve. Where had he been and what had put that glimmer in his eyes?

Ty untied his horse and led it to the livestock car.

Beau took her arm. "Let's board."

She nodded and grabbed her skirts with one hand, walking beside him to the train car with the cushioned seats. She'd noticed that about her brother, he didn't spare the money on anything. Had he made all his wealth through business dealings?

He stopped at the steps and motioned for her to go first.

She stepped up and stopped at the door. Through the small window she spotted the back of Mr. Cartwell's head. She gasped and backed up. Her arms flailed when her heels didn't find purchase. Her body tipped backwards.

She fell before Beau could grab her.

Ready to hit the hard ground, she tucked her chin to her chest and closed her eyes. She landed in the cradle of someone's arms. Opening her eyes, she gazed upon Lark's face.

"Are you hurt anywhere?" he asked, holding her tight to him as he stepped out from between the train cars.

"No. I'm fine." Her breath caught staring into his eyes. They held every emotion she wished to see in the eyes of the man she married. Her heart started to dance with his and her mind cut in. She stiffened. "Please, put me down."

He did, settling her gently on her feet.

Beau stood at the top of the stairs. "Why did you back

up?”

The reason came back to her in full clarity. “Mr. Cartwell is in there.” She pointed to the car.

Beau reached down to her. “There is nothing he can do.”

She accepted his hand and climbed the stairs, entering the car with him. She felt Lark’s presence behind her.

Beau motioned for her to sit next to the window. He took the seat beside her. Lark and Jules took the seats in front of them. Ty walked through the door and took the seat behind her and Beau. So far, Mr. Cartwell hadn’t looked to the back of the car.

Savannah scanned the interior of the train, looking for Ed. He didn’t seem to be on the train. Perhaps he’d set out on horseback to follow them.

She picked at the corner of her bodice as the train sat in the station. Would the banker turn around and see them? He would be furious with her for hitting him with the pitcher. Her stomach churned and perspiration dampened her forehead. She pulled her handkerchief from her skirt pocket and dabbed her brow. When would the train pull out of the station? Once they were moving she would feel better.

The car lurched and the wheels screeched into motion.

She stared out the window as the water tower and grass slowly crept by. The train gained speed.

The door at the back of the car opened. Savannah glanced over her shoulder and froze. Ed glared at her. His good eye was purple and puffy, a gash on his cheek made him look even scarier than before.

Sheriff Blake must have seen the fear on her face. He glanced over his shoulder then tapped Beau. “Trouble,” he said in a low voice.

Savannah faced forward.

Beau tapped Lark's shoulder. "Trouble," he repeated.

Lark nodded and spoke to Jules.

Ed walked by them, his wild eye bobbing up and down. He slid into the seat next to Mr. Cartwell. The two had their heads together for a considerable time. Ed kept peering back at them.

Did he recognize Lark as the one who injured his good eye? Fear for him, squeezed her chest. She had to admit to herself, since meeting the reverend, he had always been there for her. Saving her when she first arrived and nearly toppled off the train head first, to when they boarded here. He'd caught her when he had to have been a good ten feet away from where she backed off the platform.

Ed rose and walked back their direction. He stopped in front of Lark's seat. "I know you from somewhere?"

He couldn't know that Lark had been the one to knock him around the night before. It had been dark.

She hadn't really studied Lark this morning. She'd been too upset to care if he had injuries. From the looks of Ed, Lark had to have some telltale sign he'd been in the same fight.

"I'm the preacher in Shady Gulch. I believe I saw you there a time or two." Lark kept his tone soft and low.

"No. You look familiar from somewhere else." The man's wild eye stopped bouncing and focused on Lark. A nasty brown-toothed grin spread across his face. "You kin to the Topeka Kid? You got his eyes. Always lookin' like somethin' is goin' on inside his head."

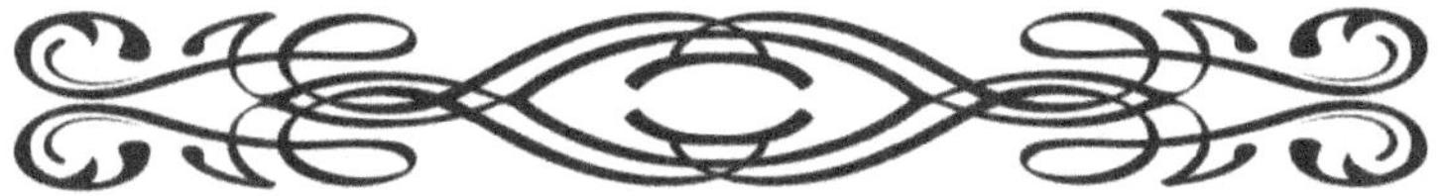

Chapter Thirty-three

Lark was torn. He liked the fact that anyone who might want revenge thought he'd died, but on the other hand, Savannah was sitting behind him. She believed him a liar and a thief.

"I've had a talk a time or two with the Topeka Kid." He waved to the empty seat across the aisle. "How do you know him?" Lark made a conscious movement of straightening his white collar. He knew how Ed was skittish around anything that had to do with religion.

The man's wild eye stared at the collar for a second before he shook his head. "Don't have the time." He glared at Savannah. "I have someone I need to talk to."

Ed walked on by but stopped beside Beau. "You the man who jumped me last night?"

"No. I did not jump you. But I understand you had my sister against her will." Beau's voice carried.

Cartwell turned in his seat, peering down the expanse of the train car.

"Watch Cartwell," Lark whispered to Jules before he

shifted to keep an eye on Ed.

The man had his hand resting on the handle of his pistol. Lark looked beyond the outlaw to Ty. He was sitting in the aisle seat, watching.

Ed had a lecherous smirk on his face. "She came along willing, didn't ya gal?"

"If you call be'n knocked out will'n." Savannah's voice also carried through the train.

Murmurs and heads turning their direction would make it hard for Ed or Cartwell to do anything.

"Tell Cartwell he owes my sister for this dress and the discomfort he caused her." Beau stood. He was a good six inches taller and twice as broad as the outlaw. "Tell him to bring it to the Silver Dollar Saloon when he arrives in Shady Gulch."

Ed's eye began bouncing as he backed up and returned to his seat next to Cartwell.

Lark released his breath and glanced at Savannah. Her pretty face relaxed. She leaned her head against Beau's shoulder. His guts tightened wishing he was the one she rested on, but he'd take his time making her see he wasn't like her mother.

"Savannah? Savannah, wake up. We're in Shady Gulch."

Beau's voice penetrated her groggy mind. Once Ed had returned to his seat, she'd relaxed and fallen asleep immediately. Her gaze sought Lark. He stood beside his seat, watching her. She dropped her gaze and took Beau's offered hand. Together she and Beau exited the train with Sheriff Blake in front and Lark and Jules following behind.

"We'll take you straight to the boarding house. I don't

want to see you in the saloon tonight," Beau said, tucking her hand through the crook of his arm.

She tried to tuck strands of wayward hair behind her ear and ignore the stares she received from the townsfolk as they walked quickly down the street. From the glance she'd caught of herself in the mirror at the boarding house where she'd bashed the pitcher over Cartwell's head, she knew she looked as if she'd been in a fight with a wildcat.

Mrs. Dearling met them at the door. "Oh, my heavens!" She started barking orders for someone to start a bath, someone to get Savannah's nightdress, all as the older woman led her toward the bathing room off the kitchen.

Beau, Lark, and Jules went into the parlor. No doubt waiting to reveal what had happened once she was soaking.

"Who did this to you?" Belle asked, helping her undress as Freedom carried in hot buckets of water.

"Mr. Cartwell and an outlaw named Ed. Remember the man in the bar the other night with one eye that looks off to the side?" Every time she closed her eyes she'd see that face.

"I thought there was something with him. He stared at you. I thought it was because he liked your music." Belle tossed the torn dress to the corner of the room and helped her step out of her underskirts. "If I see him, I'll tell Beau."

"You probably will. They followed us back here." Savannah shuddered. She didn't want to think of those two out there, waiting for a chance to catch her alone again. The two had ruined more than her dress and her pride. They'd taken her freedom.

She dropped her drawers and drew the shift up over her head.

"Oh!" exclaimed Freedom.

"What?" Savannah asked, feeling vulnerable being naked in front of the two women.

Freedom pointed. "You have a big ole bruise the size of a fist on your back and scratches all over."

"That's because when I tried to run away, the outlaw dragged me by my feet across the ground. No care to what I hit or that my skirt was hiked up over my head." Saying it stirred her rage and tamped down the humiliation. "If I see him again, he'll be sorry he ever laid his wild eye on Savannah Gentry."

With that vow on her lips and blazing in her heart, she sank into the bath and felt the sting of every scratch and bruise.

Lark stood in the boarding house parlor worrying about Savannah while trying to keep up with the conversation between Beau and the ladies of the boarding house.

"I told Savannah not to come to work tonight. Mrs. Dearling will stay with her tonight. Tomorrow, she doesn't go anywhere alone. Not until those two are behind bars or gone for good." He peered at each of the women. "If this had happened to anyone of you, I'd be giving the same order and you know Savannah would be with you day and night."

They all nodded.

"I also want all of you to travel in pairs. I don't trust them. They could try taking one of you to get to Savannah." He put a hand on each of their shoulders. "We are a family and we keep each other safe."

They all nodded and hugged one another.

"I'm going to see where they are," Lark said, unable to

think of anything other than knowing where the two men were.

"You think that's a good idea?" Beau asked.

He understood what his friend was saying. So far Ed just thought he was a relative of the Topeka Kid. He was pretty sure should the man find out he was the Topeka Kid, he'd have a gun aimed at his back. One of the men Lark had shot was Ed's brother. The leader of the gang had been the person looking to put a bullet in his back during the bank robbery.

"I'll stay low. See what Ty has to say."

Lark walked through the kitchen to leave. Savannah stepped out of the bathing room, wrapped in a cotton night gown. She hadn't dried well and the cloth clung to her damp breasts and hips. His body jerked to attention at the sight of her. He couldn't leave without speaking to her.

He walked over, close enough to catch her floral scent. "Are you really all right?"

She gulped and nodded. "I have some bruises and scratches, and…" She held up her right hand. "My wrist hurts, but I'm more angry and embarrassed than anyth'n."

That she was talking to him gave him hope she would come around. "I can send the doctor over."

"No. If my wrist doesn't get better by tomorrow, I'll go see him."

He tucked a clump of wet hair behind her ear. "And there is no need to be embarrassed. Those men are in the wrong. You have done nothing." He wanted to put a hand behind her head and kiss her. Show her he cared and would do anything for her.

She stepped back. "I'm get'n cold."

"I'll let you go. But I'll be back to check on you."

"You don't need to bother."

He took a step closer and kissed her cheek. Peering into her eyes, he said, "It's no bother."

She ducked her head and walked out of the kitchen.

Lark's heart sputtered back to life. Maybe, just maybe, there was a chance for them.

Mrs. Dearling entered the kitchen. Her gaze narrowed. "I thought you left." She busied herself putting a kettle of water on.

"I am leaving." He started for the door and spun back. "Don't let anyone in to see Savannah."

She nodded. "I won't let anyone other than you, Sheriff Blake, Beau, Jules or the ladies in here. You can count on me."

He gave the woman a hug and headed to the Sheriff's Office.

Pete sat behind the desk. Shouting came from a room in the back with the two cells.

"Who is making all that racket?" Lark asked.

"Mr. Cartwell and Ed Dellinger." Pete looked up. "Sheriff brought them in an hour ago. The old one has been yellin' ever since." He leaned forward and waved a poster. "The other one is wanted. We could get some money for him."

Lark was happy to hear the two were locked up. But he found it hard to believe the two had walked into the jail easily. "Watch yourself. Those two are sly."

"I will."

Lark left the jail and headed home. He needed to clean up. He could use some sleep, but it would depend on what notes were awaiting him. He'd have to throw himself into his work even harder to prove to Savannah he wasn't anything like his past.

Savannah slept most of the day. When she awoke it was growing dark outside her window. She put on a chemise and a cotton dress Mrs. Polzin had made for her. She didn't plan to go outside but felt wandering around inside the house in her night clothes for longer than getting from the kitchen to her bedroom was wrong.

Mrs. Dearling was in the kitchen putting together the evening meal. "There you are. Poor dear. Would you like a cup of tea?"

"Yes, please."

"Sheriff Blake came by. He has the two men locked up in his jail. He wanted to get your story about what happened. I told him we'd send for him when you were ready." Mrs. Dearling set a cup of tea in front of her.

"Thank you." It was a relief to know the men were locked up. She wasn't sure she wanted to tell him everything. She felt embarrassed to talk about what she'd gone through. Having someone there she trusted would help. Lark flashed into her mind, but she shoved him aside. She glanced at the motherly woman setting dishes on the table. The woman had to have heard all kinds of stories considering the women who had lived here.

Lottie Mae and Belle entered through the kitchen door.

"Good to see you up." Lottie Mae gave her a hug.

Belle smiled. "You look better."

These women had become the sisters she never had. She'd take one of them with her to talk to the sheriff.

"I'm feel'n much better. It's amaz'n what a little sleep can do for a person." She picked up the tea and sipped.

The two women took their seats and started eating.

"How's the saloon? Bet it's busy since it was closed last night."

Lottie Mae shook her head. "We kept it open last night."

"Without Beau and Jules? How did that go? I mean, who all kept the men from gett'n rowdy?" Savannah's respect for the women rose even higher knowing they'd run the saloon without Beau.

"I asked Manfred Albrecht to help out for the night." Lottie Mae's face deepened in color.

This must have been the person she'd hoped would bid on her basket. Savannah looked back in her memory trying to remember if he had. But she'd been so upset over seeing Mr. Cartwell she hadn't registered much of anything else at the picnic.

"And how did y'all do?" Savannah asked.

Belle waved a fork toward Lottie Mae. "She and Manfred made eyes at each other all night, but he also kept the men's hands from roaming."

"Good. Was Beau pleased y'all kept the saloon open?" She wasn't sure how her brother would feel, knowing women could do his job.

"He was pleased with the nights profits." Lottie Mae said proudly.

They finished their meals and headed out. Within minutes Freedom and Liesa walked into the kitchen. They both gave Savannah a hug.

"I am glad you're back," Liesa said, shyly.

"Me, too." Savannah ate with the two women and watched as they left with plates for Beau and Jules. A smile had settled on her face.

"You have been a light in the lives of these ladies,"

Mrs. Dearling said.

Savannah stared at her in surprise. "What do you mean? They have made me see things differently."

"They see not all women of money are like the ones who have previously been in their lives and treated them like they were worthless." Mrs. Dearling refilled Savannah's tea cup and sat down with one of her own. "You've heard their stories that brought them here, but many times it was a woman of means and society who wronged them before a man did."

This didn't surprise Savannah. She'd seen her mother ridicule a woman of little means. While she never spoke, she'd been ashamed of her mother's actions. She cringed, thinking how at first, she had been as judgmental as her mother. Now, having met the women in this house and realized not everyone had a rich husband to keep them fed and clothed and in luxuries, she had empathy for those less fortunate. The women here had taught her some things were more important than money and status.

Her mind skipped to Lark. He treated everyone equal and gave them all the same respect no matter if they were a pauper or the richest man. One thing Lark and her mother didn't have in common.

"I don't believe a person should be treated any different because they have had a harder life. Look at me. Ball gowns and servants one day and clean'n and cook'n and sell'n my ball gowns the next." She shook her head.

Gunfire boomed.

Savannah started and Mrs. Dearling squeaked.

The gunfire lasted only a minute. What could have happened?

"I'm go'n to the saloon to see." She started for the

door.

"No! Stay here. Those men could have escaped." Mrs. Dearling put herself between Savannah and the back door.

Before she could spin around and head for the front door, the back door crashed open.

Wild-Eye Ed stood in the doorway, a pistol in each hand. "Get out of my way, old woman," he said, shoving Mrs. Dearling to the side. She lost her footing and fell to the floor.

"Don't you hurt her!" Savannah hollered and moved to go to the woman.

"You stand right there. Cartwell, get in here and tie her hands," Ed called over his shoulder.

She ran for the front door.

It flew open.

Lark stood in the doorway dressed in the clothing he'd wore the first time they'd met. He looked every bit the outlaw he said he'd once been.

"Get up the stairs," he ordered, a pistol in his hand.

She faced Ed. "Don't shoot him." She didn't want to be the cause of Shady Gulch losing their preacher.

"Savannah. Get upstairs," Lark ordered, grabbing her around the waist and setting her up three steps. "Now stay. I don't want you to get hurt."

His face was determined but his eyes pleaded with her. She sat on the step.

He stared down the hallway. "What's a matter, Ed, you see a ghost?"

"I knew I'd run into you someday, Topeka Kid."

Savannah didn't like that she couldn't see what the other man was doing. All she could do was sit and listen to the conversation and watch Lark's face not give away a thing.

"How did you fall in with scum like Cartwell?" Lark asked.

"Back when you rode with us we stole from banks he wanted to ruin. Then he used his money from the robbery to set up a new bank in that town."

Savannah could believe the banker was that nasty. He probably took her father for more than he owed, too.

"I thought I recognized Cartwell as someone I'd seen you talk to after a bank robbery." Lark walked farther down the hall.

She could no longer see him. What was he trying to do? Get killed? Her heart raced. He'd come to her rescue again, but this time he could end up dead. Knowing he could be taken from her forever started her searching her heart and coming up with the fact she loved him and she believed he had changed. Her mother had never come to her rescue, let alone risked her life for her daughter.

"You know, I'm going to kill you." Ed said.

Savannah's heart stopped and lodged in her throat. "No!" she cried and flung herself down the stairs.

Shots rang through the hallway.

Hands pulled her out into the cool night air.

"Let go! Lark! I have to get to Lark!" she cried and clawed at the large arms banded around her.

"Quiet. Let him concentrate on what he needs to do." Beau's voice ordered in her ear.

Savannah's cries had pulled Lark's attention from Ed.

The first shot, caught him in his arm. His gun arm. He dropped to the floor, hoping Savannah wasn't standing behind him and that no one was behind Ed. With his left hand, he aimed and shot all the rounds from his pistol at the outlaw.

After the third shot, the man fell to the ground.

The echo of the shots died. It was eerily quiet. He heard another body drop outside the kitchen door.

He'd never forgive himself if he hit someone coming to his aid. Lark pushed to his feet and walked along the hall, blood dripping down his arm and hand. Mrs. Dearling would skin him alive for the mess he'd made.

His guilt ate at him even more when he spotted the woman in a heap on the floor by the pantry door. He knelt beside her, keeping an eye on Ed.

"What happened?" Beau asked from the door Lark had just walked through.

Before he could answer, Savannah pushed by her brother and slammed into him, knocking him onto his backside. She knelt beside him, holding his head and crying.

"I'm fine. Just a bullet in my arm."

She leaned back, saw the blood, and cried some more.

"Shhh, I'm fine." Lark put his good arm around Savannah, holding her tight. He glanced at Beau. "Someone fell outside the door. I hope to God it wasn't—"

Ty stepped through the back door. "It was Cartwell. Took one to the shoulder. He's still alive. Pete is taking him back to the jail." Ty's face was washed out.

"How did these two get out of jail?" Beau asked.

"Knocked me over the head, dragged me into the jail, and took off with the key. The first shooting was Pete using a rifle to break the lock and get me out."

"This one won't rob or hurt anyone again," Beau said, tapping Ed's body with the toe of his boot. He squat next to

Mrs. Dearling and picked her up. "Ty go get the doc. Mrs. Dearling and Lark need tended to before Cartwell."

"Headed there now." Ty disappeared.

"Come on," Lark stood, drawing Savannah to her feet beside him. He held onto her down the hallway and into the parlor. More blood for Mrs. Dearling to clean up.

He sat in a chair and pulled her onto his lap. When she'd cried out and came hurtling down the stairs, he'd feared she'd get shot. "When I put you some where you stay put," he said, and kissed her.

Her salty tears intensified his need to show her how much she meant to him.

A hand tapping his shoulder drew him out of the kiss.

"The doc and Ty are coming." Beau pulled Savannah off his lap.

The last thing Lark remembered was the doctor walking into the parlor.

Chapter Thirty-four

Savannah sat on Lark's bed. She'd stayed with him, helping Dr. Nolan take the bullet out of his arm, and now, waiting for him to wake. The doctor cautioned he'd be weak from loss of blood.

Beau had explained to her how stupid she'd been, taking Lark's attention away from Ed, causing Lark to get shot. He was hurt because of her foolishness.

But he was alive! She would thank the Lord every day that he spared Lark. And that she'd realized he had changed. He had been ready to give his life to protect her. Her mother would have never done such a selfless thing.

His head shifted and his eyes moved under his eyelids. "No. No!" he hollered, rising.

"Shhh. You're safe, tucked into your own bed." She put her hands on his shoulders, pressing him down on the mattress.

"Savannah?" he asked, his eyes opening, shutting, and opening again.

"Yes. As I live and breathe. Rest. Dr. Nolan said you

lost a lot of blood." She kissed his cheek.

"You? Are you injured?"

"I'm fine thanks to you. But my heart." She pressed a fist to her chest remembering the ache that had radiated in her chest at the sight of the two men shooting. "I nearly died see'n you shoot'n with that outlaw. I thought I'd lost you forever."

"Savannah, I know I didn't find my way to being a preacher the usual way. But I enjoy helping people and spreading the word of the Lord. And I love you. Have since the day you stumbled off the train. Once the congregation hears about my past, I may be out of a job."

He reached up with his good hand and grasped her hand. "Is there a chance you could forgive my past and keep me on the straight and narrow by becoming my wife?"

She peered into his eyes and knew, no matter where he was or what he did, she wanted to be by his side. "Yes. I would be honored to be your wife. You settled in my heart a while back as well. I just had to realize you are noth'n like my mother and her lies and thiev'n."

Savannah leaned forward, touching her lips to Lark's. After the brief kiss she said, "And there's no one who knows about your past who would tell a soul about it."

Lark couldn't believe the people who came to see him as he recovered from his wound. Everyone showed their concern and didn't say a word about Savannah practically living in his little house by the church. She arrived at dawn to cook his breakfast and tended his needs all day, returning to the boarding house well after dark.

They were enjoying their time together and realizing what being married would be like. They had gone from heated kisses to nearly bedding, but he refused to allow his carnal desires to take them into wedlock having already consummated their bodies.

Ty arrived four days after the shooting. Lark was dressed and sitting in his chair when Savannah answered the door.

"Good mawnin', Sheriff Blake," she said, waving him into the house.

Ty grinned from ear to ear. "You two are looking all husband and wifey."

Lark held out his good hand. Savannah walked over, grasped his hand, and stood by his side. "Could be because we are getting married as soon as I can write a letter to a friend to come marry us."

"Congratulations. I'd heard the rumor but thought I'd check for myself." He held out a paper. "You could use this to start your new life."

Lark released Savannah's hand and grasped the paper. He read it and stared at Ty. "What is this? Why would I get a bank draft for seventy-five dollars?"

"It's the reward for Wild-Eye Ed Dellinger. You stopped him from robbing anymore banks and trains." Ty shoved his thumbs in his gun belt and grinned like he was the one who'd received the money.

"I can't accept money for killing a man." Lark held the paper out to Ty.

"You may not, but I will." Savannah grabbed the paper. "We can get that organ and put the remain'n money in the church coffers."

"What will the congregation say?" Lark had misgivings about using blood money for the church.

"The same thing they've been say'n. You did this town

and territory a service by send'n that outlaw to his maker." Savannah walked over to the small desk he used to write his sermons and settled the paper on top of his Bible. "Thank you for bring'n this over Sheriff."

Ty tipped his hat. "You're welcome."

Savannah showed the sheriff out.

Lark held out his good hand. When she grasped it, he pulled her down onto his lap. "We need to set a date and get this wedding over with. I want to feel you lying next to me in bed and love you until the sun comes up."

A beguiling blush flushed her cheeks. "I've been think'n the same thing, Reverend."

Savannah stepped off the train holding onto Lark's hand. She couldn't stop smiling. She was Mrs. Larkin Webster, the wife and soulmate of Reverend Webster. They'd had a wedding at the church three days ago, with Lark's friend officiating. Beau had paid for their stay at the Bismarck Hotel for their honeymoon. And this morning before boarding the train to come home, they'd purchased the organ and had it loaded on the baggage car.

She wasn't surprised to see the ladies from the boarding house standing on the platform. The other person who surprised her was Beau, continuing to stare at the passengers disembarking.

"Who are you look'n for? I'm right here," she said, giving her brother a hug.

"The Pinkerton I hired to find out about Cartwell and your mother."

A man dressed like a dandy stepped off the train. He scanned the platform and walked up to Beau. "Mr. Gentry?"

"Yes." They shook hands. "And this is my sister, Mrs. Savannah Webster."

"Ma'am." The man touched the brim of his hat.

"I'm Pinkerton Agent Wilmer Brunt." He held out an envelope. "This is the reason Mr. Cartwell wanted to make your sister his wife."

Savannah reached for Lark's hand and pressed closer to Beau.

Her brother opened the envelope and pulled out several pieces of paper. His eyes scanned the missives. "Not that I don't think you are a fetching woman, but I knew there had to be another reason for Cartwell wanting to make you his wife." Beau handed the paper to her.

It was her father's will. It stated that she would receive ten thousand dollars upon his death. She studied Beau. "No one told me about this. I wouldn't have had to leave Georgia if I'd been given this."

Lark squeezed her hand. She gazed into his eyes. "But then I wouldn't have met my husband or all of you."

"Where is the money?" Beau asked the Pinkerton.

"In an account in a bank that neither Cartwell nor Mrs. Gentry knew about. From what we've pieced together, Cartwell and Varicella Gentry were working together to get the money. Once Cartwell married Miss Gentry, he planned to get his hands on the money through her. Mrs. Gentry was to get a portion for not telling her daughter about the will."

Savannah had known the day would come when she would completely shove her mother out of her life. Today was the day. Lark would have been spared the bullet in his arm and she would have been spared the kidnapping if not for her mother's greed.

Lark wrapped her in an embrace. "What do you plan to do with your money?"

"We already have an organ. I'll have to think about it." She might wish her mother hadn't kept the money from her to save them pain, but if she'd received the inheritance, she would never have met the wonderful man now in her life.

She handed the will to her husband and hugged the women from the boarding house.

"You look happy!" Freedom exclaimed, giving her a hug.

"I am happy." She reached behind her, and Lark put his hand in hers. She would never understand why a woman wouldn't want the love of a man. They had spent more time in the hotel room exploring one another than they did exploring the town. Her body hummed with contentment. She'd never been as happy as she was at this very moment.

"We have the organ," she announced and pulled Lark down the train to the baggage car. Her friends all followed them.

"This Sunday the church will be blessed with the heavenly sounds of this organ, played by my wife," Lark said. The love shining in his eyes, matched the happiness in her heart.

About the Author

Thank you for visiting Shady Gulch. I hope you enjoyed reading about the lives of the women and men of this small railroad town. Savannah and Lark are just the start of many happy couples from the Silver Dollar Saloon who will fall in love. If you liked ***Savannah***, please leave a review. It is the best way to let an author know you enjoyed their book.

All my work has Western or Native American elements in them along with hints of humor and engaging characters. My husband and I raise alfalfa hay in rural eastern Oregon. Riding horses and battling rattlesnakes, I not only write the western lifestyle, I live it.

I love to hear from fans. You can find or contact me at:
patyjag@gmail.com
or my website – www.patyjager.net

My historical western books

Silver Dollar Saloon Series

Savannah
***Lottie Mae*-** Coming soon

Halsey Brother Series

Marshal in Petticoats – Gil's story
Outlaw in Petticoats – Zeke's story
Miner in Petticoats – Ethan's story
continued

Doctor in Petticoats – Clay's story
Logger in Petticoats – Hank's story
Halsey Brothers Series – Box Set

Halsey Homecoming trilogy
Laying Claim – Jeremy's story
Staking Claim – Colin's story
Claiming a Heart – Donny's story
A Husband for Christmas - Shayla's story
Halsey Homecoming Box Set

Letters of Fate
Davis
Isaac
Brody

Other Historical Western Romance
Gambling on an Angel
Improper Pinkerton
For a Sister's Love

Historical Paranormal Romance
(Native American)
Spirit of the Mountain
Spirit of the Lake
Spirit of the Sky
Spirit Trilogy Box Set

Thank you for purchasing this Windtree Press
publication. For other books of the heart, please visit our
website at www.windtreepress.com.

For questions or more information contact us
at info@windtreepress.com.

Windtree Press
Hillsboro, OR

www.ingramcontent.com/pod-product-compliance
Lightning Source LLC
Chambersburg PA
CBHW071729190726
48292CB00003B/668